CHANGE IS GOOD

Emmy's Story, Part 20

by
Kenneth Lee McGee

I was listening to the song
"The Triangle Fire"
by The Brandos recently,
and was moved to tears because
I knew some of the horrific details
about the 1911 fire in New York City.
I borrowed a book from the library
by the author, David van Drehle,
to learn more and decided to,
in my own insignificant way,
honor the memory of the victims.

When I started writing about Emmy, Kenny
and all their friends, I thought it
would be a single book.
This is book number twenty in the series,
and I am currently outlining number twenty-one.
Thanks for the support and encouragement
to keep telling Emmy's story.

I wish to thank my wife for helping
to make these stories more relevant.
She also finds my mistakes.

Chapter One

"Change is good," Emmy said as she and the family reached their Honda Odyssey in the parking lot of the Crest Ridge United Nazarene Church.

"Why?" Kevin asked. "Did you want Pastor Tyler to leave?"

"No, but I'm not God. I don't see the big picture like He does."

"We will miss them, but it's not like we won't ever see them again." Kenny Colwell opened the side doors with his key fob, and the kids climbed in.

"Is that why Mom didn't say goodbye to Phoebe?" Isabella asked. "Are we going to visit them in Michigan?"

"One of these days, we will," Emmy said as she buckled her seatbelt.

"I wonder how much snow they get in Michigan. If we visit them this winter, maybe I can build a snowman with Grayson and David." Kevin squeezed into the third row.

"Is Pastor Wyatt going to be the next pastor?" Isabella asked. "Grace said he's going to be in charge."

Emmy turned in her seat to look at Isabella. "He will be preaching, so I guess that means he's in charge. I suspect the church board will choose to hire someone with more experience. Wyatt has never been in charge of a large church before."

"Pastor Tyler didn't have any experience when they hired him," Heather said.

Kenny edged forward in the line of traffic leaving the church to turn onto Canton Lane. "Tyler was already on the staff, and when Dr. Behren resigned suddenly, the board decided to hire Tyler as an interim leader. He surprised everyone by quickly becoming the perfect person to lead the church."

"I think he should still be the pastor," Kevin replied. "Why does this light take forever to change?"

Heather looked over her shoulder and frowned at her brother. "Get over it. He resigned and now the church has to find someone else."

1

"How long will it take to find a new pastor?" Isabella asked. "I hope whoever the church hires has a family."

"I hope the old people on the board don't decide to hire another old preacher," Kevin said.

"I hope people don't decide to leave before the new pastor comes," Emmy replied.

Kenny eased the Honda Odyssey onto Canton Lane and headed to their home in the gated community of Bristol Ridge.

"Dad, there's a squad car coming up behind us. Were you speeding?" Kevin asked.

Kenny checked the speedometer. "I'm doing forty and everyone is passing me."

Emmy laughed and said, "Maybe your father will get pulled over for going too slow."

Kevin watched as the South Hampshire squad car roared past with its lights flashing. "It's a good thing Dad was driving and not Mom. She usually drives fifty-five or faster on this road."

"I drive the same speed as other traffic," Emmy replied while turning on the radio.

Later, as Kenny turned left into Bristol Ridge, Kevin hollered, "What station are we listening to? They're playing one of Dad's new songs. They were playing church music before."

"It's WONU, the Olivet station," Emmy answered. She looked at Kenny. "Did the band bribe whoever's in charge of the station? Is that why they're playing this song?"

Kenny shook his head as pressed the remote to open the gate and rolled ahead. He waved to the guard in the security building. "I talked to someone at the station. They heard the song 'Mercy' and thought the lyrics were appropriate for today. *When Light Flashes* is the most spiritual CD the band has ever released."

"I wouldn't call it spiritual," Emmy said. "It definitely has songs that refer to God, but it's not overtly what people would call a Christian CD."

"Intentionally so," Kenny replied.

"I admit I didn't think the songs were all that great when I first heard it, but the more I listen to it, the better I like it," Heather said. "Yeah, it's still a CD by a bunch of old guys, but it's decent."

2

Kenny glanced in the rear-view mirror at the older of his twin daughters, grinned and replied, "Thanks for the vote of confidence, but I'm only forty-three. Not exactly a senior citizen yet."

"You know what I mean."

Kevin hollered, "Yeah! We like that new rapper who grew up in SoHam."

"Who is that?" Emmy asked.

"His real name is Vontez Hartnett, but his stage name is V-Hart, and he recently released his first set of tunes."

"Does he have a CD out?" Kenny asked as he turned onto the winding drive which led up the hill to their home.

"No, he puts his stuff out as individual raps, and we download them," Heather answered. "I guess he's an independent artist."

"He comes to our church. You've probably seen him, but he doesn't look like a typical rapper. He looks like all the other teens," Isabella explained.

"Do his parents come to church?" Emmy asked.

Kenny opened the garage door from the minivan. "His father is an accountant, right?"

Heather and Isabella shrugged.

"Maybe I'm thinking of someone else," Kenny said as he parked the minivan and turned it off.

Kevin waited until Isabella was mostly out of the way before he dashed past her and raced up the concrete stairs and into the mudroom.

"What's his problem?" Heather asked. "He almost knocked Isa over."

"I'm okay," Isabella said.

Kevin hung his coat on a hook and looked back. "Sorry, Isa. I didn't mean to knock you down."

"I know you can be impatient," Isabella replied.

"I think we liked you better when you were smaller than us." Heather walked up the steps and smacked Kevin's arm. "You better stop growing soon, or else you'll be bigger than Uncle Tony."

3

"Ben's the one who'll be bigger than his father. He'd be playing football if it wasn't for the stupid virus." Kevin opened the mudroom door and was greeted by Lassie, the family's five-month-old black labradoodle.

"I'm glad to see you, too, Lassie." Kevin got on his knees and allowed Lassie to lick his face. "I bet you're hungry. I hope you didn't make a mess anywhere. If you did, we will have to put you in your cage whenever we leave."

"What's for lunch?" Kenny asked closing his door.

"Ham and bean soup with corn bread," Emmy answered. "I just need to warm it up and pop the corn bread in the oven. Give me twenty minutes."

The kids headed upstairs to change clothes. After changing they gathered in the hallway.

"Let's ask Dad. I don't think he'll mind," Kevin said loudly enough for Kenny to hear as he climbed the stairs and stopped outside the master bedroom suite.

"I won't mind what?" Kenny asked.

The kids met him at the end of the hallway.

"Ask him, Kevin," Heather said.

"Since no one's using the nanny suite, can we buy a TV and sound system to put in there. It would be more convenient than going to the basement or using the family room. You and Mom use the family room more than us."

Kenny looked to the other end of the long hallway and rubbed his jaw. "I don't see an issue as long as you don't stay up all night. Do you have one in mind?"

"We could talk to Pastor Jonah. He's in charge of technology, and would know a good system to buy."

"I know a few things," Kenny said, mildly disappointed.

"Yeah, but there's a lot of new gear available now, Dad. You still use the same old amps you did twenty years ago."

"It's vintage gear, and sounds better."

"Can we buy something?" Heather asked.

"Maybe you should ask your mother."

"Dad! You're supposed to be the man of the house. You should make the decision."

4

"Okay, Isa. If you do the research and come up with a plan, I'll take a look at it and see if we can afford it."

Kevin chuckled. "Dad, we're not talking about billions of dollars like the government spends. It's just a TV and a decent sound system."

"That's good," Kenny said.

"What were you and the kids talking about?" Emmy asked a few minutes later. "Listen for the timer. Should be ten minutes." She walked into her closet, hung up her dress and put on her comfortable old jeans and a fifteen-year-old Fridays At Five sweatshirt.

Kenny sat on the edge of the bed and removed his shoes. "They want to put a TV and stereo system in the nanny suite. I told them to do some research."

"Why do we need another TV? We have two gigantic screens already."

"They don't like to go downstairs."

"I'll think about it," Emmy said. She kissed his cheek and headed for the door."

Kenny started to say something but held his tongue.

"What?" Emmy asked.

"Nothing."

"Don't nothing me. I know that look. Spill it."

"I think I should be the one to make this decision."

Emmy laughed and shook her head. "Don't tell me they used the *man-of-the-house* routine on you."

He stared at the floor and scratched his ear.

Chapter Two

"Well, if it isn't Rory Porter," Emmy said. "To what do I owe the pleasure of a phone call?"

"Hey! I texted you the other day," Rory replied.

"Texts are not phone calls. What's up, Dr. Porter?" Emmy closed her laptop and scooted her chair back from the desk in the den where she had been working on the outline for her next Claire and Ruby story.

"I tested positive yesterday. I thought you should know."

"Why? You haven't been around in forever."

"Thanks for the concern. I talked to Kenny at church Sunday. From a safe distance and I was wearing a mask."

"Sorry. Do you feel okay? Do you have to quarantine for two weeks? Do you have any symptoms?"

"I feel great other than feeling fatigued, and I can be tested again on Friday. In the meantime, I'm staying home and Rochelle is crashing at the hospital. They are so shorthanded."

"James told me the nurses at St. Bart's were working overtime every day."

"Mercy is definitely as chaotic. Nurses and staff are strained to the limit. Is Father James allowed to see people now?"

"He's the only priest allowed to visit patients, and he has to wear a hazmat suit."

"Really?" Rory asked.

"Almost, and he gets tested every couple days. I'll tell Kenny. Should he get tested again?"

"Only if he starts feeling sick. I don't think he's at risk, but I figured you should know."

"Thanks for calling, Rory. I'll let him know, and I'm sorry I didn't see you at church."

"I popped in because it was Pastor Tyler's last week. Will it take long to find a replacement?"

"It might take longer than normal because of the COVID thing. We'll see. I'm sure the board will be meeting with Dr. Schofield soon."

"Who is he?"

"He's the District Superintendent for our area. He's the one who will find candidates."

"It won't be easy to find someone as likable or personable as Tyler," Rory said.

"Tell me. I've been through pastoral changes before, and it's not easy. People have to adjust because all pastors do things a little differently."

"I need to head out," Kenny kissed Emmy once, paused and kissed her again. "I still kinda like doing that even after all these years."

"I'm so glad. Should I come with you?" she asked as Kenny grabbed his keys and coat.

"I might stop at the office before I come home."

"Where are you going, Dad?" Heather asked.

"Your grandparents are leaving for Florida today. I have to take them to the airport."

"Why are they leaving before our birthday?" Heather asked. "Did they forget about it? They aren't getting Alzheimer's, are they?"

"I don't think they forgot, but they were able to get cheap tickets. It would cost more if they waited."

"We can talk to them on the computer, I suppose," Heather said. "Tell them goodbye from us."

Kenny arrived at his parents' place and parked in the driveway alongside the two-story, brick house. He saw Fez Rivera come out of the carriage house and waved.

"How are you?" Kenny asked bumping elbows with Fez. "Has school started already?"

Fez laughed and said, "Not yet, but I came back from Wisconsin early. Your parents are letting me stay in the apartment when I don't have to be at Olivet."

"Are some of your classes in person?"

Fez nodded. "I have two classes that meet in person, but I can do the rest of them online. That saves gas. I only need to be on campus two days a week."

"Are you still working at Darby's?"

"Mr. Darby is giving me a few hours," Fez replied. "Did you know he added a drive-up window?"

"No. When did he do that?"

"During the holidays," Fez replied. "Business has picked up since then."

Kenny chuckled and then shrugged. "I never know if restaurants are open or not. The government changes the regulations every other day."

"Tell me," Fez sighed. "Our dining room is open, but Mr. Darby taped off some of the booths to keep people spread out."

"Were you coming inside?" Kenny asked as he locked the Odyssey.

"Yeah, your father wanted to show me the new security system."

Kenny opened the back door, and they stepped inside.

"I'm here! Are you ready to leave for the airport?" Kenny asked.

Ellie Colwell entered the country-style kitchen and checked the refrigerator. "We are packed. Hello, Fez. How are your parents?"

"They're doing well. My mom was kinda down after Christmas, but she's doing better now."

"Good. There's some things left in the fridge. Please use whatever you want. There's a fresh gallon of milk. I know you will drink it."

"Thanks, Mrs. Colwell," Fez replied with a smile and a chuckle.

"Kenny, can you help me take the luggage to the van?" Mr. Colwell asked.

"I'll do that," Fez said.

"Okay, and I'll show you how to use this newfangled alarm system. If you ask me, it's a waste of money. If someone wants to break in the house, they'll find a way," he said shaking his head.

"Dad, the new system will deter those who are looking for an easy house to burgle," Kenny said. "The neighborhood is changing, and you need to be aware."

"We won't be here."

"Thus the need for improved security."

"I'll keep an eye on the house," Fez said. "I'll park my car in the drive when I'm here and clear the snow if we get any."

"Thank you, Fez."

The van was loaded and Mr. Colwell gave Fez the codes for the new alarm.

"There are timers on some of the lights, and they vary from day to day."

"We added smart technology to the house. It didn't even have electricity when it was built," Kenny explained. "Are we ready now?" He checked the time. "You need to be at the airport in ninety minutes."

"Were the girls disappointed?" Ellie asked. "We won't see them on their birthday."

"They'll survive, but you need to be here next year when they turn sixteen." He shook his head. "It doesn't seem possible."

Carter laughed. "I'm not the only one getting older."

"Kristen, I thought Wyatt did a great job with the service today," Emmy said. "I enjoyed his sermon."

"Thanks. He was nervous this morning," Kristen replied.

"Why? He's been in charge when Tyler and Liz were on vacation."

"Yes, but it's different now. He will be in charge until the board hires a new pastor. There's more pressure on him." Kristen paused then asked, "Did you think the crowd was smaller today?"

Emmy giggled and said, "No, I thought everyone looked about the same size."

Kristen rolled her eyes. "You know what I meant."

"I heard one of the ushers say there were less than two hundred people here. Do you remember the days when the church would be packed with over a thousand people?"

"I remember, but it seems so long ago."

Emmy put an arm around Kristen. "Don't worry. I'm sure people didn't stay home because of Wyatt. They might have been traveling or something. He should check how many people watched online."

9

"He did say the number of people watching the livestream has been increasing gradually."

Emmy saw her kids talking to Kristen's two oldest children. "Who's watching Kayla Eve?"

"She's in the nursery," Kristen answered. "Are you always going to call her by both names, Emily Olivia?"

Emmy laughed. "No, I will try to remember to call her Kayla, or the baby."

"Wyatt doesn't call her *the baby* anymore," Kristen said.

"Is he getting better at feeding her and changing her diaper?"

Kristen smiled. "He loves to feed her, but if she has a poopy diaper, he brings her to me or Gracie."

"I've watched Grace care for her baby sister. She must be a big help."

"Yes, but she gets upset if I ask her to watch Kayla too often. She is only twelve."

Wyatt Pearson approached, sighed and said, "I'm finally ready to leave. I'm sorry it took so long, but I needed to talk to Roger Goldman about the agenda for the next church board meeting."

"Was it about the finances?" Emmy asked.

Wyatt looked at Kristen then Emmy.

Emmy waved a hand. "You don't have to answer that. It's none of my business. I'm not a board member."

"You should think about accepting a nomination, Em," Kristen said. "You're a leader of the church even if you don't have a specific role at the moment."

Emmy put her hands on her hips. "Kristen, are you trying to say I've been around for so many years that I'm now old enough to serve on the church board?"

Kristen laughed. "You're such a goof. You do realize there are a couple board members younger than you, right?"

"Yeah, but most of them are much older than us. Quite a bit older in fact."

"Age isn't really the most important qualification, Emmy," Wyatt said.

"Oh, and what exactly is the most important qualification? I'm curious because Tony's on the board, and he's such a..."

"Be nice," Kristen said.

"Mom! Can we go home now?" Kevin asked as he walked quickly toward her. "I'm starving, and have a project I need to finish before tomorrow."

"A school project? Why haven't you started before now?" Emmy asked.

Kevin shook his head as he tugged on his mother's arm. "It's not a school thing. It's something Ben and I have been working on, and we want to finish it today."

"Can you tell me what it is?" Emmy asked.

Kevin looked at Wyatt and Kristen then stared at his mom. "I'm not supposed to tell anyone, but it's nothing illegal."

"Oh, that makes me feel so much better," Emmy said shaking her head. "I better get these kids home before they starve." She waved goodbye and began walking away. "Where is your father?"

"He's waiting in the van," Isabella said.

"Do you know anything about your brother's secret project?"

"Mom, if Aunt Diane swore you to secrecy about something, would you have told your parents?"

"Of course not."

"You can't expect me to do any different," Isabella said.

"But this is different. I'm his mother."

Isabella rolled her eyes and walked outside.

"Emmy, you should come over because I am going to Facetime Liz this morning," Kristen said.

"When?" Emmy drained her coffee and set the cup in the sink.

"In ten minutes. Are you dressed?"

""Yes, but I haven't showered." Emmy shrugged and added, "It doesn't matter because she won't be able to tell."

"I hope I won't be able to tell," Kristen said.

Kristen was already talking to Liz when Emmy arrived.

11

"I took a quick shower," Emmy said. "That's why my hair is still kinda wet." She took a seat beside Kristen. "Hi, Liz. How are things in Michigan?"

"The weather has been okay, but it's snowing again today."

After talking about the weather and the kids, Emmy asked, "How is the house? Describe it to me."

"It's an older two-story, and we are close to the church. Maybe three or four minutes away. Tyler can ride his bike, or jog there."

"How many bedrooms?" Emmy asked.

"Four upstairs, and there's room for two in the basement if we need the space. There's a bathroom on both floors, and a half-bath in the basement."

Emmy looked at Kristen.

Kristen shook her head and whispered, "You better not ask how much they paid."

"We paid $190,000, and were able to close right away," Liz said.

Emmy made a face at Kristen. "I didn't have to ask. Did you use a Realtor?"

"We used Lillian Marras. She's a member of the church, and has been selling real estate over thirty years. We were fortunate to find a place close to downtown. There aren't a lot of properties for sale in town. There are new developments at the edges of town, but we wanted something close to the church."

"How old is it?" Kristen asked.

"It was built in the 1870s, but not in this location."

"What does that mean?" Emmy asked.

"One of the men from church told Tyler this house used to be on Third Avenue. It was moved here in the early 1900s, but they didn't know why."

"That's different. Do you have a lot of mature trees since it's an older neighborhood?" Emmy asked.

"Definitely. Our property has several large trees. Tyler said he doesn't look forward to cleaning leaves out of the gutters."

"Have you unpacked everything? Are you settled in?" Kristen asked.

"There are boxes in the basement we haven't touched. Tyler has done some work. We painted the whole house. It was empty for almost a year, but the previous owner was a smoker. It reeked when we first saw it."

"How big is the kitchen?" Emmy asked.

"I will show you."

Liz gave them a virtual tour of the first floor.

"You've got hardwood floors. That's good," Emmy said.

"We put new carpeting in the addition. It's going to be the playroom."

"Are you going to install cable or Internet?" Emmy asked.

Liz shook her head. "We don't plan to buy a TV, but Natty and Grayson are trying to convince their father they need one for school. Something larger than their computer monitors at least."

"Good luck with that," Emmy chuckled.

"Oh, an interesting thing happened last week."

"What?" Kristen asked.

"The fire department is on the main street kitty-cornered from us. They own the house next door and use it as their main office. They recently bought the old house north of us. Grayson saw a group of firefighters on the roof of the garage. They chopped holes in it."

"Why?" Emmy asked.

"Apparently, they plan to use the house for training and burn it at some point."

"How close is it to your house?"

"I don't know how many feet it would be. Our backyard and driveway, and their backyard and driveway separate the houses. There's an old fence that is falling down. I hope they burn it."

"The boys would love to watch. I know Kevin and Ben would. There must be another reason for them to purchase it."

"They need to expand the building where their equipment is stored."

"How are things going at the church?" Kristen asked.

"Tyler doesn't have a lot to do yet."

"Why not? He has to preach, doesn't he?" Emmy asked.

13

"Yes, but the staff and volunteers do most everything during the week. There aren't as many people on the office staff as at Crest Ridge, but the church isn't open as many hours. No one is there at all on Friday."

"Tyler won't like sitting by and doing nothing. He will get bored," Emmy said.

"He is looking for things to do. I'm making a list of projects for the house."

"Does Derby like her new home?" Emmy asked.

"She's... adjusting."

"She can't run around like before, huh?"

"Not yet. Tyler takes her for long walks in the morning and at night. We looked into putting up a fence, but the cost was prohibitive. Tyler thinks we should install one of those underground fences. They are much cheaper."

"Lassie is used to ours," Emmy said. "You wouldn't need one as long."

"That's true."

"We won't visit until you've had time to get settled," Kristen said.

"That might take a while," Liz said with a chuckle. "You can come for a visit anytime. I should go. David is bored, and wants my attention."

"It was good to talk to you, Liz," Kristen said. "Say hi to everyone for us."

Emmy looked at Kristen. "We could pay for the fence."

"True, but you have to let them live within their budget."

Chapter Three

"Mom, can we skip school today since it's our birthday?" Heather asked Wednesday morning.

"No way! I didn't get to skip school on my birthday," Kevin complained. He grabbed two doggie treats and fed Lassie.

"Did we even have school on your birthday?" Heather asked as she poured maple syrup on her blueberry pancakes. "Didn't the schools shut down sometime in March last year?"

Emmy set another platter of pancakes on the breakfast nook table. "If I remember correctly, schools shut down on your birthday, Kevin."

"Was that supposed to be my birthday present?" He grabbed three more pancakes and ignored his sisters' protests.

"I can make more," Emmy said. "Don't let Lassie eat people food. It's not good for her."

Kenny walked out of the mudroom and stood behind Emmy as she mixed more pancake batter at the kitchen island. He put his arms around her waist and kissed her neck.

"What was that for?" Emmy turned to face him.

"Do I have to have a reason to kiss my lovely wife?" He grinned and kissed her again.

"Will you guys get a room," Kevin said with a mouthful of pancakes.

Lassie sat in front of them wagging her tail. Kevin broke off a piece of pancake and slipped it to her.

Emmy pointed a wooden spatula at Kenny. "I know the difference in your kisses. That kiss means you are up to something. Spill it."

Kenny raised his eyebrows.

"Not that," Emmy whispered. "You want to buy something, or you need a favor. One of those kisses."

Kenny backed up. "It's nothing expensive."

"What is it?"

"We need a new heater in the garage."

Emmy thought about their large garage with enough room for six vehicles.

15

"Did the old one break?" Kevin asked as he rinsed his plate and set it in the sink. "I thought it felt colder in the garage when I took Lassie out for her walk this morning."

"It still works, but we need one with a larger capacity. More BTUs."

"Why? The garage isn't any bigger than when we built the house," Emmy said.

"Either it wasn't big enough when it was installed, or the winters are getting colder."

"Maybe it simply wore out, Dad," Isabella suggested.

Emmy finished the batter and made more pancakes. She set the platter on the table and asked, "How did the skating rink turn out?"

"Mom! You weren't supposed to know about it," Kevin hollered. "How did you find out?"

"Tony let it slip. Why did you keep it a secret?"

Kevin shrugged. "I thought you might get mad and think it was too dangerous."

"I went ice skating a few times when I was your age."

"Did you play hockey?"

"No. Why?"

"That's what the ice is for. Some of the guys in the neighborhood want to play hockey."

Emmy looked at Kenny. "Did you know about this?"

"About what?" Kenny asked with a straight face.

"You know what I mean." Emmy put her hands on her hips and frowned.

"Kevin and Ben might have mentioned it. I told him to be careful."

"Right! Careful. A bunch of kids on skates hitting each other with sticks. Sounds safe enough to me."

"Mom, we won't get hurt," Kevin promised.

When the kids finished eating, Emmy and Kenny sat in the breakfast nook and gazed outside. The girls busied themselves with school assignments while Kevin raced up and down the hallway in his socks pretending to be playing hockey.

16

"What are you thinking about, Em?"

"Thinking about who the church might hire to replace Liz and Tyler."

Kenny watched two squirrels race along the deck railing. "Do you have a replacement in mind?"

"Of course not. That's Dr. Schofield's job. He probably has a few candidates for consideration." She laughed as the squirrels tumbled off the railing. "You can buy a new heater for the garage, but don't try to install it yourself. Call the furnace guy from church and pay him to do it."

"I wasn't going to try."

"Good. Are you taking the kids to church tonight, or should I play taxi?"

"I didn't know they were having church tonight."

Emmy nodded. "The teens are meeting in person for the first time in a month or so. I can drive if you're too busy."

Kenny shook his head. "You don't have to put me on a guilt trip, Em. I'll take them."

"Thank you. You're such a good father," Emmy said with a grin.

"You mean I'm a sucker for giving in so easily."

"That too."

Everyone turned when they heard a knock on the mudroom door.

"Is anyone home," Father James entered carrying a stack of presents. "I was in the neighborhood, so I thought I'd stop by and see my favorite nieces."

"What about me?" Kevin asked. "Am I your favorite nephew?"

"Least favorite," Emmy said with a chuckle.

Isabella and Heather rushed to their uncle, who happened to be a priest and their mother's half-brother. He worked for the South Hampshire diocese as a hospital chaplain.

"Are those for us?" Isabella asked.

"I heard a certain set of twins were turning fifteen today."

Kevin snorted. "They are making a big deal about it, too. It's just another birthday."

17

Father James watched the twins open their gifts.

"What do you say?" Emmy asked.

"Thank you, Uncle James," Isabella said first.

"We appreciate your thoughtfulness," Heather added.

"Now I need to talk to your mother," he said seriously.

"Can we talk in here, or should we move to the den?" Emmy asked.

"The den."

Emmy followed him down the hall. He closed the door Behind her.

"What's up that you can't tell anyone else?"

"My father suffered a stroke, and I'm leaving for Kansas from here. I took a compassionate leave, and I'm not sure how long I'll be gone."

"I'm sorry about your father, but you could have told this to everyone."

"I didn't want the kids or Kenny to worry."

"We will all worry about you, and we will pray for your parents."

"Thanks, Emmy."

He waved goodbye to the kids and told them he needed to run. They barely acknowledged him leaving. Emmy decided not to mention the reason for his sudden departure.

"Mom, I'll help you with the laundry if you want," Heather said as Emmy carried a load of dirty clothes into the downstairs laundry room. She rose from the breakfast nook where she had been doing school virtually and hurried after her mother. "Are there any more loads to bring downstairs?"

Emmy set the plastic tub on the counter and looked at Heather. She tilted her head and asked, "What favor do you want? You never volunteer to help with laundry."

Heather closed the door. "I know you told me your parents wouldn't let you date until you were almost too old to want to... and how much you resented it"

"They made me wait until I was sixteen even though Diane was allowed to date at fifteen. Ancient history. I survived."

18

"Fifteen, huh?" Heather grinned and pulled one of her tops from the basket. "This is kinda clean."

Emmy turned to face Heather. "Okay, I see where this is going. Has someone asked you to go on a date?"

"Kinda in a way."

"Care to elaborate?" Emmy opened the washing machine and began loading it.

"You know Peter and I have been hanging out together..."

"Did he ask you on a date?"

"Yeah. He wants to take me out for dinner. Nowhere fancy. Maybe Darby's or some place like that."

"Good. Make sure Isabella doesn't eat one of their Polish sausages. It upset her stomach the last time."

"Mom!"

"What?" Emmy added a packet of detergent, closed the lid and started the machine.

"It's only me and Peter. He didn't ask Isa."

Emmy shook her head. "No way. You just turned fifteen today. You're too young."

"Mom!"

"Don't *Mom* me." Emmy scooted past Heather and headed to the kitchen. "Aren't you supposed to be in school?"

"It's between classes. Why am I too young? Several of my friends are allowed to date."

"Really? You're going with that?"

Heather rolled her eyes. "Okay, that's lame, but it's Peter. He's almost family, and you can trust him."

Emmy opened the fridge and grabbed the Tupperware containing the chicken salad she made for sandwiches. "It's not a matter of trusting Peter or you. I trust you both."

"Then can I go?" Heather asked.

"Go where?" Kevin asked as he grabbed the bread from the wicker basket above the new microwave. "Can you fix me a sandwich, too, Mom? I'm starving."

"You ate a bag of chips a moment ago," Isabella said from the breakfast nook.

"Half a bag. Go where?" he asked again.

19

"Peter asked me out if you must know, creep," Heather answered.

"Why?" Kevin asked while making a face. "He could ask one of the girls from church or school. Why would he want to go anywhere with you?"

"He likes her, Kevin. Are you so dense?" Isabella grabbed four plates from the cabinet. "As long as we're having lunch, I'll get the potato salad out.

"I'm teasing. Ben told me Peter asked Uncle Tony if he could take Heather out."

"Why would he ask Tony?" Emmy asked. "It's not his decision."

Kevin shrugged and grabbed the first sandwich Emmy made. "Just sayin' what Ben told me. I don't care if Peter likes Heather or not."

Kenny came up from his basement studio and sauntered into the kitchen in time to hear part of Kevin's comment.

"Did you get that?" Kevin asked his father.

"I hope Peter likes Heather. They've been hanging out with each other a lot lately," Kenny said as he eyed the chicken salad. "Can I have one, too?"

Emmy sighed. "I should open a fast food place. Would you like fries or chips with your sandwich, sir? Perhaps a pickle?"

"Skip the pickle, but potato salad would hit the spot. Did Mama Bertucci make it?"

"I made it," Emmy answered.

"I'll take some anyway."

Emmy rolled her eyes. "My potato salad is just as good."

Isabella patted her mother's shoulder. "Of course it is, Mom. It's as good even if it's different."

"Dad, can I ask you a hypothetical question?" Heather asked with a smile.

"You better explain what you mean," Kevin teased. "Dad doesn't use big words like that."

"How about I hypothetically issue you an allowance, Kevin?" Kenny turned to Heather. "What would you like to *hypothetically* ask?"

20

She looked at her mother then her father. "What would you say if you're daughter was asked to go somewhere with a trusted family friend?"

"I suppose it would depend on where and who was asking. Why?"

"Peter asked her on a date," Kevin shouted. "She's afraid to ask because you always say they can't date until they're forty or fifty."

Heather frowned at her brother. "Thanks for ruining it, creep."

Kenny looked at Heather then Emmy. "For real?"

Emmy nodded. "He wants to take Heather on a dinner date."

"What did you tell her? You said no way, right?"

"I didn't really give her an answer. I thought we should talk about it first."

Emmy used all the chicken salad for sandwiches and placed the empty container in the sink.

Kenny took a bite of his sandwich. "What's there to talk about? She and Isa are too young."

"Dad!" the twins said together.

"What? You're only thirteen, right?" Kenny asked with a shrug.

"Fathers are impossible," Heather said as she stomped away.

"Can I have Heather's sandwich since she left?" Kevin asked.

"Thanks for the ride, Dad," Kevin said as Kenny dropped the kids at church.

"Call me when you're ready to come home." Kenny looked over his shoulder at Heather and Isabella. "Are you still mad at me?"

"I'm not mad at you," Isabella replied.

Kenny looked at Heather.

"I'm not upset, but you can't treat us like children forever."

"Yes I can! I'm your father," he replied with a laugh.

21

"You know what I mean."

Kenny spotted Peter's gray Hyundai Elantra pulling into the church parking lot. "Would you like to ride home with Peter?"

Heather shook her head. "Uncle Tony won't let him drive back and forth to church with anyone other than Dotty in the car. He said there's some weird state law. Is there?"

Kenny shrugged. "There wasn't when I was that age."

"The laws have changed since electricity was invented," Heather teased. "We will text you when we're ready to be picked up."

Emmy came to bed after midnight and instead of finding Kenny sound asleep, he was sitting up with a distant look on his face.

"Can't you sleep?"

He shook his head.

"Okay. Spill it," Emmy said as she climbed under the covers.

"Should we let Peter take Heather to dinner?"

"Do you mean like a one time exception to the rule, or whenever he wants?"

"I was thinking of this Friday. Do you think he will want to take her out more than once?"

"Would you have been satisfied to take me out one time only?"

"That's different."

Emmy jabbed her elbow into his hip.

"Ow!"

"Serves you right."

"You didn't answer my question, Em."

"Would you even consider it if it wasn't Peter asking? What would you say if one of the other guys from church asked her out? What if someone asked Isa for a date?"

He shook his head as he scooted under the covers. "No way. Isa is too young."

Emmy tilted her head as she stared incredulously.

"Isa is a child."

22

"You do realize they are the same age, right? Okay, Heather is a few minutes older, but... you know what I mean."

"I know they're twins, but their personalities are so different."

"Not as much as you'd like to think. Isa is quieter, but she... never mind. Can we talk about this in the morning? I need my beauty sleep."

Kenny grinned and put a hand on her stomach. "You don't need much sleep to stay beautiful in my eyes."

"Can we wait until morning?" Emmy asked.

Kenny shook his head then grinned.

"Heather, your mother and I talked about this date thing with Peter, and we made a decision," Kenny said at breakfast. "Would you like to hear it?"

Heather looked at her mother, who was still heating the hash browns. "What did you decide about my life?"

"Heather, don't cop an attitude now," Isabella whispered.

"I want to hear it," Kevin hollered from the pantry. "Is this cereal still good? It's been in here for ages."

"Taste it and see," Heather suggested.

He took a bite. "Stale." He tossed the box in the garbage. "I'm waiting."

"We decided to let you go with Peter tomorrow night, but that doesn't mean you are free to accept dates with other boys. We know and trust Peter."

"So, if I find a trusted older man you guys know, am I allowed to date him?"

Kenny looked at Emmy for help.

"Don't answer, Dad. It's a trick question," Kevin said.

Emmy stood at the end of the table still holding the knife she used to cut up the onions and peppers. "One date with Peter. Then we'll discuss your future dating privileges at a later time. Since we are allowing you to go out with Peter, Isabella will be afforded the same option."

Kevin laughed.

"What's so funny?" Heather asked.

23

"Why would Peter want to date Isa? Why would she want to go out with him?"

"We didn't mean Peter would be allowed to ask Isa on a date," Kenny explained.

Isabella shook her head. "Doesn't matter. I'm not ready to go on a solo date. I'm happy to hang out with friends in a group setting. But can I have a rain check in case I meet a hot hunk?"

"No!" Kenny yelled. "Neither of you are dating hot guys."

"Fine! I'll tell Peter he's not a hunk," Heather said.

"Is that what you're wearing on your date?" Kevin asked when Heather came downstairs Friday evening.

"What did you expect me to wear?"

Emmy frowned at Kevin then smiled at Heather. "You look fine, dear. Will you be warm enough in that top?"

"Mom! I have a coat, and what's wrong with this top? You said I look good in dark colors."

Kenny walked into the family room. "Do we need to take a picture of you and Peter on your first date? How about a video?"

"Dad!" Heather rolled her eyes.

"Mom, don't let Dad get all weird when Peter gets here," Isabella said.

Emmy adjusted Heather's top then said, "I don't think we need any pictures tonight, but if he asks you to the prom, that's a different story."

"Since you're going to Darby's, can you bring back a couple chili dogs?" Kevin asked.

"No way, and we might not go to Darby's. We might decide on pizza instead."

"I recommend Kerry Lynn's Pizza and Pasta," Kenny said. "They have the best in town."

When Peter arrived, everyone followed Heather to the garage and waved as they left.

"Do you feel older, Em?" Kenny asked. "One of our babies is going on a date."

Kevin and Isabella rolled their eyes.

"Did your parents make a fuss about tonight?" Heather asked as Peter drove out of Bristol Ridge.

"Not really. Ben and Taylor tried to razz me, but Mom and Dad didn't try to take pictures or anything."

"My father wanted to make a video, but Mom talked him out of it."

"Why is this any different that the other times we've gone somewhere?" Peter asked.

"Isn't it different? You said I should consider it a real date."

Peter turned to smile at her. "If I'm totally honest, I considered some of the times we went to Darby's real dates. Even if Dotty or Isa were with us."

"That's sweet, I think," Heather whispered as she grabbed his hand.

Everyone was in the family room when Heather returned. For a moment, no one looked up or said anything to Heather about her evening.

Finally, Kevin hollered, "How was your date? Mom said we shouldn't ask about it, and treat you like normal, but I want to know how it went. Did you have fun?" He looked at his father. "See? I didn't ask if he kissed her."

Isabella threw a small pillow at her brother. "It's none of your business if he kissed her."

"Do you want to tell us about your evening?" Emmy asked.

Heather sat on the couch between her mother and Isabella. "There's not a lot to tell."

"Where did you go?" Kevin asked.

"Kerry Lynn's Pizza and Pasta like Dad suggested." She looked at her father. "Thanks for the suggestion. We split one of their deluxe pizzas and a pitcher of Dr Pepper."

"Did you bring any back, or did you eat it all?" Kevin asked.

"Peter took the box home."

"Thanks a lot."

"We can order a pizza tomorrow if you want one that much, Kevin," Emmy promised.

25

"Thanks, Mom." Kevin stared at his sister. "What did you guys talk about? You did talk to each other, right?"

"Of course we did, creep," Heather answered making a face at him. "We didn't talk about anything that would interest you though."

"Did he ask you for another date?" Isabella asked quietly.

Kenny heard the question and sat up straighter in his recliner. "We agreed to one date, Heather."

"Fine! He did ask if I would want to go shopping or see a movie. Are theaters even open now?"

"The place in the mall is open, but you have to wear a mask and sit far apart," Isabella answered with a giggle.

Kevin grinned and asked, "Would you want to go if you can't sit next to each other and hold hands?"

"Grow up!" Heather replied. She looked at her father. "Will you consider letting Peter take me out again? You know I will be safe with him."

Kenny looked at Emmy for a moment. "We will have to think about it. Maybe Isa could go to a show with you and Peter."

"No way!" Isabella exclaimed shaking her hands. "I've heard the stories of Grandma making Mom go on Aunt Diane's dates. No way you're making me spy on Heather and Peter."

"It was rather awkward for both of us," Emmy said with a sigh. "We will pray about it, Heather."

"I already did," Kevin said with a straight face.

"Get out! You did not," Heather replied.

Kevin nodded. "Did too."

"Did you get an answer?" Emmy asked knowing Kevin would have a smart remark.

"I did, and God told me you guys should see the new Jason Bourne movie and take me with."

"Ha! Ha! There's no new Bourne movie."

"There might be this year, and I want to see it."

Chapter Four

Emmy looked around the sanctuary of Crest Ridge United Nazarene and poked Kenny in the side. "There are even fewer people here than last week, and last week's attendance was pretty low."

"Do you think it's due to the virus, or the fact we don't have a pastor?" he asked.

"I'm sure it's because of the virus. I hope people aren't staying home because Tyler and Liz left."

"Maybe you shouldn't say anything to Kristen. She and Wyatt are probably tackling enough matters without having to worry about declining attendance."

Emmy watched Kristen talking to some of the older church ladies. "Did you ever think Kristen would be a pastor's wife?"

Kenny whispered back, "I never thought about it because she was married to John."

"I think there's still some resentment from the older women because Wyatt married a divorced lady. I heard Mrs. Thompkins say a Nazarene pastor should never be allowed to marry someone who was divorced."

"Mrs. Thompkins has strong opinions about everything," Kenny said. "And she's not shy about voicing them."

"Kristen was really upset about Liz leaving. They had grown so close." Emmy smiled as Kristen took a seat in the second row of chairs. *You used to always sit in the back because you were afraid to sit up front. You've changed so much over the last couple years.*

"Mom, we got texts from Pastor Wiley," Isabella said.

Emmy looked up from her laptop. "What about?"

"Two teens tested positive for COVID, and he's canceling all teen meetings for the rest of the month."

"Did he say who was positive?"

"He didn't, but I talked to Noemi and she heard from a friend..."

"Who was it?" Emmy asked impatiently.

27

Isabella answered, "Two new kids. Heather and I haven't really talked to them, but I kinda know who they are."

"Maybe you should get tested."

Isabella shook her head. "Not unless we have to. Would you call Rochelle, and ask her what we should do? Maybe Uncle Rory knows."

"I'll call Rory first to see how busy Rochelle is. I heard both hospitals are swamped with new cases."

"Thanks, Mom. Don't forget." Isabella rushed away.

A few minutes later Rochelle Porter called.

"Hi, Rochelle, how are things at Mercy?" Emmy asked.

Rochelle wiped her forehead. "Today has been less chaotic than the last few, but it's still busy. Rory told me about the positive test at church."

"Heather and Isa assured me they didn't have close contact with either teen. Should I be worried about them anyway? Should they get tested?"

"Not unless they start showing symptoms. They aren't feeling ill, are they?" Rochelle, a nurse at SoHam's Mercy Hospital, asked.

"No, they're as healthy as horses. They haven't lost their appetites or anything."

"They should be fine. You might keep them at home for a few days."

Emmy chuckled and replied, "That's easy enough since school is virtual."

"Call me if things change."

"I will. You take care of yourself, Rochelle," Emmy said.

"What time is your board meeting?" Emmy asked Friday evening while browning hamburger.

"Seven," Tony answered. "Are you going to crash the meeting? Why am I on speaker phone?"

"I'm making dinner, so I need both hands. No, I won't be there, but people are allowed to attend and just listen, right?"

"True, but the meetings are usually so boring that no one shows up other than board members."

"I heard Dr. Schofield is going to be there. Do you think he has any pastoral candidates, or is it too early?" She turned the heat down on the stove and began chopping green onions and tomatoes.

Kevin wandered into the kitchen and checked the stove. "Tacos?"

"Yes. Can you grab two cans of refried beans from the pantry, please?"

He found the refried beans and hollered, "What about diced chiles?"

"Two small cans or one large one," she replied over her shoulder, "Does the board have anyone in mind?"

Kevin set them on the counter and listened to the conversation.

"Not really, and no one I've talked to appears to be in a hurry. At least the older board members. I think the younger, or newer, people might be more impatient."

"You guys need to hire the right person to lead the church." She set the knife down.

"Duh!" Tony stared at his phone. "Thanks for the advice, Emmy. We never would have thought of that."

She sighed and replied, "I know you will, but I feel better if I keep after you."

"How long will it take to find the new preacher?" Kevin asked as he snagged one of the cherry tomatoes.

"It might take longer than usual because of the world situation," Tony answered.

"People are blaming everything on the virus." Kevin shook his head while walking away. "They need to get over it."

After Kevin was out of sight, Emmy asked, "Does Wyatt have a chance to be hired as the senior pastor? Tyler was on the staff when he was hired."

"I can't say for sure, but I haven't heard anyone suggest it. I think they are okay with him being an interim pastor, but... I don't know, Em." Tony shrugged as he walked into his family room and sat in his large leather recliner.

"Yeah, I get the same feeling."

"He hasn't been ruled out. He has strengths," Tony said.

29

"Wyatt is really good at explaining the Bible and leading class and small groups, but he's not as engaging as Tyler. Let me know how the meeting goes. I need to get dinner ready before Kevin starves."

Dr. Schofield set his briefcase on the conference table, adjusted his face mask and bumped elbows with Roger Goldman. "It's good to see you, Roger. How has the church fared since Tyler and Liz left?"

"It's only been two Sundays, and Pastor Wyatt has done his best. I'm sure you are aware of his capabilities," Roger said while going over the latest financial report. "He is not prepared to lead a church of this size especially under current circumstances."

Dr. Schofield nodded. "Frankly, I thought he would go with Tyler to Michigan, and I would have to find an experienced interim pastor to lead the church."

"You might still need to look into that," Roger whispered as more board members entered the room.

Dr. Schofield greeted everyone enthusiastically and even remembered a few names.

"It's not easy to recognize everyone while they are wearing a mask," Dylan Michaelis chuckled.

Within a few minutes all board members, who were able, had arrived.

"Is there enough room at this table to maintain social distancing?" Dr. Schofield asked as he counted the people.

"We usually meet in here, but I thought we could use one of the adult classrooms tonight," Carol Wisnewski, the board secretary, offered. "There are four large tables set up in there."

Dr. Schofield picked up his briefcase and followed Carol down the hall. She flipped on the lights.

"This room will work better," Dr. Schofield said.

"I thought so," Carol replied.

"Is this everyone? Should we get started?" Dr. Schofield asked five minutes later.

"Yes," Carol answered. "Three people are working tonight, and Mike Fisker's wife is in the hospital in South Carolina."

Dr. Schofield opened the meeting with a prayer and talked for a few minutes about the steps the church would need to follow to find the right pastor.

"We do not want to rush the process. God knows who the next leader of this church will be, and we need to pray for guidance from the Holy Spirit. Does anyone have questions about this process? I know several of you have been through the replacement of a pastor." He glanced around the room. "Some of you were on the board when Dr. Ausland was here."

The board members discussed the process for a time, and Dr. Schofield answered their questions.

"Let me ask this." He looked around the tables. "What kind of a pastor would you like to see? Tyler was young and inexperienced, but your previous pastors have been older, experienced leaders. Where did you see the next pastor falling into the spectrum?"

When no one spoke up, Bill Griffith said, "I doubt if we could find another rookie pastor like Tyler. He was an exceptionally gifted minister for someone without leadership experience." He saw nods from a number of fellow board members. "To be safe this time, I suggest we look for a senior pastor with ten to twenty years of experience leading a large church."

"Personally, I'd rather see someone older," Martin Stackhouse said. "Being older myself, I feel more comfortable with someone the age of Dr. Behren or Dr. Ausland."

Ryan Deighton smiled and said, "I understand your feelings, but I feel the opposite. Being in my twenties, I would relate better to a younger pastor."

"The next pastor should have a young family," Tanya Paduchik added.

Marley Menconi laughed and said, "It would be nice if he, or she, has strong family connections to Illinois."

Though the board members had differing opinions, they agreed the new pastor would face a challenge returning the church to its pre-COVID status.

"How was the board meeting?" Emmy asked.

Tony chuckled. "How did you know it was over? I just got in my truck to head home."

Emmy shrugged and answered, "Carol texted me. Did you decide on anything?"

"We decided not to start Sunday School for now."

"Okay, but I meant about a new pastor."

"Dr. Schofield cautioned us that the process might take longer than normal..."

"Because of COVID," Emmy interrupted.

"That, and he doesn't want the church to make a hasty decision. He will begin looking for candidates, and he wants the church to follow some steps."

" Dr. Schofield has a different approach than the last district superintendent. He is super hyper, and the previous one was really laid back."

"Dr. Schofield was surprised Wyatt didn't go to Michigan with Tyler."

"Wyatt can't leave!" Emmy shouted into her phone.

"Why not?"

"That would mean Krissy would have to move away, and I won't let that happen."

"You're such a goof, Emmy," Tony chuckled.

Chapter Five

"Mom, why are all the band guys here? Are they going to do another virtual concert soon?" Heather asked when Emmy walked into the kitchen.

Kevin got up from the island and headed down the hallway toward the basement door. "I'm going to listen."

"You get back here, Kevin Michael!" Emmy hollered. "You are in school."

Kevin trudged back to the kitchen. "It's so boring. It's Monday, and I'm already dying of cabin fever. When can we go back to school for real? I am so freaking tired of staring at a computer."

"Soon, I hope," Emmy answered.

"What's going on with Daddy's band?" Isabella asked. "Are they going to record a new tune?"

"Not that I know. They're meeting here to talk about their future."

"Are they going to retire?" Heather asked. "They aren't old enough to get senior citizen discounts." She grinned at Isabella.

"If they disband, will Dad have to get a real job?" Kevin asked. "Does he have any skills beside playing guitar?"

"They aren't going to retire or disband," Emmy answered. "Their contract with Steward Music is ending, and they need to decide if they want to re-sign or whatever."

The members of Fridays At Five gathered in the control room of Kenny's state-of-the-art, basement recording studio and caught up on family news.

"How's Andy doing?" Jeff Rawlings asked.

The bands' longtime, and only, manager was currently spending the winter in Phoenix and had recently undergone surgery on his vocal cords.

"He texted a couple days ago," Kenny replied. "He's frustrated because he's not supposed to talk above a whisper."

Jeremy Lenhart laughed and said, "We all know how much he loves to talk."

Dave Persching looked at Paul Joseph and asked, "How are Tommy and Sabrina? When is she due?"

P.J., who joined the band in 2005, smiled and said, "They are doing great, and she's due at the end of July. I can't wait to be a grandpa and spoil the baby."

Adam Vicini, an original member of The Only Hope Band, joined Fridays At Five in 2012. He laughed, pointed at P.J. and said, "You are like a grandfather to Alex. He sees you and Teresa more than he sees his real grandparents."

"We love to babysit Kinsey and Alex," P.J. said. "I usually make Teresa change his diaper though."

A few minutes later Kenny brought up the subject of touring.

Jeff looked around. "I don't know about you guys, but I have enough projects to keep me busy for the next ten years."

"You didn't have to buy another house to restore," Dave said.

"How many homes have you restored in Timberline Heights?" Jeremy asked.

"This is number six," Jeff answered quickly, but then tapped his chin. "Maybe seven. I can't keep track. The point is if we didn't, or aren't allowed, to tour this year, it would be okay with me. Frances will keep me busy with her honey-do lists."

"You love working on old homes, Jeff," Kenny said.

"True."

"Claudia and I are going to be in Australia for half the year," Dave said. He was engaged to Claudia Hall, a twenty-three-year-old Australian supermodel.

"Do you have a date for the wedding?" Jeff asked. "Or is it going to be a last minute thing in order to keep it private?"

"March 6," Dave answered. "We're going to spend a few months down under. She wants to buy a house in New Zealand."

Kenny slapped his knee. "I guess that settles it. We can't tour until the fall at the earliest."

"If that's the case, let's take the whole year off," Jeremy said.

"Okay with me," Jeff replied.

"What should we do about our touring staff?" P.J. asked. "We can't afford to pay everyone to do nothing."

"I hate to mention this, but I believe we need to lay off everyone except for the staff in the office. Most of the full-timers can collect unemployment if they haven't already found new positions."

The other guys agreed.

"What should we do about our contract with Mr. Kesson?" Kenny asked.

Max Kesson owned the Steward Music Group to which the band had been signed throughout their entire existence.

"A lot of bands are going independent," Adam said.

"I can see the advantages of that," Jeff said.

"We do own our recordings," Kenny said. "We license them to Steward Music now. We could continue to do that with the back catalog and release new material on our own label."

"We should let the lawyers and bean counters know. They might blow a gasket if we go independent," Dave said. He had always been the most business-minded of the guys.

The discussion lasted another thirty minutes, and the guys decided to take a year off, and not renew their contract with Steward Music.

"Who wants to tell Mr. Kesson?" Jeff asked.

"We could make Andy do it," Jeremy said.

Kenny raised a hand. "I'll take care of it. I don't think it will be a surprise. He might be relieved because he can sell the company and retire for good."

"When?" Jeff asked.

"I can see him Wednesday."

"What will you tell him?" Emmy asked as Kenny grabbed his wallet, keys and coat.

Kenny shrugged. "The truth, I guess. It's a band decision and nothing against him."

She straightened his collar and said, "If the independent thing doesn't work out, you could always re-sign with Mr. Kesson, or another label."

Kenny drove to the Steward Music Group building, turned off the car and waited a few seconds before getting out. He took a deep breath, put on his mask and headed inside. He was greeted by a new receptionist and directed to Mr. Kesson's office. The door was open, so Kenny knocked and entered. He saw Max Kesson talking on the phone with his feet on the edge of his desk. Kenny noticed the worn cowboy boots and faded jeans and flannel shirt.

Mr. Kesson ended the call and sat up. "How have you been? You can take off that mask. I hate the idea of wearing mine, so I refuse to go anywhere that requires one."

Kenny approached and shook hands with the man who owned and ran the company that had signed Fridays At Five to a recording contract in 1995.

"How's the family?" Mr. Kesson asked.

"Doing good. The kids are getting older and growing up too fast."

They caught up on family for a couple minutes.

"Have a seat," Mr. Kesson said pointing to one of the chairs in front of his desk. "I assume you're here to talk about the contract, right?"

"I am, and I'm sorry to say the guys want to try our luck as an independent band."

Mr. Kesson waved dismissively. "I don't blame you, and, frankly, I'm glad. The business has changed so much. I'm ready to get out. I've had a few offers for the company, and now's the perfect time to accept one. I'm ready to retire and spend my days in the Caribbean on my boat. I bought a new one." He pointed to a photo on the wall to his right. "I will let the attorneys and accountants know. They can do all the legal stuff." He stood up and offered a hand. "It's been a great ride, hasn't it?"

"That it has," Kenny said. "I can't see us ever signing with another label. The guys are keeping busy with projects outside of music."

"What will you do?"

Kenny told him about the property in Idaho.

"I have been to Mr. Robertson's ranch. If yours is close to his, it will be a great place to get away from it all."

36

"If you get tired of sailing around the islands, you're welcome to come out to Idaho," Kenny said.

"What time are we supposed to meet everyone?" Emmy asked as she got dressed Friday morning. She put on faded jeans and a new sweater.

Kenny finished brushing his teeth and walked out of his bathroom. "We're supposed to be there at nine to sign the contracts."

Emmy plopped onto her back on the bed. "Can you believe we are buying a ranch in Idaho?"

Kenny sat on the bed, patted her knee, smiled and said, "And paying cash."

Emmy sat up. "Can we afford it? $875,000 is a lot of money."

"We have to think of it as an investment, and yes, Em, we can afford it. Even though 2020 sucked for bands, our investments didn't take a hit. We actually made more money than in 2019."

"I still feel kinda guilty buying a place so far away. It's not like we can spend the weekend in Idaho and come back to SoHam during the week."

"You might not think it's a possibility now, but in the future after the kids are grown, we might spend half the year in Idaho."

"Can we take Lassie to Idaho?" Kevin asked with a mouthful of scrambled eggs.

"I suppose," Kenny answered.

"We can't put her in a kennel if she can't go with us," Heather insisted.

"We could ask Uncle Tony to keep her," Isabella suggested.

"We don't have to decide now. It will be summer before we actually go to Idaho," Kenny said.

"What is the name of the town and river?" Kevin asked.

"It's the Big Lost River, and the ranch isn't in town."

"What's the closest town?"

Kenny thought for a moment. "I suppose Ketchum Forks would be the closest town of a decent size."

"How many acres?"

"Fifty or so," Kenny answered. "It's in a valley with mountains on two sides."

"Does the house have electricity and indoor plumbing?" Heather asked.

"It would be so cool if it didn't," Kevin said. "We could live like that family in Alaska. They have to chop firewood every day and hunt for their food. They have to haul water from the river and don't have to take baths every day. They might go for weeks without taking a bath!"

Heather and Isabella stared at their mother.

"The house has all the modern necessities," Emmy said. "You will have your own bedroom and bathroom."

"Can we make Kevin live in a shack?" Heather asked.

"No!"

"Why not?" Kevin asked. "I wouldn't mind. I can learn to be a real mountain man."

"You plainly want to smell like one," Heather said.

"Can I chop firewood instead of going to pretend school?" Kevin asked.

Emmy shook her head. "No. You have to do your schoolwork, and we buy our firewood from a guy who knows how to chop it and age it correctly."

Kenny and Emmy signed the contracts. The money was wired to the seller, and they left the attorney's office as owners of a valuable property in Idaho.

"I feel so bad because Mr. Robertson won't be here to share the excitement," Emmy said. "I hope the family keeps his place."

"Which one?" Kenny asked pulling out of the parking lot.

"The one in Idaho."

"It's hard to say what will happen to his properties. I'm sure it's all in his will."

"I have a feeling the neighborhood will be changing this year," Emmy said staring out the window at the falling snow.

Chapter Six

"Who was on the phone?" Emmy asked when Kenny walked into the den. "I'm having trouble with the outline for the next Claire and Ruby story. I might need your input."

"I don't know anything about writing." He paused a few feet from her and looked at her laptop.

"You have written a thousand songs. You know a little about writing."

"That's different."

"Who were you talking to? You didn't answer me."

"It was Adam."

Emmy spun in her desk chair. "Are the kids okay?"

"I suppose."

"Why did he call? Do I have to drag it out of you?"

"He wanted to know how I would feel if he took a job with Steward Music."

"Why? What did you tell him? He doesn't need money, does he?"

Kenny shook his head. "He's okay financially. He's not exactly rich, but he has a good income from the band. I told him to take the job since we're not doing anything this year."

"What kind of job is it? Is he going to be a session musician or a producer?" Emmy stood up and played air guitar. "I would let him produce a CD for me if I ever record again."

"No. It's an office job. He will be working with accounts or something."

Emmy made a face. "Sounds boring. He's still part of the band, right?"

"Of course. Why wouldn't he be?"

"Just making sure." She paused then added, "What about The Only Hope's new CD? Is it ever going to be released?"

"Yes, but the vinyl is holding everything up. It could have been released months ago, but they wanted the vinyl version to be available at the same time. I told him the manufacturer has it on their schedule, but because it's a low-volume project, it's not a priority."

"It's their decision, but I would release the CD now and the vinyl can wait," Emmy said. "The public can be rather fickle."

"Hey! I have an idea for your book."

Emmy tilted her head and stared at him. "What?"

"Maybe Claire and Ruby could be on one of those TV shows and get signed to a recording contract. They could become huge stars..."

"Thanks, but no thanks," Emmy said sitting at her desk again. "I want to keep the series rooted in reality."

"We need a ride to church," Heather said at dinner. "Tonight is our first in-person meeting since Pastor Wiley shut everything down."

"Isn't it too soon to meet in person?" Emmy asked.

"It's been over two weeks, and no one else has gotten sick."

Isabella added, "We have to keep our masks on the whole time and maintain a distance of six feet, or whatever the rules are. Someone will take our temperature before we're allowed inside the building."

"Can't they take your temperature inside?" Emmy asked. "It's still below freezing. I can't remember the last time we had a cold spell that lasted so long."

"I love it," Kevin said. "We've gotten close to thirty inches of snow already. Have you seen how high the piles are at the end of the street? They're great for sledding, and they won't melt until the middle of summer."

"It's supposed to snow again this weekend," Kenny said as he took a piece of fried chicken. "One forecast called for eight to ten inches, but that's what they said last week."

Kevin took two pieces of chicken. "Yeah! They really blew it. We didn't get more than a sprinkling. Are there more mashed potatoes, Mom?"

"Sorry, but that's it. I ran out. I could always make the packaged potatoes."

"Don't bother," Kevin said. "They aren't as good as homemade."

"I will drop the kids at the church," Kenny said later. "Tony offered to pick them up, but there's not enough room in his truck."

"We need a small bus to transport kids," Emmy said.

"We could lease a tour bus," Kenny said with a chuckle. "No one is using them, and companies are offering great deals."

"Yeah, I bet they're great in the snow and ice," Emmy replied with a smirk.

"How did it go?" Emmy asked when the kids returned.

Isabella sat beside her mother on the couch.

Emmy paused the YouTube video she was watching. "You look upset. What happened?"

"There were less than twenty kids there tonight. Eight of us from Bristol Ridge. Sure, it's cold, and I can see how that might keep some people home, but come on! Bundle up and live your life. Pastor Wiley took the time to prepare a lesson and Brenda made brownies and hot chocolate. Some people infuriate me so much I could strangle them. They complain about not having anything to do, and when there is something, they stay home and make excuses."

"Maybe more kids will be there next week," Emmy said.

Isabella snuggled against her mother. "You're always an optimist, Mom. I hope you're right."

Kevin woke up early Saturday and looked out his windows. "Holy cow! It's like a blizzard. Maybe the weatherman was right for a change." He dressed quickly and raced downstairs. He looked out the family room windows. "There's gotta be eight to ten inches on the deck already. This is great." He put on his boots, coat, gloves and stocking cap and went out the garage service door. "It's blowing so hard I can't see the guesthouse."

The winter storm dumped twelve inches of snow in the northern parts of South Hampshire. Bristol Ridge received fourteen inches in less than ten hours. By the time the rest of the family was eating breakfast, the wind had eased up, but the snow kept falling.

"There's no way we're going anywhere today," Emmy said. "At least we have enough food in the house."

41

Kevin added ketchup to his eggs and hash browns. "I heard the city plows go through earlier, but the wind is blowing the snow right back. Uncle Tony plowed the driveway and over to the guesthouse, but he'll have to do it again when the snow stops."

"What were you doing outside? Isn't it below zero with the windchill?" Isabella asked.

"I was totally bundled up," Kevin answered. "The only thing exposed were my eyeballs." He looked at his mother. "Can your eyeballs get frostbite or freeze?"

"I don't think so, but I wouldn't want to put it to the test."

Kenny's and Emmy's cell phones chirped simultaneously. Emmy checked hers first.

"Church is canceled."

"Yep! Wyatt sent a text to everyone on the list," Kenny said. "I hope someone calls those people without cell phones or computers."

"The seniors have a list of people they call, but I seriously doubt anyone will try to make it to church tomorrow. Most people won't be able to leave their neighborhoods," Emmy said as she added apricot jam to her wheat toast.

"Dad, can we take the snowmobiles out later?" Kevin asked. "I'm old enough, and big enough, to operate Mom's machine by myself now."

"Maybe."

Emmy looked out the window as the wind howled. "If you do, you can't stay out too long. I don't care how well you're bundled up. It's too dangerous to be outside. Don't even think about playing hockey again."

"It wasn't my fault that kid broke his arm," Kevin said.

"Tony never should have allowed the neighborhood kids to use the skating rink. Now he might get sued."

"I'll see if Ben and Uncle Tony are going out," Kevin said. He finished his breakfast and ran upstairs to get his phone. He texted Ben and received an answer immediately. Kevin ran downstairs, raced down the hall and slid into the kitchen. "Ben said they're going snowmobiling when his dad gets done plowing driveways."

Emmy looked at Kenny. "If you go out, check on Bobby and Shay. Make sure they have enough food and stuff. I wouldn't want baby Karissa to starve."

Two hours later Tony and Ben roared up the driveway on their machines. Kenny and Kevin were waiting inside the garage while their machines warmed up.

"Sloane warned me not to stay out more than an hour," Tony said.

"Yeah, Mom said kinda the same thing," Kevin answered. "We have to check the guesthouse to make sure Bobby and Shay are all right."

"I was out a couple days ago, and the trails are in good shape." Tony chuckled and added, "At least they were then. This wind might have knocked over some trees. It's certainly created some mighty tall snowdrifts."

The group of four snowmobiles left with Tony in the lead, the boys in the middle, and Kenny bringing up the rear. They raced to the guesthouse and found Bobby using his snowblower to clear his sidewalks.

"You guys doing okay?" Kenny asked. "Emmy is concerned about the baby."

Bobby waved at the front porch. "We're doing fine. I stocked up on supplies earlier in the week. Karissa loves watching the snow." Bobby pointed to the front yard. "I made a snowman yesterday, but the wind blew it over. Shay brought Karissa out for a few minutes to see it. She jabbered and pointed and had fun."

"Let us know if you need anything."

"Will do," Bobby replied.

The guys took off and Bobby fired up the snowblower again.

Emmy opened the mudroom door leading to the garage and stood at the top of the steps with hands on hips and a scowl on her face.

"Mom! It was great! I jumped the creek," Kevin said.

"You've been out over two hours."

"Really? I lost track of time," Kenny said as he kissed Emmy's cheek. "It wasn't too bad in the woods. The wind is worse by the street. Oh, we talked to Bobby. They're okay. I told him to call if they need anything."

"I'll make some hot chocolate. You guys better drink something hot to warm your innards."

"Did you guys do anything special yesterday?" Emmy asked Kristen Monday evening.

"Not really. Wyatt tried to get the snowblower started, but couldn't."

"Ours works. Kenny could come over and clear your sidewalk," Emmy offered.

"He doesn't need to," Kristen said. "Tony came by a couple hours ago and cleared the driveway again. It's the third time he's plowed since this storm hit."

Emmy looked outside. "I can't believe it's still snowing. Our outdoor thermometer is registering five below. I thought it was too cold to snow."

"Wyatt canceled all the small group meetings until Wednesday. Reed Shafer and his maintenance guys are struggling to keep the parking lots cleared. At least all the furnaces are working, and we haven't had any issues with frozen pipes like a couple years ago."

"I didn't know the church's pipes froze."

"It doesn't happen often," Kristen said.

"I guess I don't think about the stuff you and Wyatt have to take care of."

"It can be rather hectic. Merely getting the mail can be an adventure. Luckily, Bill Griffith lives less than a mile away. He and Reed take turns checking the buildings."

"It's a shame the old house burned down."

"Do you mean the one along Canton Lane?"

"Yes. I remember when Liz and Tyler lived there. We helped them move in."

"That seems like ages ago."

"I know what you mean."

44

"It would be convenient to have one of the staff living there, but it really needed a lot of work. If you ask me, the church is better off without it," Kristen said. "Oh, by the way, the board had a Zoom meeting earlier. They decided to cancel the early service temporarily because of low attendance. It didn't make sense to keep it going for less than fifty people."

"I'm sure the attendance will pick up once the weather gets better," Emmy said. "I know some of the older people won't leave their homes if it snows or gets too cold."

"Wyatt won't let me go anywhere until it warms up. He is concerned about Kayla."

"I don't blame him. It's too cold to take a baby anywhere. She's only five months old, and needs to build up her immune system."

Kristen heard Kayla crying on the baby monitor. "I better let you go, Em. I can hear Kayla. She is probably hungry."

"I'll talk to you later. Let me know if you need anything," Emmy said. She heard Kevin putting away his gear in the mudroom. "Kevin Michael! Come here!"

"What's up, Mom?"

"Were you playing hockey again? I thought I told you not to."

"We weren't playing hockey," he said.

"What were you doing all this time? In the dark, no less."

Kevin stood in front of her. "Okay, we were using the ice, but not for hockey."

"What for then?"

"Have you ever heard of curling?"

"Yes, and I watched it once for five minutes. Boring." Emmy laughed and asked, "Are you telling me you were pushing hockey pucks down the ice like you were playing shuffleboard?"

He shook his head and grinned. "Nope! We were using boulders. They crash better."

Chapter Seven

"Please, Mr. Rigoni, come in and make yourself comfortable," Brady Robertson said as the attorney for his late father arrived at the house.

"Thank you, Brady, and please call me Gordie. Mr. Rigoni was my father."

Brady took Gordie's hat and gloves and set them on the weathered oak cabinet. He hung the coat on the matching coat rack. "Did you have any trouble with the roads? At least the snow has stopped."

"The main streets are clear, but there is still snow and ice on some of the side streets."

"The plows have been going through Bristol Ridge several times a day," Brady said. "My wife refuses to drive in this weather."

"I'm sorry for your loss," Gordie said. "I know you've heard that too many times."

"It is still appreciated. Mona is waiting in the front parlor with Bennett."

"How is she coping?"

Brady sighed and answered, "She has many friends who keep her busy."

Gordie followed Brady into the front parlor, which could have been a set from *Gone With The Wind*.

He approached the couch where Mona and Bennett were sitting.

"Thank you for coming, Gordie," Mona said. "We could have come to the office."

"No reason for you to brave this weather, Mrs. Robertson." He nodded at Bennett. "Again, I'm sorry for your loss."

"Thank you," Mona replied.

"Would you like some tea or coffee?" Brady asked.

"Coffee, but only if it's already made."

Brady grinned and said, "I will tell the maid to bring some."

Mona smiled and laughed quietly.

46

Gordie looked from Brady to Mona and back to Brady. "I'm missing something. You've never had a maid before."

"Emmy has been coming over to help clean the house and make meals. I call her the *maid* to tease her," Brady said about his sister-in-law. "Diane encouraged me to tease her."

Bennett rang the vintage butler's bell, and Brady poked his head into the hallway.

"Are you ready for the coffee?" Emmy hollered from the kitchen.

"Yes, please," Brady replied.

Emmy glided along the polished hardwood floors in thick, gray woolen socks and appeared in the parlor a moment later. Her curly, dark hair was tied back by a red and white checkerboard scarf. She wore faded jeans and an old Fridays At Five sweatshirt. She set the tray on the buffet and looked up at the two large portraits of Bill and Mona.

"Emmy, this is Gordie Rigoni. His father was Bill's attorney for years," Mona said.

"It's good to see you again, Gordie," Emmy said with a grin. "Please forgive my appearance. I've been cleaning the house."

Gordie smiled and noticed the ripped knees in her jeans.

"She insists on doing it," Bennett said. "Her house is cleaner than the operating rooms at St. Bart's Hospital."

Emmy giggled then shook her head. "I used to keep it clean, but I gave up. I have three teenagers now."

Gordie smiled and said, "I understand. I have three boys."

Emmy headed back to the kitchen. After taking time for the coffee and chitchat, Gordie removed a folder from his briefcase.

"There are no surprises in this, Mona. You and Mr. Robertson revised it last summer." He looked at the sons. "For an estate of this size, it would, at times, take years to go through the probate court." He smiled and continued, "Mr. Robertson wisely placed most of his assets in trusts. The actual estate to probate is... well, to be blunt... less than two million dollars." He looked at everyone. "All of his properties were held jointly with Mrs. Robertson and belong to her. Have you given any thought about this house?"

47

Emmy appeared in the doorway and asked. "Would anyone like more coffee?" She put a hand to her mouth. "Sorry. I didn't mean to butt in on private business." She turned to walk away.

"Please stay. You should hear this, Emmy." Mona patted the couch next to her and Emmy sat. "Gordie was asking about the house. I've already told Brady and Bennett. You should know, too."

Emmy bit her lip and put her hands on her knees.

"I've decided to sell the house. It is much too large for one person, and I would like to be closer to my children and grandchildren. I hope you understand."

Emmy grabbed Mona's hand and squeezed it. "I totally understand, but we will miss you. The girls think of you as their grandmother, and Kevin..." Emmy's voice caught.

Mona squeezed Emmy's hand. "Kevin Michael and Bill were very close."

"It might take quite a long time to sell it in this market. There aren't many buyers looking for a home in this price range," Bennett said.

"This is true," Gordie said.

"I want to sell it to a family," Mona said. "I don't want it to become a museum. It needs to be lived in."

"What about the place in Idaho and the ranch in Hawaii?" Emmy asked. "Am I being too nosy?"

"Not at all," Mona answered. "The Idaho property will stay in the family, and the ranch in Hawaii will become Galen's property."

Galen Easton and his wife, Frieda, were the caretakers of Mr. Robertson's thousand acre ranch on the island of Maui. Galen had worked for Mr. Robertson more than forty years in one capacity or other. They met in the army and were lifelong friends. He was with Mr. Robertson at the time of his fatal heart attack.

"That's fitting," Emmy said.

"He wants to start a dude ranch," Brady added. "It's the perfect location."

"Mr. Robertson did specify his collection of cars would be sold at auction with the proceeds to be split between St. Bart's and Mercy Hospital," Gordie said.

"One of the cars belongs to Emmy," Brady said. "Dad was storing it for her, but it is hers."

Gordie read more about the collection. "Ah, yes. The 1958 Packard Hawk is listed separately."

"What should I do with it?" Emmy asked. "It cost a lot to restore."

"You should keep it, Emmy," Brady suggested. "I've never been into old cars like Dad. Keep it and give it to Kevin when he's older."

"Okay, I won't sell it."

"I want to travel as soon as it's feasible," Mona said. "Both of my husbands loved to travel, and I want to see as much of the world as I can while I still have my health."

"You don't mean alone, do you?" Emmy asked.

Mona shook her head. "Rosco and Teresa will accompany me."

Rosco Sandchek headed security for the Robertson family. He and Bill Robertson graduated from Theodore Roosevelt High together, and had been friends since getting into a fight in the second grade.

"Good! I would worry if you were traveling alone," Emmy said. "Rosco is the best at what he does."

After a short discussion about taxes, Gordie stood up.

"If you have any questions, please call. I will file this soon. The press may call, but you can refer them to my office. They are always curious about Mr. Robertson's holdings."

"Thank you, Gordie."

Brady escorted him to the door.

"I don't blame you for wanting to sell this place," Emmy said as she held onto Mona's arm. "I know the perfect person to help."

"I appreciate the offer, but Mr. Carter already has the house listed. Privately. For a decent price. He will make sure the buyers are qualified. I believe he has a couple families in mind."

"I forgot about him. He was the man who helped me and Diane when Mr. Robertson bought the house on Hickory Street for us."

"He's retired, but offered to find a buyer for me as a final favor to Bill."

Emmy got up and grabbed the tray with the coffee cups. "I'll finish cleaning the kitchen before I head home."

"You don't have to work so hard, dear."

"I don't mind. You and Mr. Robertson have done so much for us over the years. This is a way for me to repay your kindness and generosity."

"Here they are, Emmy." Brady handed her the keys to the Hawk the next afternoon. "Are you going to give it a name?"

She grinned and said, "I'm going to call it Fortune, and I promise to take good care of her."

She followed Brady to the building housing the car collection and the place where Mr. Robertson suffered his second, and fatal, heart attack.

"I know it's none of my business, but I kinda hope the new owners tear this building down."

"I can understand your feelings, but the memories will fade. I'm sure the new owners will find a use for it."

Emmy walked up to the car and ran a hand along the chrome which glistened under the lights. "It does look like a car from the future."

"You should get in and start her up," Brady suggested. "Remember it's got a supercharger under the hood."

"I don't plan to drive it like a race car." She got in and cranked down the window.

Brady laughed because he knew her reputation for speeding. He listened as she started the car and let it idle.

"I'm certainly not a mechanic, but it sounds pretty good for such an old car," Emmy shouted.

"I'll open the garage door. Don't get a ticket."

Emmy waited until Brady was out of the way. Then she slipped the transmission into drive and edged the car out of the building. Brady closed the overhead door and stepped outside to watch her drive away. He grinned as she gave it some gas and spun the rear tires on the asphalt.

"Later, Brady," she hollered though he could not hear her.

She waved at the security guard, left Bristol Ridge and turned onto Hough Street. She put thirty miles on the car before returning home. Kenny and the kids were outside when she parked by the garage.

Kevin sprinted to the car. "Mom! This is the new, old car Mr. Robertson restored for you, right?"

Emmy got out, smiled and ran a hand along the chrome. "Yes. What do you think?"

"It looks both old-fashioned and futuristic."

Kenny and the twins joined Emmy and Kevin.

"Can we go for a ride?" Isabella asked.

"Maybe later. Some of the roads are still icy, and I don't want to put too many miles on it," Emmy said with a grin.

"What's so funny?" Heather asked.

"I was thinking about Mr. Souchek."

"Who?" Isabella asked.

Kenny put his hands on Emmy's shoulders. "Should I tell them the story, or do you want to?"

"You can tell them," she whispered.

"What story?" Kevin asked.

Kenny grinned and said, "It involves this car, a birdcage and a dead bird named Fortune."

"If this is going to take long, could we go inside?" Heather asked. "I'm freezing."

They moved to the breakfast nook and Kenny tapped his jaw for a moment. "This is what happened."

The twins sat on the edge of their chairs and Kevin put his elbows on the table.

"'I don't want a dead bird,' your mother screamed," Kenny said with a laugh.

"Wait! What are you talking about?" Kevin asked. "I thought you were going to tell us about the old car."

"I will get there, but this is how it starts," Kenny explained.

"Can you skip to the part about the car?" Kevin asked.

"No, you better tell them the whole story," Emmy suggested.

51

"Okay, I will," Kenny said and then closed his eyes. "It happened like this..."

"Dad!" the kids yelled.

"Don't make it into a drama," Heather said.

"Okay. One day we got a letter from the office of Bushell, Strohmeyer and Plimpton. They were attorneys. I handed the letter to your mother as she walked into the kitchen. She stared at it and asked what could it be about? She thought we might be getting sued or something."

"You probably said something like 'I think the only way to find out is to open it.'"

"His exact words," Emmy nodded.

"She opened the letter and we read it together."

"I hadn't thought about Mr. Souchek for several years," Emmy said.

"Who was he?" Kevin asked.

"He was the old man who lived next door when I was a little girl. He and his wife treated me like a grandchild," Emmy explained. "I barely remember him and his wife."

"Should I continue?" Kenny asked.

"If you insist," Emmy replied.

"He passed away at least five or six years before we received the letter, so I wondered why this attorney would need to see your mother in his office as soon as convenient." Kenny paused then tried to imitate Emmy's voice. "I have no idea, but maybe we should call this number."

The kids groaned.

"Dad, please tell the story without the sound effects," Isabella said. "We understand it's a flashback."

"Okay, I wanted you to know who was talking."

"Get to the car," Kevin said.

"We called the attorney and set up an appointment for the next morning. We drove to downtown SoHam, found the office in the old Palace Theater Building, and were shown into Mike Bushell's office."

"I finally realized why I recognized the name. Annie O'Dell used to work for him," Emmy added.

52

"Mom! Let Dad get this over with," Kevin whined.

"Sorry." She zipped her mouth closed.

"Mr. Bushell handles the legal side of Annie's career now. Anyway, he offered coffee, which we declined, and we talked about Mr. Souchek for a time. He finally mentioned the letter. We were rather curious about it."

"It didn't appear we were getting sued," Emmy said. "All I could think it might be about was the old doll his wife gave me years ago. I told Mr. Bushell I still had it, if I needed to give it back. Mrs. Souchek said it was the only doll she had growing up during the depression."

"Mr. Bushell said it wasn't about a doll."

"I remember now," Emmy said waving her hands. "Mr. Souchek passed away in 2004. Seventeen years ago plus a couple months."

Kevin waved his hands. "Wait a second! This happened before any of us were born?"

"Yes," Emmy answered. "Let your father finish the story."

"Sorry, Dad. I won't interrupt again."

Kenny smiled and resumed the story.

"Mr. Bushell explained how the will directed his estate be divided among any living relatives on his side of the family who could prove kinship. He specified a time limit of five years. That limit had passed, and the estate was probated..."

Emmy listened as Kenny explained all the legalities involved with closing the estate.

"Cut the boring part, Dad," Kevin said with a sigh.

"Fine. So each of the relatives received a check for $1,200, give or take. The judge closed the estate, and Mr. Bushell said only a couple things remained. Mr. Souchek had specifically bestowed two items to be held in safe keeping until such time as required... blah, blah, blah." Kenny looked at the kids. "There was the automobile that had been stored in his garage and a birdcage."

"A birdcage!" the kids shouted together.

"Mr. Bushell asked if we remembered anything about a car, and your mother said she remembered he drove a beat up old Ford. She wondered why he would leave it to her."

Emmy added, "Mr. Bushell showed us a photograph of Mr. Souchek's garage, and said it wasn't about the old Ford."

"That's good," Kevin said.

"He asked if I could see the old tarp under all the junk in the photo."

"Junk?" Kevin asked.

"He was what we would call a hoarder now," Emmy explained. "He used to brag about some fancy old car under it. I snuck into his garage and peeked under the tarp one day. The car was a piece of junk like all the other stuff around it."

Kenny laughed. "I remember Mr. Bushell shook his head and smiled like a circus clown."

"What? It wasn't just a piece of junk?" Kevin asked.

Kenny shook his head. "Mr. Bushell held up a piece of paper and said it was the title to that piece of junk. He explained it was actually a 1958 Packard Hawk with a supercharged V8 engine. I kinda understood it was a rare car, but your mother didn't have a clue."

Emmy shrugged and said, "I asked if it was mine, and wondered if it even ran."

"He nodded, said it ran and offered to have it appraised. We declined, and he asked your mother what she planned to do with it. I think he might have offered to buy it."

"I said no to his offer. I thought if Mr. Souchek wanted me to have it, I would keep it out of respect."

"Mr. Bushell said that left only the birdcage."

"He had songbirds in a cage in the dining room and called each one Fortune," Emmy explained. "When they would die he would have them stuffed, or whatever you call it, and replace them. His wife always made fun of that."

"Anyway, Mr. Bushell paused to add suspense or drama, then he said, and I remember his exact words. He whispered, 'Mr. Souchek left his *Fortune* to you, Emmy.'"

"Is that when Mom screamed 'Get out! I don't want a dead bird'?" Heather asked.

The girls looked at their mother and she nodded.

"I wouldn't want a dead bird, either," Heather said.

"Let Dad finish," Kevin said. "I want to hear about the dead birds."

"Unfortunately, or perhaps fortunately, Mr. Bushell didn't mean one of the birds. He meant the actual birdcage. He stood up, walked to a cabinet and pulled out an ordinary looking birdcage and said 'This is what he left you along with its contents.'"

Emmy giggled and added, "I said the contents better not be those stuffed birds."

"Mr. Bushell explained how Mr. Souchek left detailed instructions about the cage itself. It was built with a false bottom barely large enough to hold a letter passed down from his great-great grandfather."

"Are you saying the birdcage was an antique and worth some money?" Kevin asked.

Kenny shook his head. "No, the cage wasn't worth more than a few dollars. However, Mr. Bushell said he had a copy of a letter contained in the birdcage. He explained the original was now in a safe place to keep it from disintegrating. He waved his hands and said it had been authenticated by experts and that was why it needed to be kept in a secure place. He opened a drawer and pulled it out. The copy, I mean. He slid it across the table to us. We peered closely at the letter and read part of it. I looked up and said it read like some kind of legal document. It was all legalese to me."

"Me, too," Emmy added.

"Mr. Bushell smiled and said the document was simply a reply to another attorney. He mentioned the signature."

Emmy smiled and said, "I took a closer look and said the signature was faded and kinda difficult to make out. All I could read clearly was the letter *A* followed by a scribbled name. Your father realized the implication first."

The kids stared at their father.

"I did realize it first," he said proudly. "I grabbed the copy and took a closer look. I stared at it for a moment then took a deep breath and said 'It says Lincoln, Em. A Lincoln.'"

"You mean like President Abraham Lincoln?" Isabella asked.

Kenny and Emmy smiled as they nodded.

"No way!" Kevin exclaimed.

"Yes, way," Kenny said with a grin.

"Cool!"

"Mr. Bushell smiled and explained the letter was dated February of 1840 which made it one of the oldest, if not the oldest, known signature of President Lincoln." Kenny looked at Emmy and asked, "Do you remember what you said?"

She laughed and answered, "I said 'That must be worth more than a birdcage.'"

"I rolled my eyes, and Mr. Bushell nearly choked."

"Did it really happen that way?" Kevin asked.

Kenny held up a hand. "That's the truth and nothing but the truth."

Emmy shook her head and rolled her eyes.

"Are we going to Sunday School?" Isabella asked several days later. "We have to wear masks if we do."

"Duh!" Kevin exclaimed. "We're supposed to wear masks everywhere. I am so sick of the stupid things. I'd hate to wear them for the rest of my life, and why are you in my room?"

"I followed Mom in here."

"I seriously doubt that's likely, Kevin," Emmy said as she checked his closet for a clean dress shirt. "Wear this and find a clean pair of pants."

"Jeans?" he asked.

"If you insist, but your sisters are wearing dresses."

Kevin made a face at Isabella. "They'll freeze their legs off. I'm going to wear something to keep me warm."

"In case you haven't noticed, we have leggings on."

"We need to leave in thirty minutes," Emmy said as she straightened the collar of Isabella's dress.

Richard Cornejo stood behind the podium as the people found seats. When everyone was seated and the small talk over, he addressed the group. "Thank you for coming to our first class in almost a year. I will pick up where we left off back in March." He saw the confused faces and laughed. "I'm joking."

56

"That's a relief," Robby Collins said with a laugh.

"I have no idea where we were. I do want to talk about the direction of this class. I have a few options, but I am open to suggestions." He looked around the room and mentally tallied a total of fifteen people in a class that, in pre-COVID time, would have averaged close to thirty.

"I want to hear more about eschatology. I've been watching some YouTube videos, and find them fascinating," Jim Rosek said.

Stella Rosek nudged his shoulder. "You told me you thought they were a load of hooey."

Most of the class laughed.

"I did not!" Jim insisted. "I merely stated it was a total reversal of everything I've been taught in my lifetime."

"It does require a shift in the paradigm," Richard said. "I've been studying the Olivet Discourse, and seeing it from a different perspective. We can talk about it later."

Emmy spotted Kristen ahead of her in the hallway after the class and hurried to catch up.

"Which class were you in?" Emmy asked.

"Wyatt's, of course. You must have gone to Richard's class. How was it?"

"Enlightening to say the least. It's so good to be able to attend a class again. I truly believe everyone should attend one."

"I agree, but some people think an hour for church is too long."

"Is Kayla in the nursery?" Emmy asked.

Kristen grinned and said, "Oh, she's around here somewhere. I'm not sure who is taking care of her."

Emmy grabbed Kristen's arm and they stopped walking. "Are you..."

"Of course not. Terry Marjai is watching her. I wanted her to take a look at a rash."

"Where?" Emmy asked.

"A diaper rash. Nothing too serious, I hope."

Emmy waved dismissively. "All babies get a diaper rash at some point. You shouldn't worry."

57

Chapter Eight

"Where are you going?" Maxwell Grandison asked his older brother.

"I need to get out of the house," Mason answered. "I'm going to check out the neighborhood."

"In this weather?"

"Yeah, I have to get out before I go stir-crazy."

"It's below zero out there. It will be dark in an hour."

"No, it's not, and I don't plan to go out without a coat, you idiot."

Conrad and Farrah Grandison had purchased a piece of property in Bristol Ridge the previous winter. They razed the existing home, and replaced it with a contemporary structure of glass and steel hidden from sight of the road. The family moved into their new home after the holidays. Their two sons, Mason and Maxwell, enrolled in Reagan High School. Though younger by a year, and not particularly thought of as handsome by the girls at school, Maxwell was the more outgoing and popular of the brothers. Mason struggled to make friends and spent most of his spare time locked in his room surfing the dark web.

"Suit yourself. Mom and Dad won't be home until Friday night. Don't expect me to search for your frozen body in the woods if you don't come home." Maxwell turned his attention back to his English essay.

Mason put on his winter layers and stuffed his cell phone in a pocket of his fur-lined parka. In another pocket he stuffed his flask now filled with his father's expensive brandy. He glanced at his boots, but left them behind and headed outside in street shoes. He took two steps off the rear deck of the house, slipped on the icy sidewalk and fell into a snowdrift. He swore loudly as he struggled to get up and returned inside.

"Back already?" Maxwell asked.

"No, I slipped on the stupid ice," Mason replied.

"Was that why I heard you swearing?"

"I almost split my skull open. That's why I yelled. I wasn't talking to myself again."

He put on his boots, picked out a heavier pair of gloves and left again. He pulled his stocking cap snugly over his ears, covered that with the hood of his black parka and kept his hands in his pockets. He reached a snowmobile track at the back of their property and paused to choose a direction to walk. He saw deeper snow to the west, so he turned and began trudging to the east. He knew there were other houses in the neighborhood, but none could be seen through the deep woods even in winter.

He made his way up and down hills and tumbled down a steep slope when he tripped over a tree branch. He caught himself in time before crashing into a semi-frozen river. He watched the river for a time while drinking from his flask. He heard the roar of snowmobiles and saw two headlights coming toward him. He ducked behind a tree and waited until he could no longer hear the machines. He kept to the path, but stumbled over a hidden log. He got up, swore and kicked the log.

Eventually, the path turned to the south. He relied on the moon for enough light to keep on the trail. Mason thought he could hear music from somewhere, but couldn't see any lights. He left the track and entered a thick grove of Douglas Fir trees and lost his sense of direction. He pushed his way through the deep snow drifts and eventually found himself at the edge of someone's backyard. He hesitated a moment when he heard the snowmobiles again. He dropped to his knees as the two machines roared through the yard and raced off in the other direction. He could see the rear of the house situated on top of the hill. He shivered for a second.

"Crap! I don't want to backtrack along the trail to get home. It's too far."

He decided to cut across the yard and return home on the street. He had only taken a dozen steps when he saw a light inside the house. He froze for a second before dropping to the ground. When he looked toward the house again, he could see someone talking on a phone and pacing in and out of view in front of the doors leading to the rear deck. He took another sip from his flask and watched for a time. He didn't move until the figure's back was to him.

"It's a girl, but I could see her better if I move closer."

59

He dashed closer and dove to the ground behind a mound of snow. He realized he was hiding behind a snowman and laughed. He peered around Frosty, as he instantly named the snowman, and gazed at the house.

"Holy crap! She's hot!"

He stared for a moment before remembering his cell phone. He removed his glove, took out the phone and began taking pictures. The girl disappeared, and he checked the images.

"I don't know who you are, but you're a fox, and I want to get to know you."

He replaced his phone, put his glove on and, by keeping to the edge of the yard, made his way to the street. He climbed over the snow and tumbled into the road. He got to his feet, guessed his house was in the opposite direction of the security guard's shack and took off running in that direction.

Maxwell heard the rear door open and hollered, "Is that you Mason?"

"Are you expecting someone else?"

"Just wondered. How was your walk? Did you see anything interesting?"

Mason pulled out his phone. "You could say that."

For the next two afternoons Mason trudged through the snow back to the place where he saw the girl. He didn't spot her, but saw three younger boys repairing the snowman. He returned home, locked himself in his room and booted up his computer. Within an hour, he found the information he craved.

"Gotcha!" He pointed at his monitor then slapped his desk. "I know who you are, Dorothy Bertucci, or Dotty, or whatever people call you. You look so cute in your fancy dress and I love your smile. Are those dimples? I bet your eyes are green, but it doesn't matter. I love your hair. We may not know each other yet, but I'll fix that." He stared into space for a moment. "What kind of scam can I use to get inside your house?"

Every idea he came up with had too many flaws.

"It's okay. I can be patient," he whispered as he stared at his favorite photo of her.

60

Chapter Nine

"How did the auction go?" Emmy asked. "Did it raise a lot of money?"

Diane took another sip of tea before answering, "I suppose it would depend on what you consider a lot of money."

"Did it raise over a million dollars? That would be a lot."

"Nowhere close, Em."

"How much?"

"The final total after the auction house took their cut was slightly over $420,000," Diane said.

"That's not too bad, I guess." Emmy flipped on the light in the pantry and did a quick inventory of the canned soups. "How many cars were sold?"

"Sixteen. Brady bought the 1958 Chrysler Imperial because it was Bill's first car."

"I won't ask how much he paid because I don't want to be nosy," Emmy said slowly.

Diane rolled her eyes then laughed. "Don't give me that crap, little sister. I might as well tell you otherwise you'll pester me until I cave."

"You don't have to tell me."

"Fine. I won't tell you," Diane said stifling a laugh.

"Diane!" Emmy exclaimed, stretching out the name.

"I love torturing you, Em. He paid $35,000."

"That's not too much, I suppose. So, the money gets split between the two hospitals, right?" Emmy walked out of the pantry.

"Those were Bill's instructions. He didn't want to play favorites."

"If St. Bart's expands, will they name it after Mr. Robertson?" Emmy turned off the pantry light, but stepped back inside to retrieve her inventory sheet. She stood in the dark.

"You know he would never allow that," Diane said. "One of the stipulations when he donated money was that his name could not be used. He didn't want the attention."

"Yeah, he liked to do things anonymously."

Emmy heard footsteps and Kevin appeared in the doorway.

"Mom, what are you doing on the phone in the pantry with the light off?"

"I was talking to my sister, and I had the light on earlier."

"Whatever. What's for dinner?" he asked.

Emmy moved past him and whispered, "I don't want to cook. We can order out."

"I can't think of a single instance where he donated money and allowed someone to attach his name to the project," Diane said.

"Now that he's gone, maybe we can change that."

Diane shook her head. "Don't even try, Em. You knew him better than that. He wouldn't like it."

"I guess you're right, but I think people should know more about him. They should know how generous he was and stuff."

Diane laughed and said, "Maybe someone could write a book about him."

"That would be a great idea," Emmy said as her eyes sparkled. "Who could we talk into doing it?"

Diane tapped her mouth a few times. "Who do we know who writes books? Who knew Bill well enough to take it on?"

"Hey! Are you suggesting I write it?"

"Duh! You would be the perfect person to do it."

"I write fiction," Emmy reminded Diane.

"You wrote a book about your band. That wasn't fiction."

"No, but..."

"No excuses. If you want there to be a book, you have to write it. I'm sure Mona, Brady and Bennett will give you enough background."

"I'll think about it," Emmy said.

Kevin held up the latest menu from Kerry Lynn's Pizza and Pasta.

Emmy saw the menu and nodded as she walked out of the kitchen and down the hallway to the den. "I'll think about it, but I won't do it unless Mona agrees."

"I'm sure she will, and I might buy a copy."

"Great! I'm almost guaranteed to sell a dozen copies."

"Sloane told me you had a private meeting with Glenn Rosenthal today. Did he finally wise up and fire you?" Emmy teased Tony over the phone Friday night.

"You're such a riot, brat," Tony said without answering her question.

"Well, are you going to tell me why you had to meet with the company's CEO or not?"

After a successful football career with the Chicago Bears, Tony Bertucci had worked for his father and uncle's construction company, Bertucci & Keasling Construction, until it was sold out of the family. He now worked for another SoHam company, Liberty Manufacturing.

"Didn't Sloane tell you?" Tony asked.

"Yeah, but I think she was joking."

"Why?"

Emmy giggled and said, "Because she said Mr. Rosenthal promoted you. Why on earth would he do that? You don't know anything about manufacturing. All you know how to do is sit on the couch and watch football."

Tony waited until she was quiet for several seconds. "Are you finished with the verbal abuse?"

"I suppose. What is your title now?"

"I am the senior vice-president in charge of customer relations."

"What does that mean? What do you have to do? Do you answer the phone when a customer complains?" she asked with a giggle.

"No, brat. Basically, I am responsible for dealing with the major clients..."

"Clients? Do you mean customers?"

"We refer to the major customers as clients. Those contracts can be worth millions of dollars."

"And they put you in charge of buying dinner for these *clients*, huh?"

"Yeah, I have to take them to Darby's for chili dogs and fries," he joked.

"Will you have to travel?"

63

"Occasionally, but not too often."

"Too bad for Sloane."

"Why do you say that?"

She grinned and replied, "Because she likes it when you're gone."

"Tell me again why I bother talking to you."

"Because I'm your favorite person in the world. Other than your family, I mean."

He shook his head. "I'll talk to you later. I have to order a pizza for one of our best customers."

"Peter's here. I'm leaving." Heather grabbed her coat from the mudroom. "Save me a slice of pizza." She scooted out before anyone could respond.

"Where's she going?" Kevin asked as he grabbed another slice of pizza. He picked off the black olives and put them back in the box.

"Peter is taking her to a movie, and don't ask why?" Isabella answered.

"What are they going to see? I'd like to see the new Mark Damon movie."

"I think Heather wants to see *Raya and the Last Dragon*."

"Why? Isn't that a cartoon?"

Isabella rolled her eyes. "It's not a cartoon. It's an animated movie."

Kevin shrugged. "What's the difference? It's probably a stupid movie."

"She probably thinks the movies you like are stupid," Isabella said with a frown. "Peter asked me if I wanted to go."

"Why would he want you along on a date?" Kevin took a bite of pizza and stared at her.

"I don't think he really wanted me along. Aunt Sloane or Uncle Tony probably made him ask."

"Figures."

"Mom told Heather she had to be home by nine o'clock. She tried to talk her into staying home and watching a movie here, but Heather complained."

"We don't have any new movies, and it sucks to watch the old stuff on the streaming service."

"You could convince Mom to order something to watch on cable."

"I've tried, but she says they cost too much, and I should read or do something constructive with my time instead of watching the TV in the nanny suite."

"I thought you'd already be asleep," Emmy said when she climbed into bed shortly after midnight. She scooted close to Kenny and moved his arm around her.

"I tried, but I can't get to sleep."

"Do you need some help?" she asked.

"Not that kind," he replied.

"What's on your mind?" She sat up and looked at him.

"I'm bored. There's nothing for me to do. The band is taking the year off, so there's no need to write songs, practice my guitar or anything. I need something to stimulate my creative juices."

"You could help me write a book about Mr. Robertson," she suggested while rubbing his shoulder.

"I can't write a book. I need to do something with music."

She slipped under the covers and turned on her side. "I'm sure you'll think of something. I'll see you in the morning."

"What time did Heather get home?" He turned off the reading light. "Did she say anything about her evening?"

"She was home before nine if that's what you want to know."

"She needs a curfew. She's only fifteen."

"I agree, but nine o'clock on a Friday night is a bit too strict. The movie didn't end until eight thirty."

He turned the light back on. "Didn't you have a curfew when you were fifteen?"

"Yes, but it wasn't so early, and I could always sneak out after my parents fell asleep."

"At least we live in a two-story house."

"Heather made popcorn when they got home. She, Peter and Isa headed downstairs to watch TV."

"What time did he leave?"

"Ten thirty. Give or take. Why?"

"I'm concerned. I am her father, you know."

"Yes, but you can't lock her in her room until she's forty. It's probably illegal." She kissed his cheek and whispered, "I'm not fifteen anymore..."

"Genna Ademilola said there were only ninety-seven people at church this morning. She heard several people tested positive this past week," Emmy said as she was making lunch.

"Maybe we should consider heading to Idaho until the situation stabilizes," Kenny said.

"I don't want to get stuck in Idaho. What would we do if we fly out there, and the governor decides to close the state? Let's stay home for now."

The church board met via Zoom Monday evening and, after learning eight people with close ties to the church tested positive during the week, voted unanimously to suspend all in-person gatherings for a minimum of two weeks.

"Are we not going to have church at all?" Sloane asked when Tony returned from the basement and told her the result of the meeting.

"Pastor Rebecca is going to have a smaller worship team use the sanctuary to livestream, and Pastor Wyatt will do the message from his office. Tyler's office, I mean. That way only a few people will have to meet at the church. If no one else is positive, the church will open in two weeks."

"So, it will be live and not recorded, huh?"

"Yes, but it will still be available on Facebook and YouTube later."

Chapter Ten

"Adam, I have good news," Kenny said. "The vinyl is ready to ship. *This Is Our Time* will be available for purchase tomorrow."

"That's great," Adam replied, but then chuckled. "Too bad it will die on the racks. We can't tour to support the new project, and we don't have enough followers on social media to sell more than a handful of copies."

"I wish I could do a media blitz for the band, but times have changed."

"It's not your fault, Kenny. Sooner or later, this pandemic will run its course, and bands will get back on the road. I'm afraid in our case it will be too little, too late. The guys have moved on. They have jobs and families to support. We might be able to do a few concerts locally, but our days of full-time touring are over."

"As soon as it's feasible, we can do a re-release party," Kenny said.

"I hope you eventually recover your costs," Adam said. "Bristol Woods Records shouldn't suffer because of the pandemic."

"I'm not concerned with that. I do think your project deserves to be heard."

"We did put our best effort into it."

"There are some amazing songs on the recording," Kenny said.

"Why are you smiling like you just did something naughty?" Emmy asked when Kenny rushed into the den.

"Mr. Kesson was on the phone. Guess what?" Kenny raised his eyebrows up and down imitating Groucho Marx.

Emmy rolled her eyes. "What? Tell me, and stop doing that silly impression. No one remembers that TV show."

"People still remember it and the movies," Kenny said.

"Whatever. What did Mr. Kesson say?"

"I have an opportunity to exercise my creative mind."

"How? Did he show you a new chord on your guitar, and now you want to practice until you get it right?"

Kenny pulled her hair away from her neck and kissed her. "Nope. Better than that."

She waited for a time. "Well, are you going to tell me, or do I have to torture the info out of you?"

"I don't want you to get mad when I tell you."

"What did you do? Tell me."

He straightened up, and Emmy spun her chair around to face him.

"You'll only make it worse if you don't tell me."

"A few months ago Mr. Kesson signed a new band. He told me they're really good, and I watched a video of them performing before the pandemic hit." He ran a hand through his collar-length hair. "They are kind of a cross between a Beatles-like band and someone like Kill The Prophets."

"Who? I've never heard of them."

"You've heard of the Beatles, Em."

"No, you goof. The other band. What was their name?"

"Kill The Prophets. Ask the girls or Kevin. They'll know who they are."

"What kind of a name is that? Are they a punk band?" Emmy spun her chair back to face the desk.

Kenny scratched his jaw. "No, they aren't exactly punk. More like a Louisiana swamp-bayou band except they're from Nebraska."

"That doesn't make any sense."

"Fogerty's music has a swamp vibe to it, and he's from somewhere in California."

"So, what does Mr. Kesson want you to do for this band? You haven't told me their name yet."

"It's Agenda Harmony, and he wants me to produce their debut album."

"That's cool. No one's using your studio now. The timing is perfect. Now go away. I need to work on the outline for Mr. Robertson's book."

"There's kinda this one other little thing I should tell you," Kenny said slowly.

"So tell me," she answered without looking at him.

"It's kinda important."

She waited for him to continue, but he didn't. She turned sideways.

"Spill it."

"The band's from England."

She shrugged. "So what. I don't care if they're from Mars as long as it keeps you from being bored out of your skull and pestering me while I'm trying to work."

"They're from the London area, and Mr. Kesson told them they could use a local studio."

"Fine. They can either use your studio, or one of the Steward Music Group's studios."

"No. London local, I mean," Kenny said then cringed.

She stared at him. "You have to go to London to produce them?"

"Yes. I'm glad you agree."

"I wasn't agreeing. I was asking a question. Why can't they come here? Why should you have to travel halfway across the world?"

"London isn't halfway..."

"It's not SoHam."

"It's only eight hours away by plane."

"Oh, that's better. I thought you'd have to take a submarine to get there."

"Emmy," he said slowly.

"Have you already accepted the job?"

"No, but I told him I'd let him know by tomorrow. I really want to do it."

"And how long do you anticipate you might be in England? I assume this will take longer than a couple days."

"They've booked three months at Abbey Road."

"Three months!" She sprang out of her chair like she'd been ejected from a fighter jet. "You're going to leave us for three months with a worldwide pandemic going on? What if you get the virus and have to stay in London for a year or longer? What will we do?"

"Em, it's only three months at the most."

69

"Fine! Go ahead and desert us. We will survive without you."

By the evening Emmy had cooled off and reluctantly given her approval for Kenny to take the job in London.

"Did you tell Mr. Kesson you were going to London?" Emmy asked as she cleared the dinner table.

Kenny carried the plates to the sink. "I told him you didn't like the idea, but you grudgingly gave me permission to be gone."

"Three months at the most. Not one day longer. How soon are you leaving?"

"The company booked a flight for this Saturday. I get to fly first-class."

"Big deal. You guys charter a plane when you travel."

"Not anymore. If we were on tour now, we'd be traveling in a bus."

"I'm going to let you tell the kids you're leaving," Emmy said as she rinsed the plates and handed them to Kenny to put in the dishwasher. "I won't be the bearer of bad news."

"Em, I kinda told them before I mentioned it to you."

She frowned with hands on her hips. "You did what?"

"Well, I knew they wouldn't mind, but I wasn't sure how you'd react."

"What did they say?"

He closed the dishwasher. "They want to go with me. I told them they couldn't because of school. They said they could go to school anywhere because it's... you know."

"They are not going to England for three months. I'm not staying here by myself."

"You could come with me. We could turn it into a vacation," he suggested.

"No way. Travel in England is probably more restricted than here. I'm only letting you go because I know how bored you get. You have to promise you'll finish the project ASAP."

"I'll try, but I have a feeling this band will take the full three months."

"Do you have your passport and everything?" Emmy asked as Kenny brought the last piece of luggage downstairs.

"In my pocket along with my photo ID, my money and a note from you allowing me to travel."

"Very funny," she said making a face.

"Can we ride to the airport?" Kevin asked. "I want to stop..."

"No! We are not stopping anywhere," Emmy said. "You can say goodbye here."

The girls hugged their father then returned to their cell phones.

"I promise to Skype or whatever the latest technology is at least once a day," Kenny said.

"Once a week will be okay," Heather said.

Kevin waited until his sisters weren't looking before he hugged his father.

"Kevin, you aren't too old to hug your father," Emmy said. "I'll be back in a couple hours."

She drove Kenny to O'Hare and kissed him before letting him out of the BMW X3.

"That's a sample of what you'll be missing. You better not sample anyone else's lips."

"I wouldn't think of it, Em."

"Call me when you arrive. Don't text. I want to hear your voice."

"I will," he promised. Then he kissed her again.

She called Father James on her way home.

"Go back. Why did you take him to the airport? You cut out on me."

"He's going to London for three months."

"Why?"

She explained the reason.

"I am surprised you agreed."

"The only reason I did was because the band isn't doing anything, and he was so bored. At least this will keep him busy, and it's only three months at the most."

"Should I come over after church tomorrow to console you?" he asked.

"Yes, please. I will need a shoulder to cry on."

"Why are we having meat loaf and cheesy potatoes for lunch?" Kevin asked. "How long will it take? I'm starving."

Emmy grabbed a bottle of ketchup. "Thirty minutes. Can you wait, or will you starve to death?"

"I'll eat an apple or something. You didn't tell me why you're making Dad's favorite meal. Did he really not go to England?"

"It's also my brother's favorite meal," Emmy answered as she put the baked beans in the other oven.

"Is Uncle James coming over for lunch?" Isabella asked walking into the kitchen to grab a bottle of water. "Is he home from wherever he's been hiding?"

"We haven't seen him since our birthday," Heather added.

"He's home, and I will let him explain where he's been."

Emmy and Diane's half-brother, Father James Boyanov, had been adopted and raised by his Russian immigrant parents in Topeka, Kansas. He entered the priesthood after college and didn't meet his half-sisters until ten years ago. His existence was a shock to both Diane and Emmy.

Father James arrived moments after Emmy took the food out of the ovens.

"Your timing is impeccable," Emmy said.

"Do I smell my favorites?" He smiled and hugged Emmy as the kids rushed into the kitchen from the family room.

"Hey! Did you hear about Dad going to London?" Kevin asked.

"I heard," Father James answered.

"Where have you been?" Isabella hugged him. "Mom wouldn't tell us."

Father James stared at Emmy. "You could have told them. It's not like I'm a Russian spy."

"You should have told them before you disappeared so quickly," Emmy said. "Lunch is ready."

Heather led her uncle to the breakfast nook. "What have you been doing if you weren't spying?"

"Heather, he can't tell us what he was spying on," Kevin said as he set the baked beans on a hot pad on the island. "He'd have to kill us if we knew."

"You've been watching too many spy movies," Emmy said as she sliced the meatloaf.

"I'll tell you after we start eating," Father James said.

Several minutes later everyone's plate was filled and the kids were ready to listen.

"My father had a stroke, and I've been taking care of him."

"I'm sorry," Isabella said. "Is he doing all right? Will there be lasting problems? There was a girl at school last year whose grandmother had a stroke and she died."

"Isabella! Why did you mention that?" Emmy asked.

"Sorry, but I remember feeling sad."

"He lost use of his arm, and had trouble walking. I felt I should be there while he recuperated."

"Is he doing better now?" Heather asked. "What about your mother? Can she take care of him? She's pretty old."

"I tried to talk them into selling the house and moving, but they wouldn't consider it."

"You could hire someone to be a caretaker," Emmy said.

He shrugged. "I am a poor..."

"Don't give me that crap," Emmy said. "Hire someone and don't worry about the cost."

"You better do what she says, Uncle James," Isabella said. "She can be rather stubborn."

"They won't stand for someone coming to the house."

"Make them see the benefits," Emmy said. "Your mother has worked hard all her life. You need to convince her it's her time to be pampered."

Kevin looked disappointed. "So, you've been in Kansas this whole time, huh? Big deal."

Emmy grinned and said, "You should have told them you were spying on the Russians."

"What did you want to tell us, Mom?" Isabella asked later that evening. "Is it important? Did you talk to Daddy?"

"I did."

"Are you still mad because he left?"

"I'm not mad, but I will miss him."

"Where is he staying?"

"He's renting a flat in St. John's Wood. It's close to the studio."

"I looked it up. Abbey Roads is where the Beatles recorded. It's pretty neat Daddy is there."

"Yes, but I have other news. Your school is going to open for classes. Mr. Robertson... Bennett, I mean... sent an email to all the parents informing us that classes will meet in person, but the parents have the option of continuing with virtual classes." Emmy looked at Isabella with a straight face. "Which do you prefer?"

"Do you even have to ask?" Isabella said with a grin. "I am so tired of virtual school."

Heather and Kevin heard part of the conversation and stood in Isabella's doorway.

"I'm with Isa," Heather said.

"If they get to start real school, can I go back, too?" Kevin asked.

Emmy shook her head. "Sorry Kevin, but the church hasn't opened its school yet. You will have to keep doing pretend school."

Chapter Eleven

"I hate to bother you, Mona, but I'm calling to inform you the will has been filed," Gordie Rigoni said as he entered the elevator. "I'm not sure how it happened, but the press was waiting. I promised to answer their questions before I leave. I hope you don't mind."

"Not at all. If you answer their questions, they will be less inclined to call me," Mona replied.

He chuckled and said, "I'm sure they will want some numbers as to the size of the estate. I won't give specific details, but I will tell them the bulk of the estate was put into trusts."

"Bill wanted to protect the estate as much as possible. I know there will be taxes to pay, but not nearly as much as there could have been."

"I will keep you informed about the progress."

Mona asked, "Will I need to appear in court?"

"I don't anticipate any circumstance requiring your appearance."

"Good. I want to see the grandchildren soon."

Mr. Rigoni met with representatives of the local press and a few reporters from national publications. He explained the precautions Mr. Robertson had taken and asked them to respect the family's privacy. He answered the questions he could without divulging too many details.

Wyatt was sitting at his desk Tuesday morning, working on his next sermon when the phone rang. He checked the caller ID. "Hello, Dr. Schofield, how are you? I heard you sprained an ankle while shoveling snow."

Dr. Schofield chuckled. "I was trying to clear the sidewalk and slipped on the ice. I should have used the snowblower, but it wouldn't start. My ankle is getting better, but I have to wear a boot for another week."

They talked about the weather and church attendance for several minutes.

"Okay, now I will tell you the good news," Dr. Schofield said.

Wyatt could picture the smile on Dr. Schofield's face.

"I have a candidate to present to the church!" Dr. Schofield exclaimed.

"That was quick," Wyatt replied. "Who is it? What can you tell me about him? I'm assuming it's a man."

"It is. His name is Dr. Marius Kohler. He is from New York originally, but has spent the last twenty years serving on the mission field in Kenya. He feels a call to return to the States, and is seeking the opportunity to serve as a senior pastor."

"What else can you tell me about him?" Wyatt asked.

"I will email you all the information I have. I am familiar with the name, but have never met Dr. Kohler."

Wyatt and Dr. Schofield talked for quite some time about Dr. Kohler and the church's situation.

"I will get in touch with the board today," Wyatt said. "Some are working and may not see the email until this evening."

"Please let me know if they would like to interview Dr. Kohler."

"Is he available?" Wyatt asked.

"He is," Dr. Schofield answered. "He is currently in California."

"Can I assume there are other churches hoping to interview him?"

"Yes. I can tell you he will be entertaining several offers."

"I'll get back to you quickly," Wyatt said.

Wyatt emailed the church board with the information and requested a quick reply. All but two of the board members responded within a couple hours. Wyatt sent a second email with the coordinates for a Zoom meeting that evening.

"I would like to thank everyone for your timely responses," Wyatt said as board members *entered* the Zoom meeting. He made sure everyone who had responded was ready for the meeting.

"Has everyone taken the opportunity to read Dr. Kohler's resume? It is quite impressive."

"I was at work all day," Ramon Warlito replied. "But I can read it now."

"Let's take a few minutes so everyone can read the information. Dr. Schofield did tell me we might want to act quickly, but he also reminded me the board should not make a hasty decision."

"From the photograph he looks to be in his fifties," LaShae Mabry said. "His children are adults."

Wyatt checked the biographical information again. "Yes. He and his wife are both fifty-five. Both sons are pastors in Kenya, and they have five grandchildren so far."

"Will we have a chance to listen to one of his messages?" Ryan Deighton asked. "Preferably in English."

"There are links in the email," Wyatt answered. "I listened to two messages this afternoon."

"Does he have an accent? Could you understand him?" Leona Ortiz asked.

Roger Goldman chuckled and said, "Leona, he is probably as easy to understand as you."

"I'm sorry if I sometimes revert to Spanish when I get flustered."

After scrutinizing the biographical information, the board listened to a segment of one of Dr. Kohler's messages.

"What does everyone think?" Wyatt asked.

"He reminds me of Dr. Behren," Dylan Michaelis said.

After a discussion, the board took several minutes to pray about Dr. Kohler.

"Do you want to pursue an interview?" Wyatt looked at each board member. "Should we take a vote?"

Richard Cornejo said, "I think we should proceed."

"Can we interview him in person?" Genna Ademilola asked. "I don't think a Zoom interview would enable us to get to know him well enough to make a decision."

"I agree," Terry Marjai said. "We should interview his wife, too."

The board voted to schedule an interview if it could be done in person.

"I will let Dr. Schofield know, and try to set up an interview as soon as possible," Wyatt said. "In the meantime, we should be praying for guidance."

The board governing the Crest Ridge United Nazarene School met in person and decided to reopen since the other schools in SoHam were opening. An email was sent to all parents explaining the decision and listing the guidelines for their child's safe return. Emmy was not surprised when Kevin jumped at the chance to return to school.

"I am so glad we're having church in person tomorrow," Emmy told Kristen Saturday afternoon. "I hope everyone knows."

Wyatt sent emails to everyone and called those without a computer. He said it felt odd to preach to a camera instead of people."

"He did a good job," Emmy said. "I about busted a gut when he started preaching with his mask on."

"He told me he did it for a laugh, but I think he forgot to take it off."

"It was funny," Emmy said.

"Have you talked to Kenny this week?" Kristen asked.

"Twice. He called Wednesday, but forgot about the time difference. He woke me up in the middle of the night. He's such a goof. He said he's over the jet lag and found a good restaurant close to the hotel."

"Do the kids miss him as much as you?"

Emmy giggled and said, "They miss him, but not like I do."

Kristen sighed. "You will survive without... you know."

"Sure, but that doesn't mean I have to like it." Emmy paused then said, "Can I ask you something, Krissy?"

Kristen laughed. "When did you become shy about asking me something? What is on your mind?"

"Okay. Heather talked to Dotty, and Dotty mentioned hearing Tony and Sloane talking about an interview with a new pastor. Is it true? Is the board going to interview someone already? Is it a secret? Are we not supposed to know?"

"It's not supposed to be a secret, but Wyatt doesn't want everyone to focus on it."

"When?"

"Dr. Schofield set it up for this Friday."

"Do you know who it is? Can you tell me anything about him, or her, or do I have to torture Tony for the info?"

Kristen divulged all the information she knew. Emmy asked a dozen questions before hanging up.

"Were you talking to Emmy?" Wyatt asked.

"Yes, and she knows about the interview," Kristen answered.

"I was not planning to mention it tomorrow, but maybe I should."

"Everyone will hear about it soon enough. You should remind them the selection of a new pastor takes time."

After the worship team left the platform Sunday morning, Wyatt took his place at the podium and removed his mask. "It is so good to see all of you this morning. It has not been easy to preach to a camera." He waited until the congregation stopped laughing. "I want to caution you to keep the safety of our people in mind and urge everyone to wear their mask when you leave. We do not want a recurrence of what happened before. I do want to let you know I have talked to everyone who tested positive, and they are all doing well. No one was hospitalized, or suffered too much. Mrs. Menconi's mother is still in the nursing home, but doing much better. We need to continue to pray for her and the others." He paused and looked at the people scattered around the sanctuary. "Before I get into the message, I want to inform you the board will be interviewing a candidate to replace Tyler this week. I would ask you to pray for the Lord's guidance in this process. I would ask you not to assume the board is moving too fast... "

"Did you know about this, Mom?" Heather asked quietly.

"Yes, but I didn't say anything because it's just an interview."

"I hope they find someone like Pastor Tyler, and not an old guy."

79

"I'm sure the board will not hire someone who doesn't meet your approval," Emmy replied with a grin.

"Who is taking us to school tomorrow?" Kevin asked after the service ended. "I could ride my bike."

"I will talk to Kristen and Sloane, and we will figure out who's taking who," Emmy said. "I can't wait until you are old enough to drive."

Kevin grinned. "I'll remind you of that when I turn sixteen."

"What time is the board meeting?" Emmy jumped down from the barstool when Tony got home after work Friday.

"Seven. Why? Are you planning to crash it, and why are you here?" Tony asked as he loosened his tie and removed his suit coat. "Your house is across the road."

"I came over to talk to Mama. She said her back was hurting. Did you know that?"

Tony looked at Sloane, who nodded. "Of course I knew it."

Emmy poked his side. "You did not. She never complains about anything. I noticed her grimace when she turned, so I asked her. You need to take her to the doctor. Now, what about the meeting? Do you have questions to ask this guy?"

"Pastor Rebecca kinda assigned us things to ask if the interview bogs down." He walked over to his wife and kissed her as Emmy watched. "Do you miss Kenny?"

"Who?" Emmy teased.

"Thought so. Heather told Noemi you've been kinda cranky all week."

"I have not!" Emmy insisted. "I can survive three months without seeing him."

"Yeah, sure."

"You better tell me what happens tonight. I don't want to wait until Sunday to find out the board hired a new pastor."

"It's only the first interview, brat. I'm sure the board isn't going to rush into anything."

"Make sure they don't," Emmy said.

"It's a pleasure to meet you, Dr. Kohler," Wyatt said later that evening. "May I take your coat?"

Dr. Kohler smiled as he removed his heavy coat. "I'm still not used to the cold. I haven't seen this much snow in the last thirty years." He handed the coat to Wyatt, who hung it up on the coatrack in the corner of the office.

Dr. Schofield rushed into the office while talking on his cell phone. He ended the call and smiled. "That was our pastor from the new Korean church in Deercreek Estates. He and his wife welcomed a baby girl into the world an hour ago. Dr. Kohler, have you met Pastor Wyatt?"

"Yes, I have," Dr. Kohler answered while looking at the photos on the wall of previous pastors.

"Can I get you some water, or something else?" Wyatt asked. "How was your flight?"

"Uneventful. Nothing for me, thank you." He pointed to one of the photos. "I know Dr. Ausland. How is he doing? I heard he was suffering from arthritis."

"He did mention it, but also said his doctor prescribed a new medication."

After a few minutes, Dr. Schofield asked, "Where are we going to conduct the interview? We will need one of the larger rooms."

"Yes, and I believe everyone is here already. I will let you take over, Dr. Schofield." Wyatt led the way.

Dr. Kohler quietly surveyed the room full of people as Dr. Schofield enthusiastically greeted everyone.

"If everyone can take a seat, we will begin," Wyatt said a few minutes later.

Dr. Schofield briefly introduced Dr. Kohler and then asked the board members to introduce themselves and explain their role in the church. Tony watched Dr. Kohler while the board members did as asked.

"As you can see, Dr. Kohler, there is quite a diversification among the board," Dr. Schofield said. "They have done an admirable job in keeping the church focused during a challenging situation."

Dr. Schofield disclosed more about Dr. Kohler's background before allowing him to address the group.

An hour later, Dr. Schofield thanked the board for their time.

"You should take time to pray about, and discuss, the next step. I do not want to rush this process, and I will not let the church proceed until the Holy Spirit tells me it is what God desires."

Dr. Schofield, Dr. Kohler and Wyatt left and the board members began talking among themselves.

Roger Goldman glanced at Dylan Michaelis, then said, "I don't think Dr. Kohler is the right man to lead this church. He is certainly qualified, and I don't doubt his intelligence or spirituality."

"I got the sense he was looking at this as an opportunity to take over a large church and kinda coast into retirement," Tanya Paduchik said.

Several of the other board members nodded in agreement.

"I didn't feel the Holy Spirit telling me this was the right person to lead us," Richard Cornejo said. "I'm sure Dr. Kohler would be an excellent senior pastor..."

"Just not for us," Robby Collins said.

Wyatt returned and listened as the board continued their discussion. When the conversations ended, Wyatt sighed and said, "I sense you might not feel as confident in Dr. Kohler as Dr. Schofield does. Is that correct?"

After listening to those who wanted to voice an opinion, Wyatt asked the group, "Should I let Dr. Schofield know he needs to continue his search?"

"Yes," Carol Wisnewski said. "I don't think we need to take a secret vote."

Roger Goldman said, "I think we need to keep searching."

"I will inform Dr. Schofield," Wyatt said. "I respect your decision to keep searching. Maybe I shouldn't say anything, but I totally agree."

Wyatt waited until everyone left before he sent an email to Dr. Schofield.

Dr. Schofield immediately responded to Wyatt's email. He expressed disappointment, but also the firm belief God would provide the right leader for the church. He also added the news that Dr. Kohler decided to accept the position of senior pastor at the Santa Barbara Church of the Nazarene.

"Why are you up so early?" Emmy asked as she slumped onto the island barstool next to Kevin. "It's only seven, and this is Saturday."

"I've been up since six. Do you need some coffee, Mom?"

"Yes, please."

Kevin started the coffee.

"What are you doing?" Emmy looked at the notebook next to Kevin's textbook.

He smiled and replied, "My science teacher gave us homework, and I'm working on it."

She stared at him. "Without complaining?"

He nodded. "It's great to finally have homework like in the old days."

"I hated homework. I did everything I could to finish it at school."

"How could you do that? Even if you had a study hall, it probably wouldn't have been the last class of the day."

Emmy grinned and admitted, "I tried to schedule something easy for my last class, and if I could get away with it, I would work on my homework instead of paying attention to the teacher."

"Thanks for the inspiration, Mom. I'm glad you were a devious kid."

Chapter Twelve

"Kristen, why are you crying?" Emmy put her arms around her best friend after church. "Did something happen?"

Kristen used a tissue to dry her eyes. "There weren't many people in church today, but half of them bombarded Wyatt with questions about the interview. They want to know why the board didn't hire Dr. Kohler, and some of them even accused him of sabotaging the interview."

"He shouldn't listen to those people." Emmy rubbed Kristen's back.

"I heard one of the senior members tell another it was Wyatt's fault the attendance and financial giving are down."

Emmy rolled her eyes. "What is he supposed to do? He can't drag them to church or force them to give. I can't believe how some people can be so heartless."

"I'm almost to the point where I am hoping the board finds a new pastor quickly, and one who brings his own staff."

"You can't mean that!"

Kristen sighed. "No, I guess not, but it has not been easy since Tyler and Liz left."

"I talked to Tony about Dr. Kohler, and he said there were only three or four people who wanted to interview him a second time. I don't care how long it takes the church to find the right person to lead our church. God knows who is supposed to replace Tyler."

"Did you have a chance to say goodbye to Mona?" Diane asked Monday shortly before noon. "Am I on speaker?"

"Yes, I'm making sandwiches for the kids." Emmy grabbed a loaf of wheat bread from the wicker basket. "I saw her this morning. She mentioned a couple buyers were interested in the house. Did you know that?"

"Brady said three families have toured the house."

"In person?" Emmy opened the container of chicken salad. "I didn't know they were allowed to do that anymore."

"A virtual tour," Diane replied.

"Can anybody see the house virtually?"

"No, they have to be qualified first. Mr. Carter and Mr. Rigoni are handling that. Once they are qualified, they receive a code to do the virtual tour."

"I hope Mona can sell the house, but in one way, I hope she stays."

"She insists the house is too big for her and would rather see a family living in it."

"I can understand, but there can't be too many families who can afford it."

"There are a few," Diane said. "Brady just got home. I better let you go."

"Wait a second! Mona told me she and the Sandcheks will be quarantined for ten days before she can visit her family. Is that true?"

Diane shrugged. "I guess so, but I think California has some weird regulations about travel and quarantining. I know they were required to be tested and were all negative. I don't see why they need to self-quarantine. I can't wait for this virus thing to disappear so we can return to normal."

"I don't know if life will ever be normal again," Emmy whispered.

"Do you think this is the right thing to do?" Mona asked Brady on the phone. She was still self-isolating in a rented condominium in Lompoc Grove, California. Her son, daughter and their families lived in this quaint town along the coast. "If I sign the offer, the house will be sold out of the family."

Brady rubbed his jaw, ignoring the two day growth of beard, and quickly read the contract again. "It is a good offer, Mona. I don't think he was supposed to tell us, but Mr. Rigoni did a background check on the family. He didn't find any reason to think they would not be a good fit in the neighborhood."

"I let Rosco see the contract. He's not an attorney, but he knows enough about real estate sales to voice an opinion. He thought I should push for a later closing, but I won't have any trouble being out of the house by the end of the month."

"According to the contract, the buyers are purchasing the house and all the furnishings. Is that what you want?" Brady asked.

"Mr. Rigoni talked to the buyers' attorney and told them which items I would be taking. They have another home in Scottsdale and were looking for a furnished home to buy. I think they might also have a vacation home in Montana."

"Do I need to make arrangements to have whatever furnishings you want put into storage?"

"Rosco and Teresa will handle it. They will be back in SoHam before the closing. Will you miss the house?"

"I won't miss the house, but I will miss Dad and you," Brady answered. "Bennett is even less attached to the house."

"Okay, I'm going to sign the contract, and a courier will pick it up. It will be sent overnight to Mr. Rigoni. He will go over it, and pass it along to Gordon Carter."

"Will you return to SoHam for the closing?" Brady asked.

"Probably not. Mr. Rigoni will do everything in his power to ensure the sale is handled privately. I'm not sure I want to meet the buyers, but I am curious about them."

"That's understandable. I know there are four teenagers in the family, but I don't know the exact ages. The mother is a rather famous defense attorney. I'm sure you would recognize the name if I told you."

Mona shook her head. "Don't tell me, Brady. What about the father?"

"He is the founder and CEO of... maybe I shouldn't tell you the name of the company."

"Would I recognize it?"

Brady chuckled. "Oh yeah! You would definitely recognize the name, and you have probably met the father. Dad spent time with him in Alaska."

Mona waved her hands and shook her head. "No! Don't tell me. Not now. I will probably find out at some point, but I'm not ready yet."

"I'll tell Diane not to tell Emmy the name of the family."

Mona laughed. "Good luck with that."

"Is Grandma coming over today?" Mona's youngest grandchild asked. "She's been quarantined for so many days. I know she must be getting anxious to see us."

Reid Moneywell smiled and ruffled his younger son's red hair. "She will be here in about an hour. Did you clean your room?"

"Mom said I didn't need to."

"Don't you want to let your grandmother see it?"

"Sure, but I want her to see it in its natural state."

"Messy, you mean, huh?"

Skyler Moneywell grinned.

Alexandra Moneywell rolled her eyes and sighed. "Skyler, you need to clean your room. At the very least, pick up your dirty clothes. I walked past it earlier and it smells."

"Not to me," Skyler said.

Kofi Moneywell listened to his younger siblings then shook his head. "Dad, are Aunt Janet and Uncle Ellery picking Grandma up?"

Reid nodded. "Your aunt insisted."

"I hope she doesn't let Uncle Ellery drive."

"Your uncle doesn't drive anymore because of his leg," Reid said. "Though he's probably still a better driver than my sister."

Ninety minutes later a silver minivan pulled into the driveway. Skyler raced outside. Followed closely by Alexandra and Kofi. They reached the side of the Chrysler Pacifica before Mona could open the sliding door. The kids waved and waited for their grandmother.

"Mom, don't make a big deal about Ellery being stuck at the office. He will meet us for dinner," Janet Lujack said.

Mona smiled at her three other grandchildren as the door opened.

"Grandma! I'm so glad you were finally allowed out of quarantine jail," Skyler teased.

Mona hugged all three kids at the same time. "Believe me. It felt like I was in solitary confinement. I'm so happy to see you."

"So are we," Alexandra said.

87

She glanced over her shoulder at Elias and Jessie. "I'm glad to see all of my grandchildren." She waved at Reid and Helena, who were approaching.

Janet turned off the minivan, turned in her seat, frowned at her children and hissed, "Please don't embarrass me with your horrible behavior again. You can be civil to your aunt and uncle and don't instigate an argument."

"We never start a fight," Elias answered.

Elias and Jessie Lujack were a few years older than the Moneywell kids and took advantage of the fact to foment a confrontation whenever the families socialized.

"Then it shouldn't be impossible to act civilized today," Janet said with a hard stare.

The adults gathered in the large country-style kitchen of Reid and Helena's two-story home to talk while the cousins took over the downstairs family room. Elias challenged Kofi to a game of pool. Alexandra tried to start a conversation about school with Jessie, who feigned interest for a time. Skyler resumed playing a game on his iPad.

"Would you like something to drink?" Helena offered Mona and Janet.

"I would like a glass of wine," Janet said. "The kids gave me a headache at lunch.

"Anything for you, Mona?" Helena asked.

Mona waved. "I'm good. Thank you."

Janet drank her glass of wine and then rambled on about her week and the struggles she endured. Mona listened politely to her daughter. She caught Reid's eye and winked to let him know she knew Janet loved to be the center of attention.

"Where are we going for dinner?" Janet asked later. "I need to text Ellery the location. He promised to leave the office by six."

"Mom, do you have a preference?"

"What was the name of the Mexican restaurant we went to last year. Bill bragged about it to Brady and Diane."

"Mony Rosales," Reid answered. "We can eat there without a reservation."

88

"That's okay with me as long as you let Ellery pick up the check," Janet said.

Reid knew which battles to fight and this was not one of them. His sister would try to flaunt her financial and social status at every opportunity.

"If you will excuse me, I need to freshen up," Mona said. She left to use a bathroom and also to text Rosco the location of dinner.

Elias and Jessie complained about the food and slow service after dinner. Mona took a deep breath and thought about the kids back in SoHam. She looked at her daughter and son-in-law hoping one of them would say something to their children.

"I thought my enchiladas were fantastic," Reid said.

"Thanks for buying dinner, Uncle Ellery. You always buy for everyone. Thank you so much," Alexandra said politely. She knew she could twist him around her finger with a bit of flattery. She looked at her aunt and smiled as insincerely as she could.

Mona had spotted Rosco and Teresa at a table in the back when she arrived. Now that dinner was over, she was ready to return to her condo.

Reid knew Rosco and also spotted him. "Mom, you look tired. Are you ready to go home?"

"It's been a long day, and I do feel tired."

"We can give you a ride home," Janet offered. "Or you could stay with us. We have plenty of empty rooms. I pay the maids to keep them clean even though no one stays overnight. That's the price I pay for living in such a large home."

"Thank you, but I don't want to trouble you," Mona said without further explanation.

"Ellery, please get the van. I'm ready to leave."

Ellery did as his wife ordered.

"We are supposed to meet some friends in Santa Maria this weekend, Mom, but we will be back Sunday night. We can get together for lunch Monday," Janet said.

Mona nodded and smiled. She waved to Elias and Jessie and took a deep breath when they left.

"Mom, do you need a ride, or will you be okay?" Reid asked. He glanced over his shoulder toward the Sandcheks.

Mona smiled, leaned closer to Reid and whispered, "You were always the smart one. I will be fine. Please don't tell your sister, but a visit with her is only slightly more pleasant than getting a root canal."

Reid laughed. "Your secret is safe with me. We will be home all weekend if you want to stop by."

"I will call you tomorrow to arrange a time," Mona said. She nodded at Rosco, who rose immediately.

"How was your day?" Teresa asked Mona as Rosco pulled out of the parking lot. "Be honest."

Mona took a deep breath and stared out the rear passenger window. "Do I have to?"

Teresa chuckled. "That bad, huh?"

"Reid and his family are easy to get along with. I don't mind spending time with them." She looked at Rosco. "You've met Janet before, and I know you will never say anything, but a day with her can be like a week listening to that obnoxious politician who does the TV show. I can't think of his name, but you know who I mean."

Rosco nodded.

Mona stared out the window again for a time.

"The food was excellent as always," Teresa said. "Mr. Robertson always knew the best places to eat."

"Not if you ask Elias and Jessie, but then they were born complaining." Mona thought about a way to avoid her daughter and her children for a moment.

"A dollar for your thoughts," Teresa said with a grin.

"Oh, are my thoughts worth that much now?" Mona asked. "I was hoping I didn't make a hasty decision about selling the house. The thought of spending most of my time in California doesn't sound as appealing now for some reason."

"You can travel anywhere you want, Mona. No matter where you are, SoHam will not be more than a flight away," Teresa said.

Chapter Thirteen

"An ambulance just took Mama to St. Bart's," Tony said then held the phone away from his ear.

"What? Why? What did you do, Tony?" Emmy hollered.

"I didn't do anything."

"What happened? Tell me it wasn't a heart attack."

"No, her heart is fine, but she fell in her bedroom and might have broken a hip," he replied.

"How did she fall? Did she trip on something? How can you tell she broke her hip?" Emmy rattled off the questions rapidly as only she could.

"If you give me a chance to explain, I will."

"Go ahead." Emmy took a deep breath. *Dear Lord, please make sure Mama is okay.*

"Okay, it happened about a half hour ago. Sloane was in the kitchen and heard a crash. Then she heard Mama moaning, so she ran back to her rooms and found her on the floor by her dresser. She tried to get up, but couldn't. Sloane told her not to move and ran back to the kitchen and called 9-1-1. Then she hollered for me."

"Where were you when this happened?"

"In the family room watching SportsCenter. I jumped out of my recliner and nearly tripped over the table. I knew something was up because Sloane was talking to someone and giving out health information. She pointed to Mama's rooms, so I ran back there and saw her. She insisted she was all right and wanted me to help her up. I heard Sloane holler to not move her and the ambulance was on its way."

"Okay, I'm going to get dressed and head to St. Bart's."

"You can't," Tony said.

"Why not? Genna told me they're allowing visitors now."

"It's one visitor a day, Emmy."

"Then I'll sneak in like before."

Tony shook his head. "You can't. I'm going later. Sloane is pretty sure she will be admitted and might be there for a week or longer."

"Okay, you can go today, but I will go during the week. Call me when you know anything."

"It might be pretty late."

"I don't care," Emmy shouted.

Emmy checked the time when her phone rang that night.

"Are you still at the hospital? It's almost ten o'clock. How is Mama doing? Is she in a lot of pain? What did the doctor say?"

Tony waited until he was sure Emmy was finished with her questions.

"Are you there?" she asked.

"I'm here."

"Are you going to answer me?"

"I'm finally on my way home. It took some time for them to do the x-rays and stuff, but she is in a room now. They are giving her something for pain, and her doctor saw her. He told me they will insert a pin in a day or two and she'll most likely be in the hospital for a week. It depends on how soon she's able to move around."

"Did she get anything to eat? She was probably in too much pain to think about it."

"I'm not sure. They might not let her eat if they're doing surgery in the morning," he answered.

"Make sure she eats as soon as she can. Did you call Kristen or Pastor Rebecca?"

"I didn't, but Sloane did. She called Marco and talked to him."

"I haven't seen your brother in ages. Is he coming home?"

"Probably not. Besides teaching his classes at Johns Hopkins, he is working on another PH.D."

"Why?"

"It's who he is. He is either teaching, doing research or taking more classes. He's the perfect combination of an absent-minded professor and a professional student."

"He should come home more often. Thanks for calling. I will be praying for her doctor and the nurses who are caring for her. Keep me informed, or else I'll pester you to death."

"I saw your text about Mama Bertucci. How is she doing?" Kenny asked Sunday as he sat on the edge of his hotel room bed.

"Okay, I guess. They're going to insert a pin in her hip tomorrow, so at least the surgery shouldn't be too complicated."

"Did you find out why she fell?"

"No. I'm not sure she remembers how it happened. How was your week? Are you ready to come home? Do you miss me? The bed is lonely without you."

"Geez, Mom," Kevin said making a face. "If you're going to get all mushy, could you not do it at the table. We're trying to eat lunch."

Emmy made a face at Kevin and stood up. The twins looked at each other and giggled.

"I miss everyone, but I really enjoy working with this band. They're so talented."

Emmy walked down the hall and leaned against the wall. "If they're so talented, why do they need you?"

"I'm here for my experience in the studio. I've suggested a few things they didn't think about."

Emmy moved to the stairs and sat on the third one. "Tell me more."

Kenny talked for nearly thirty minutes about the recording sessions.

"Have you taken time to do any sightseeing? You are in one of the most famous cities in the world."

"I went to a blues club and listened to a few sets."

"Who did you see?"

He shrugged. "I don't remember their name. It was a four-piece band, and the lead singer was decent. No original material though."

"You should check out the free museums," Emmy suggested as she got up and moved to the den. "Take a day and get out of the city. Go to the Cotswolds or somewhere."

"Where?"

"Check a map. You could check out the channel coast. Do you remember the BBC show we watched about that weird doctor? The show is filmed in a real town on the coast."

"I vaguely remember the show, but I'd rather stay in the city. There are so many parts of London I've never seen."

"Are you going to check out the pubs?" Emmy plopped onto the couch and put her feet on the back.

"Most of the places we eat dinner are pubs."

"We who?"

"I've been hanging out with the guys in the band, and their wives and girlfriends join us sometimes."

Emmy questioned him about the band members, and he told her what he knew about their background.

"Are their *groupies* cute?"

"Em, they aren't groupies. Three of the guys are married, and the other two are practically engaged."

"So, you aren't interested in the women, huh?" She suppressed a giggle.

"No! Why would you think that?"

"Just making sure you aren't looking for a replacement."

Kenny knew she was rattling his cage, so he answered, "Well, there are a lot of younger women around. You aren't as young as you used to be."

She sat up quickly. "Neither are you."

He laughed. "I'm teasing. I haven't met anyone I'd consider a possible replacement."

"You better not be looking too hard, buster."

"I won't. Anything new with the kids?"

"Heather went to another show with Peter. She said there were only six people in the theater."

"Should we limit the time they spend together? She's only fifteen."

Emmy sighed then rolled her eyes. "You do realize she will be fifteen until next year, right? You don't have to remind me."

"Okay, but they see each other all the time."

"They don't see each other as often as we did. We saw each other every day until you graduated and started college. Even after that, we saw each other more than Heather sees Peter. They talk on the phone, or text, probably every day, but she only saw him in person three times this week."

"That you know of," Kenny said.

"She doesn't sneak out of the house like I did."

"You never had to sneak out to see me, did you?"

"Not to see you. Just Rory," Emmy admitted. "If you try to limit how often they see each other, you might face a rebellion."

"She can't rebel. We are her parents."

"Please don't make it into a big deal."

Emmy turned the conversation to the subject of the church and school.

"It must have been really bad for Kevin to actually want to go to school," Kenny chuckled. "Are you carpooling with anyone?"

"We've tried to work out a schedule, but so far Kristen and Sloane have been taking their kids, and I've been taking ours. We could send them to public school, and they could ride the bus," Emmy said.

"I won't be gone forever, and when I get back, I will do my share of playing school bus."

"I'm counting on it."

"Mama is out of surgery," Tony said. "She's back in her room, and the doctor said everything went well. He wants her to start walking tomorrow."

"That soon?"

"He wants her to take a few steps. She doesn't have to walk down the hall yet."

"Did you take a day off work, Mr. Vice-President?" Emmy asked with a giggle.

"I'm taking most of the week off."

"How will the company survive without you?" she asked sarcastically.

"You are such a comedian. What day would you like to visit? And don't say every day."

"How about Wednesday?"

"Wait!" Tony checked the calendar on the wall by the whiteboard. "That's her birthday. I should see her on her birthday. You can go Thursday."

"Fine. Be that way. Wednesday is Grace's birthday, too. She will be thirteen. Did you remember?"

"Of course," Tony said.

Emmy laughed. "You did not. I always know when you're telling a fib."

"How am I supposed to remember everyone's birthday? I have a hard enough time remembering my own kids' birthdays."

"It's okay. Sloane should be grateful you have a brain left at all. You played a lot of football."

"Yeah, but I always wore a helmet, brat."

"The kids signed a card for Mama, and I put it in the mail. It was a combination *Get Well* and *Happy Birthday* card."

"Where did you find a card like that?" Tony scratched his head.

"I created it on the computer. You should keep up on current technology. Oh, wait. You still use a flip phone."

"Yeah, and my old cell phone is seconds away from shutting down."

"Call me later and tell me how she's feeling."

"Daddy's home," Wyatt announced as he walked into the kitchen.

"This is a surprise. Why are you home?" Kristen asked while feeding Kayla a bottle. "You've been staying at the church all day on Tuesday to write your sermon."

"Aren't you happy to see me?" He kissed his wife and talked to his daughter. "Daddy is so happy to see his pumpkin."

"She doesn't know what a pumpkin is," Kristen said with a smile. "Are you home for the day, or only long enough to fix lunch?"

"I can stay home if I want. I'm the boss, remember?"

"Don't let it go to your head. I was planning to have a sandwich for lunch, but if you want to heat up the leftovers from last night, I will share with you."

"Are you hungry now?"

"Yes, but let me finish with Kayla. She should take a nap."

While Kayla napped, Kristen and Wyatt ate lunch.

96

"Dr. Schofield called this morning," Wyatt said between bites.

"Did he have good news?"

"He has another candidate for the board to consider."

"Can you tell me about this candidate, or is it top secret?"

"It's not classified information. I emailed the board with his resume and links to a couple sermons."

"What do you think? Will they be more likely to accept this one?"

"I have a feeling he will check all the boxes."

Kristen waited until Wyatt finished eating, then asked, "Can you tell me his name, or should I talk to one of the board members?"

He pointed at her and said, "I knew you would ask, so I wrote it down."

"You could have made a copy of his resume. It probably has his bio."

"Right. I have a copy in my briefcase. Which is at the office." He pulled a slip of paper from a pocket and unfolded it. "His name is Grady Howe. He's married with three kids."

"Does his wife have a name? How about the kids?"

"Piper is the wife, and the kids are Asher, Corey and Ashlyn."

"Could you take a stab at their ages, please?"

He checked the paper. "The boys are teenagers. Fifteen and thirteen if my math is correct. The daughter is a lot younger. Her name is Ashlyn and she is five. There are photos on the resume. They look like a happy family."

All the board members responded to Wyatt by the end of the evening. They voted unanimously to schedule an interview as soon as practical. He emailed Dr. Schofield, and after several emails back and forth an interview was scheduled for Friday evening at the church.

"That's settled," Wyatt said slipping into bed with Kristen. "The board will interview Grady and Piper this Friday."

"Will Dr. Schofield be there? Do you need to attend?" Kristen asked after closing her book.

"Yes and yes."

"Did you remember tomorrow is Gracie's birthday?"

"I did, and it's also Mrs. Bertucci's birthday."

"I feel so bad Mama will turn seventy-seven at St. Bart's. Tony told the nurses tomorrow is her birthday, so they promised to do something special for her."

Wyatt moved onto his back and stared at the ceiling. "Gracie will be a teenager in the morning."

"Yes, but I don't think it will change her much. She is still a little girl in many ways."

"Do you think John will call?"

"He called today, but only talked for a few minutes. He did drop a card in the mail. It will take her years to forgive her father for leaving us."

"Was she happy to hear from him?"

"I think so, but she didn't have a lot to say. She considers you her father now."

"That means a lot to me." He moved his arm under Kristen and pulled her close. "Are you going to bake a cake?"

Kristen laughed. "I have never baked a cake anyone would want to eat. I ordered one from Sainsbury's. I will pick it up in the morning. Grace invited her cousins over after school. A card came in the mail from Natalie today. She was so pleased Natalie remembered her birthday."

"I remember when Natalie was born. It's hard to think of her as a teenager already."

"Kayla will be in school before you know it," Kristen teased.

"I don't want to think about that."

"You don't have to sing," Mama said when the staff brought her a small cake with unlit candles.

"We insist. You won't have to blow out the candles, but you can make a wish."

Mama smiled, and tried not to cringe or make a face, while listening to the worst version of "Happy Birthday To You" she could remember.

"You received a dozen cards today," her nurse said while cutting the cake. "And to help you celebrate this afternoon, we are going to get you out of bed and let you walk to the nurses' station. Doesn't that sound like fun?"

Mama checked the ledge holding the cards and two stuffed animals before looking at her nurse. "I know you have to make me walk even though it hurts, but it will be better for me in the long run."

Kristen limited Grace's after-school party to no more than fifteen of her girlfriends and cousins. The highlight of the party was Kristen bringing Kayla Eve to the family room and letting the girls see her.

"How are you feeling today, Mama?" Emmy asked. She removed her jacket and set it and her purse on the counter. She moved to the side of the bed. "I made Tony let me be your visitor for today. Are they treating you all right? Has my brother seen you? He told me he would stop in."

Mama used the remote to raise the back of the bed so she could see Emmy easier. "The nurses and everyone are so nice. They almost make a stay in the hospital a pleasure."

Emmy looked at the window ledge with the cards and two plants. "Did you have a nice birthday party?"

"I did. They brought up a cake, and I made sure they ate all of it. Your brother stopped by, and we talked for a long time. I learned about his father's stroke."

"He will be ninety next year," Emmy said. "He is doing much better now, but he has to use a walker."

Emmy stayed long enough to join Mama and the physical therapist on a walk to the end of the hall and back.

"I will try to sneak back in if you're still here on the weekend." Emmy kissed Mama's forehead and slipped away.

Mama smiled as Emmy left. Then she sighed and pressed the call button. It was time for more pain medication.

Chapter Fourteen

"Dr. Schofield is running a few minutes late because of an accident," Wyatt told the board members. "He picked up the Howes at the airport this afternoon and has spent a few hours with them."

Roger Goldman read Grady Howe's resume again then held up the letter Grady included. "I don't know what the rest of you think, but I am impressed by his letter."

Several other board members commented on the letter and the conversations continued until Dr. Schofield rushed into the room.

"I apologize for being late, but we made it safely. Did Pastor Wyatt tell you we were nearly involved in an accident?" He looked around the room and tried to put names to the faces.

"We are glad you are safe," Wyatt said.

"Okay, in case you may not know them, I want to formally introduce Grady and Piper Howe..."

Thirty minutes later everyone knew where Grady and Piper grew up, how they met, when they became followers of Christ and why they felt the Holy Spirit calling them to Crest Ridge United Nazarene.

Roger Goldman whispered to Dylan Michaelis, "I believe we are talking to our next pastor."

"I think you are right," Dylan responded with a smile.

Carol Wisnewski smiled and nodded in agreement.

"Who let you in the house?" Tony asked.

Emmy smacked his arm. "Sloane texted me that Mama was home, and I waited an hour before coming over."

"That must have taken a great sacrifice. Usually, you would rush right over."

Emmy moved around the kitchen island and looked in the direction of Mama's rooms down a hallway leading to the rear wing of the house. "Is she sleeping?"

Tony shook his head. "She is tired, but she knew you would rush over to pester her."

Sloane shook her head. "Emmy is not a pest. Mama is awake. I checked on her a few minutes ago. She wants to see you."

Emmy stuck out her tongue at Tony and brushed past him. She gave him an elbow to the stomach for calling her a pest and hurried to Mama's bedroom.

"I expected you earlier." Mama held out her arms for a hug.

"I thought I should wait and give the kids a chance to see you first. It wasn't easy to be patient." Emmy adjusted the blanket and sat on the edge of the bed. "I was surprised when Sloane texted you were coming home today. I thought it would be Monday at the earliest."

"My doctor kicked me out because he wanted to leave on vacation. He plays golf in South Carolina."

"How long will you have to do therapy?"

"Six weeks or so," Mama answered.

"Does it hurt when you're in bed?"

Mama shook her head. "No, and the pain isn't too much when I have to get up."

Emmy shook a finger at Mama. "You are such a lousy liar. I can see the pain in your eyes. You shouldn't try to do too much. Now that you're older, it will take longer for everything to heal. Let Tony and Sloane take care of you instead of you taking care of them."

Mama started to protest, but Emmy stopped her with a wave.

"I know it goes against your nature to let someone take care of you, but I insist."

Mama smiled. "You would have made a great nurse, or a doctor."

"Maybe, but I would suffer for my patients."

Emmy kept her visit with Mama short.

"I will see you later. Take it easy this weekend because you will have to start therapy Monday."

Emmy tracked down Tony in the family room.

"Okay, I want all the details about the interview last night." She sat on the couch across from Tony and crossed her arms over her chest. "Talk. Now."

101

Tony muted the TV. "You should come to the board meetings so I don't have to go over them with you."

"I'm not on the board."

"What do you want to know? I assume you've read the resume."

"I have. I know they are both like forty, and I know the sons are teenagers. Their daughter is so cute. Were the kids there last night?"

Tony laughed. "No, we didn't think we needed to interview them."

"Shut up! I didn't mean it like that." Emmy sat Indian-style on the couch and made a face at Tony. "Is the board going to offer them the position? Did you like them?"

"We are considering a second interview, so it's likely we will offer him the position."

"How long has he been at their church in Ohio? I asked Chase Hillman if he knew anything about the Howes, but he only knew the name."

"Isn't Pastor Chase in Toledo?" Tony asked.

"Yeah."

"Toledo is a long way from Waverly Grove. I would be surprised if Chase and Grady knew each other."

"Where is Waverly Grove? Is that the name of the church, or the town?"

"It's somewhere outside of Cincinnati, and it's both the name of the town and the church. Waverly Grove First Nazarene to be exact."

"How long were they there?" Emmy glanced at the basketball highlights on the TV. "Whoa! That was an in-your-face slam dunk."

"Ten years if I remember right. They were at a smaller church in the Akron area after college, then he was the pastor at a church in the Columbus area before Waverly Grove. What else do you need to know, Ms. Nosy?"

"Nothing. I suppose I'll get to know them better if they become our new pastors."

"Maybe I should tell you so you aren't blindsided..."

"What?"

"If he takes the position, it wouldn't surprise me if he brings some of his current staff."

"So, Wyatt may have to resign, huh?"

"It's possible."

"But it's not written in stone yet, right?"

"Not yet, and he hasn't been offered the position."

"But unless they really blow it at a second interview, he's probably going to be our next pastor, right?"

"That's the way it looks."

Emmy bit her lip. "I'm not sure how I feel about that."

"I'll let you know when the second interview is scheduled."

"Why are we doing our grocery shopping on Saturday?" Kristen asked. She picked up three packages of salad, inspected them and discarded one.

""We don't normally shop on Saturday, but I was running out of food and you said this was the only day Wyatt could be home with Kayla." Emmy grabbed a bag of red potatoes and a bag of yellow onions and tossed them in her cart. "Plus, I wanted to talk to you about the new pastor."

Kristen bumped Emmy's cart with hers. "I knew you had an ulterior motive. He is not officially the new pastor yet."

"I know, but it's probably going to happen."

"Wyatt talked to several members of the board, and they think he will be offered the position."

Emmy followed Kristen around the corner to the bread aisle.

"I heard a rumor he might want to bring some of his current staff with him. Do you know anything about that?"

"It often happens with pastors of larger churches."

Emmy grabbed two loaves of bread. "It didn't happen when Tyler was hired."

"That was a unique situation. He was not given a choice in the matter. He didn't have a staff."

"Dr. Behren didn't bring anyone from California that I remember."

"Maybe they didn't want to move to the Midwest." Kristen placed a box of donuts in her cart when Emmy wasn't looking.

"The new pastor better not try to bring someone to replace Wyatt," Emmy said. "Or Pastor Rebecca."

"Once the new pastor is hired by the board, they are allowed to hire people. The board doesn't have a choice. They can set salaries, I think."

An hour later both ladies pushed overflowing carts to the checkout area.

"There's an open one here, Kristen. Only two people in line."

Kristen followed Emmy to register twelve.

"Will Dr. Schofield be there for the second interview?" Emmy asked as she faced Kristen while leaning against her cart.

"Stop it, Em. You are going to bump into the lady ahead of you," Kristen said with a frown. "I am pretty sure he will be present. If the board votes to offer Grady the position, it would be Dr. Schofield who presents the formal offer to him."

"Will the new guy make more money than Tyler? He's older with more experience."

Kristen shrugged and motioned for Emmy to turn around. "I never knew how much Tyler was paid. Wyatt knew but he never told me. The finance team will decide on a salary package for the next pastor."

Emmy waited until Kristen was checked out.

"I saw those donuts," Emmy said with a click of her tongue. "You said you were trying to eat healthier."

"The donuts are a reward for eating healthy during the week."

"Yeah, sure."

They walked out and loaded the groceries into Kristen's Acura RDX. Kristen pulled out of the parking lot, but was caught by a red light two blocks away.

"If I tell you something, you can not repeat it to a soul," Kristen said while they waited for the light to change.

Emmy giggled and said, "It must be something juicy. Tell me."

104

Kristen rolled her eyes. "Grow up, Em. Wyatt talked to Tyler about a position."

Emmy punched the dash. "No way! Tell me he didn't."

"He thinks it is a strong possibility Grady will bring someone from Ohio."

"He needs to get to know Wyatt before he makes a decision."

"I'll be back as soon as I can." Wyatt kissed Kristen and left for the second interview of Grady and Piper Howe. He opened the locked church door, turned off the alarm and noticed all the lights were off. "The maintenance guys must have the night off." He flipped on some lights and headed to the large classroom where the board would conduct the interview.

Thirty minutes later Dr. Schofield opened the meeting with a prayer.

"I am so pleased we are here for a second meeting with Grady and Piper." He looked at the people around the room. "I will turn the meeting over to the board." He turned his head to Carol Wisnewski. "Fire away."

The next hour was spent asking questions by both the board and Grady and Piper.

"I believe we are ready to vote," Carol said to Dr. Schofield.

He stood up. "I will give Grady and Piper a tour of the property while you discuss your options."

After Dr. Schofield and the Howes were out of the room, Roger said, "Do we need to take a secret vote, or can we do this the easy way?"

Carol waved and shook her head. "We need to take a vote. I have slips of paper. We can make this very simple. Write yes if you want to offer the position to Grady. Write no if you do not want to offer him the position. Does everyone understand?" She glanced around the room and saw one of the board members frown. "Okay, I will pass out the *ballots*."

The votes were collected and Carol and Terry Marjai counted them.

105

"Okay, we have a total of eighteen votes. Seventeen are yes, and there is one no vote. I believe we want to offer the position to Grady. Roger, does the finance team have a salary package ready?"

"Yes, and we believe it is a very generous package. It is a bit more than we budgeted, but I am sure God will meet our needs."

"I will text Dr. Schofield with our decision," Carol said.

A few minutes later he returned with Grady and Piper.

"Grady, the board has voted overwhelmingly to offer the position of senior pastor to you and Piper. You are allowed time to pray about this before you give us your answer. Do you have any more questions for the board?"

Grady smiled and shook his head. "We will pray and get back to you as soon as we know this is truly God's plan for the church."

"Would you like to see the salary package now?" Dr. Schofield asked.

"I suppose I should, but I am sure it will be a fair offer."

Roger passed the salary package to Dr. Schofield, who looked at the numbers before handing it to Grady.

Grady clenched his jaw when he saw the numbers. "This is certainly a generous offer."

After the meeting Carol talked to Grady and Piper about their plans for the weekend.

"We planned to stay in the area tonight and possibly tomorrow," Piper replied.

"In that case, the church has an agreement with the nearby Hampton Inn to furnish a room for visiting pastors."

Grady looked at Piper. "We don't have family in the area, so we were planning to stay at a hotel."

"I will call the desk and let them know you are coming."

After receiving an email from Grady Howe Saturday morning, Carol Wisnewski set up a Zoom meeting between Dr. Schofield, Roger Goldman, Grady and Piper Howe, and herself for twelve thirty that afternoon.

"I believe everyone is in the room," Carol said after Grady and Piper joined the meeting.

"Let me pray and we will begin," Dr. Schofield said.

After the prayer, Dr. Schofield let Grady make his announcement.

Grady smiled and said, "Piper and I feel God is telling us to accept the position of senior pastor at Crest Ridge United Nazarene. The board made us feel incredibly welcome."

"That is great news," Dr. Schofield said. "Are you prepared to preach in the morning? That will give the congregation a chance to meet you and Piper."

"I am ready, and we planned to spend another night in Crest Ridge. We called our children and informed them of our decision. They are looking forward to the move."

Dr. Schofield nodded and smiled. "Carol, will you make an announcement in the morning service. Of course, the congregation will have a choice, and the voting needs to be announced for two weeks prior. I have complete confidence the church will decide in favor after the board has overwhelmingly given Grady and Piper their endorsement."

"I hope this isn't getting ahead of everything, but if the congregation votes in favor, I will share the news with my current church. I will remain at Waverly Grove to start their transition period. Four weeks has been the standard in our district after announcing your resignation."

"That would mean you could start on June 20."

"We haven't taken a vacation in the last ten months. Would it be possible to delay our first Sunday to the beginning of July?"

Dr. Schofield nodded and asked, "Carol, Roger, would the church mind if Grady and Piper take a well deserved vacation?"

"I am sure they could take a month if they need," Roger said. He checked his phone. "The first Sunday in July is the Fourth. Perhaps, your first week could be July 11."

"Two weeks will be sufficient, but since the Fourth is a Sunday, we could start the following week. We might visit family and take a few days to pack for the move."

"We need to talk about housing," Dr. Schofield said.

Carol nodded and said, "The church doesn't own a parsonage, but we have provided housing for full-time staff. Tyler and Liz owned a home, and they have agreed to sell it to the church's new pastor should they be interested. The house is about five minutes away."

"We would be interested," Piper said.

"I have one more item we should discuss," Grady said. "Again, I apologize if I'm being presumptuous, but I want to put it out there right away."

"Go ahead," Roger said.

"I have three staff members who have been with me for years. I would like to bring them with us. They are all willing to relocate. I realize this means some current staff members will be inconvenienced."

"The staff resigned when Tyler left," Carol said. "The board rehired them for the transition period with the understanding their future employment would be up to the new senior pastor."

"What positions will be affected?" Roger asked.

"I have an associate pastor, a youth pastor and a worship leader."

Carol looked at Roger's square on her laptop. "That means Wyatt, Daryl and Rebecca will be affected."

"If I remember correctly, two staff members chose not to stay after Tyler left. Am I correct?" Dr. Schofield asked.

"Yes," Carol said. "Wade Dickinson was our childrens' pastor. He took a senior pastor's position in Carmi, Indiana, and Pastor Milhuff decided to retire because of his health."

"We would need to fill those positions," Grady said.

"We have a Hispanic pastor," Roger said.

"Is he, or she, willing to continue?" Grady asked.

"Yes," Carol answered.

"We can discuss the staff after the church votes," Dr. Schofield said.

"I will send an email to the church to let them know Pastor Grady will be here in the morning," Carol said and the meeting was over.

Chapter Fifteen

"Is that the new preacher?" Kevin asked as he followed Emmy into the sanctuary. He pointed to Grady and Piper who were talking to Dr. Schofield.

"It looks like them, but they aren't officially our new pastors. The church has to vote on them."

"I'm an official member. Do I get a vote?" he asked.

"You need to be fifteen before you can vote." Emmy waved to Tony and Sloane, who were on the other side of the sanctuary.

"Heather and Isa can vote," Kevin said.

"Yes."

"Mom! Are you listening to me?"

Emmy turned to him. "I'm sorry. I was looking for Kristen and Wyatt."

Kevin scanned the crowd without trying to be discreet. "I don't see them. They should be here by now."

"Kristen said they might not be here today, but I didn't think she was serious."

"Why?"

"She said they might run over to see Liz and Tyler," Emmy answered shifting her attention to Dr. Schofield and the couple in front.

"Zach said Pastor Wyatt might get fired. Did he screw up? Is that why they aren't here?" Kevin asked.

Emmy jerked her attention back to her son, leaned close and whispered, "Kevin Michael, how can you say that? Pastor Wyatt did not screw up."

He shrugged. "Don't blame me. I'm just sayin' what I heard. Some people think it's Pastor Wyatt's fault there aren't many people coming to church. One of the older ladies said he wasn't very good at preaching. She said he sounded bland and boring."

"You shouldn't believe everything you hear, and those people should not engage in gossip."

"So Pastor Wyatt won't get fired, huh?"

"You can't tell your friends, but it is possible the new pastor might bring his own people to fill out the staff."

109

"That's got to suck for Pastor Wyatt. I don't think he's a terrible preacher. He doesn't talk real long like some of them."

The worship team took their positions on the platform. Emmy grinned and waved hesitantly at Heather and Isabella. She saw Heather roll her eyes and nudge Isabella.

"Mom, don't embarrass them," Kevin whispered.

Pastor Rebecca started playing the piano, and the service started. After the worship team finished, Carol Wisnewski came out from the side of the platform and grabbed one of the handheld wireless mics.

"Some of you may have already heard, but this is the official announcement. The board voted to offer the position of senior pastor to Grady Howe at our meeting Friday. You as the church will have the opportunity to meet Grady and Piper, and in two weeks we will vote on whether to accept them or not." She nodded to Dr. Schofield. "Dr. Schofield is going to introduce them to you."

Carol waited until Dr. Schofield and Grady and Piper were next to her before she handed the microphone to Dr. Schofield. He introduced Grady and Piper and cited his experience as a senior pastor.

"Pastor Grady has consented to preach this morning, and after the service you will have a chance to meet them and ask questions."

"Okay, he was pretty good at preaching," Kevin whispered to his mother after the service. "He was funny and didn't stand in one spot like Pastor Wyatt."

"Does that mean you would vote for him if you were old enough?" Emmy asked.

"Sure. Why not? Plus, he's got a couple boys my age."

"Emmy, you should be so proud of the twins," Rebecca Deighton said after the service. "They practically did the whole service by themselves."

"They are certainly not as nervous as I was when I first joined the worship team."

"I can't imagine you being nervous," Pastor Rebecca said. "How did you like Pastor Grady's message?"

"I enjoyed it," Emmy replied then glanced around and whispered, "How do you feel about him bringing his own staff?"

"I don't mind."

"You might be replaced."

"Yes, but we aren't leaving the church. In fact, there is an opening in the office. Lois Crawford needs one more part-timer."

"Are you interested? That's totally different than leading the worship team."

"Yes, but the hours will be flexible, and the money will be enough for us to get by."

"Do you need to wait until the new pastor starts officially before you can get hired?"

Rebecca shrugged. "Not really. Mrs. Crawford is normally allowed to hire her own staff, and Roger Goldman said he would insist I be hired immediately if I'm let go as worship pastor. "

"If Mr. Goldman wants it done, it usually happens," Emmy said.

Emmy listened as Dr. Schofield announced the *town hall meeting* would start in a few minutes.

"Mom, do we have to stay for this?" Kevin asked.

"No, I suppose not. We will have plenty of time to get to know them."

"Did you guys go to Alexandria Rapids Sunday?" Emmy asked when Kristen called Wednesday morning.

"Yes, we did, and Liz said to say hello. Everyone is healthy and adjusting to their new home. Do you have time for coffee after we take the kids to school?"

"I always have time for you," Emmy answered.

Emmy drove to Kristen's house after dropping the kids at their schools. She walked into the kitchen and saw Kristen feeding Kayla.

"Can I do that?" Emmy reached out for Kayla, who grinned when she saw Emmy.

"How can I refuse."

Emmy took Kayla and sat next to Kristen. "What's on your mind? How are Liz and everyone doing? You didn't answer me."

"Yes, I did. They are all well and feeling right at home."

"Did you make it there in time for church?" Emmy asked while making faces at Kayla.

"We did," Kristen said then looked away.

"Okay, spill it. What's going on?"

"Tyler offered Wyatt the position of senior associate pastor."

"Too bad it's so far away. You can't commute from here to Michigan."

"We won't be commuting, Em."

Emmy stopped looking at Kayla and stared at Kristen.

"It will be basically the same position Wyatt has here. The money will be less, but the cost of living is quite a bit lower."

"You can't leave me, Krissy," Emmy whispered. "We've been best friends forever."

"That will not change, Emmy."

"What if Grady doesn't bring someone to replace Wyatt?"

"Doesn't matter. Tyler needed Wyatt to replace the guy who retired last year. He has been working too many hours on administrative things. Wyatt is so much better than Tyler at taking care of those details."

"Is there anything I can say to change your mind?"

Kristen shook her head and stretched out her arms to hug Emmy.

After crying on Kristen's shoulder for a time, Emmy straightened up. "Are you at least staying until the new guy takes over?"

"Yes. Wyatt told Carol Wisnewski and Mr. Goldman he will be leaving when Grady starts."

"Are we supposed to keep this secret until them?" Emmy asked.

Kristen shook her head. "No, this doesn't need to be a secret."

Emmy sighed and took a deep breath. "I guess you will need to buy a house in Michigan, huh?"

"A house would be better than a tent in Liz and Tyler's backyard," Kristen teased. "Actually, one of the local men offered one of his apartments until we find a house."

"I can't see you living in an apartment. You lived in a dorm at North Park, but you ran home a lot."

"It might not be easy to find a house in Alexandria Rapids, but Liz said she would keep her eyes open."

"Hey, Mom! Guess what I saw," Kevin hollered as he ran into the house. He didn't hear his mother, so he sprinted down the hallway and slid into the family room. "Heather, where's Mom?"

"The last time I saw her she was upstairs doing laundry."

"Thanks." Kevin dashed around the corner and stomped up the stairs. He almost slipped going around the corner but caught his balance by grabbing the railing. He slowed down as he passed the bedrooms. "Mom, where are you?"

"In the laundry room," she answered.

Kevin stood in the doorway. "Guess what I saw while I was mountain biking."

"What? A bear?"

"No! I saw a moving van unloading stuff at Mr. Robertson's house. The new family is moving in."

"Did you see them?"

He shook his head. "All I saw were the guys unloading the truck."

Emmy added a detergent packet to the washer, closed the lid and started it. "We should welcome them to the neighborhood."

"Yeah. I want to meet them. I can take them for a ride on the trails. Should I stake out the house?"

"I don't think that will be necessary. We know they will arrive in the next couple days." Emmy handed Kevin a basket of folded laundry. "Put your clothes away. When was the last time we changed your sheets?"

He shrugged. "It's been a while."

"Strip your bed and bring the sheets and pillowcases in here. I will make your bed later. I should let Kristen and Sloane know about the new neighbors."

113

After texting Kristen and Sloane, a plan came together. They would welcome the new family the next day.

"Kevin, come here," Emmy said later that evening from the den.

"What, Mom? I'm playing a game with Ben."

Emmy got up and walked to the family room. "After school tomorrow will you check to see if the new neighbors have arrived?"

Kevin paused his game and grinned. "Are you asking me to spy on them?"

"Yes. I want to know they are here before we go over there to greet them."

"Should I wear camouflage so I don't get spotted?"

"Don't be silly," she replied. She turned to walk away. "Wear your black coat."

Kevin walked into the kitchen as Emmy was standing in the pantry with hands on hips.

"I'm here to give my report," he said seriously.

"Did you see anyone? Would you like chili or tacos for dinner?" She held a can of refried beans in on hand and chili beans in the other.

"Tacos." He pointed to the refried beans. "Are you ready to hear my report?"

"Yes, sergeant. What did you learn about the opposition? What is their position?"

"Mom, I'm a spy, not a sergeant."

"Sorry. Should I call you 009?"

He put his hands on her shoulders. "I spotted two teenage boys come out of the house and walk to the garage. They apparently knew the code to get inside."

"Did you see anyone else?"

"No, but I did see two cars in the driveway. Are you going to pester them today?"

She ducked under his arms and escaped the pantry. "We are not going to pester them. We want to welcome them to the neighborhood."

"Maybe you should wait until the weekend. You know. Give them a chance to unpack and settle in a bit."

"I suppose they might need some time to get settled."

"How did you get in touch with them?" Emmy asked as Sloane drove up the driveway to the Robertson house.

Sloane laughed and answered, "Simple. I called Brady. He knows the family. He and Diane stopped by the house Wednesday. He told them we would visit soon."

"So, they know we're coming, right?"

"Yes, Emmy, and here we are." Sloane stopped in front of the portico and turned off the Toyota Sienna. She looked over her shoulder at Emmy in the middle row. "Are you going to talk to them, or are you going to be shy?"

"I'll talk."

Kristen laughed. "Once you start talking, you never stop."

Emmy made a face at her friends, grabbed the bowl of taco salad and hopped out. She walked around the minivan and stopped suddenly as the front door opened.

"Are you coming, or are you pretending to be a statue?" Sloane asked. She waved as the parents of the new family stepped out of the house to greet them.

"You go first," Emmy said. She followed Sloane and Kristen up the steps. "Diane didn't tell me she knows the family."

"Greetings! And welcome to Bristol Ridge. I'm Sloane Bertucci. I live in the first house on the right after the security gate."

"I am Jansen Knechtel, and this is my wife Evina Ortega." He shook hands with Sloane and Kristen.

"I am Kristen Pearson. We live next door to Sloane and Tony."

Evina laughed and looked in the direction of the other houses. "Next door takes on a new meaning in Bristol Ridge. One cannot see the other houses, and I doubt it changes much in winter. I grew up in the city. I could hear my neighbors sneeze." She smiled and then waved at Sloane and Kristen.

Then all four of them looked at Emmy.

115

Jansen was the first to sense her shyness, so he smiled and said, "You must be Diane's sister, Emmy. She told us you make the best taco salad in the country."

"Are you going to say something, Em?" Sloane asked.

Emmy stepped forward and handed the large yellow Tupperware bowl to Evina. "I hope you like taco salad. I didn't make this batch as spicy as I would for my kids."

Evina took the bowl. "I am sure it will be fantastic. Let's go inside, and I will make coffee."

"If you excuse me, I need to make a couple calls," Jansen said. He headed to the den and the ladies followed Evina into the kitchen.

Emmy took a seat at the island but then she stood quickly. "Sorry. I shouldn't make myself at home."

"Please. Make yourself at home. I know you and the late Mr. Robertson were close. Would everyone like coffee?"

Several minutes later they sat at the island drinking coffee and snacking on pastries.

"I suppose you are curious about who we are," Evina said. "I will go first then I want to hear about your families."

"We know you are one of the best defense attorneys in the country," Sloane said. "And your husband owns the Knechtel-Parkhurst Group. I now know they are a large real estate company, but I had never heard of it until Tony clued me in."

"What is the company known for?" Emmy asked. "They don't sell houses, do they?"

Evina waved and Emmy noticed she had a ring on each finger. "They buy and sell skyscrapers all over the world."

"How many kids do you have?" Emmy asked.

"Four. Three boys and one girl. Colten, Gage, Jalen and Hadley." Evina gave them a brief bio of her children. Emmy was surprised the kids were finished with their school year already.

"Hadley is the same age as my daughter, Grace," Kristen said. "Where will they go to school?"

"Colten will be attending Stanford in the fall, and the other three will attend the Barclay Academy. I understand Bennett Robertson is the headmaster."

"He is, and they will be your neighbors if Marissa ever stops making changes to the monstrosity next door," Emmy said.

Evina chuckled. "Your sister told me everything about the building process. Is it true she fired the first three contractors?"

"I heard they quit because they couldn't deal with Marissa," Emmy said. "She insists on a bigger and fancier house than Mr. Robertson's." She put a hand to her mouth. "Sorry. It will take me a while to stop thinking of this as their house."

"That's quite all right. It will take us time to get used to it."

"I heard you have three other homes," Sloane said.

"We own property in Sedona, a ranch in Montana and a condo on St. Kitts in addition to this one," Evina said. "This will be our primary home, but I travel often."

"Several neighbors live here part-time," Sloane said.

"Hadley! Don't be shy. Come and meet our neighbors," Evina said when Hadley popped her head around the corner of the kitchen.

Hadley walked around the island and stood next to her mother.

Evina put an arm around Hadley's waist. "Kristen has a daughter your age, and Emmy has a son whose birthday is only a few days earlier than yours."

Hadley smiled but didn't speak.

"I have six kids all together, and two of the boys are close to your age," Sloane said.

"Hadley plays the violin. She wants to make it a career," Evina looked at Emmy. "Your husband is a musician, correct?"

Emmy nodded. "Yes. He plays guitar in a local rock band."

Sloane and Kristen laughed.

"What?" Emmy asked.

"Em, you make it sound like he plays in a bar band for tips," Kristen said.

"He is currently in London producing a new band," Sloane said. She grinned and added, "Emmy misses him a lot."

Emmy made a face at Sloane.

"Jansen and I often spend several weeks in different parts of the globe. I know how you feel."

117

"I need to practice," Hadley said. "It was a pleasure to meet you." She hurried away.

"Where are you from originally?" Emmy asked.

"I was born in New York City, but my parents were from Puerto Rico. I went to Columbia for my bachelor degree and law school. I started my career with a mega firm, but left after three years and opened my own practice. I earned a reputation along the way and here I am."

"How did you meet Jansen?" Sloane asked.

"In court," Evina said with a grin.

"Were you his lawyer?" Emmy asked.

"No, I was defending his brother."

"Oh, I just realized you have different last names," Emmy said.

"I used my maiden name professionally, and decided not to change it when we married. I can assure you we are legally married." Evina's laugh came from deep inside and her eyes sparkled.

"Emmy can be quite curious at times," Sloane said.

"Is Mr. Knechtel from New York?" Emmy asked

"Jansen's family is from Boston." Evina used her best Boston accent. "They are old money, and my family is new money and not a lot of it compared to his. Old and new money don't mix well in Boston society. His family threatened to disown him when he married me."

"Has that changed?" Kristen asked.

"Fame has a way of erasing prejudices."

Chapter Sixteen

"How did you vote?" Kevin asked his sisters.

"I'm not telling you," Heather said. "It's none of your business."

"I voted for him," Isabella said. "I talked to Asher and Corey before church. They seem like good guys."

"Oooh! Are you interested in one of them?" Kevin asked.

"Grow up, Kevin. Are you interested in Hadley?" Isabella asked.

"No! She's weird. She plays her violin ten hours a day."

"Hush!" Emmy said. "Listen to Wyatt."

After Wyatt finished, Carol Wisnewski walked up the steps to the platform and grabbed one of the wireless mics to address the congregation. "The board didn't want you to wonder, or wait to get the results in an email, so here are the results of the vote." She looked out at the people gathered in the sanctuary. "I'm glad we had a decent number of voting members here today. This was an important decision for the church."

"Amen!" one of the older members said.

"Okay, there were 112 ballots cast with 105 yes votes and 7 no votes. I will pass along the results to Dr. Schofield, and he can inform Pastor Grady." She chuckled and said, "I am relatively sure Pastor Grady will accept the position of senior pastor. The plan is for July 11 to be their first Sunday."

Emmy smiled and high-fived Kevin. "I knew the church would like Grady and Piper. Now if there was a way we could convince Kristen and Wyatt not to move to Michigan."

"But I thought he already took a position at Pastor Tyler's church," Kevin said.

"Yeah, he did."

"Emmy, could Zach and Gracie stay with you while I go to Michigan with Wyatt?" Kristen asked Tuesday morning.

"Sure. What about Kayla?" Emmy asked.

"She is going with us, but I don't want Zach and Grace to miss school."

"When are you going, and how long will you be gone?"

Kristen checked the calendar on the fridge. "We are leaving in the morning after Wyatt takes the kids to school, and we plan to stay until Friday. Possibly Saturday, but we will be back by Saturday evening at the latest."

"The kids are always welcome to stay here. Are you going to look for a house?"

"Yes. Liz talked to a lady from the church who is a real estate agent. She has several listings to show us."

"Don't you need to sell your house before you buy another one?" Emmy asked. "You still have a mortgage."

"As long as we stay within a certain range, we can afford to buy before we sell this one."

"You could always use the money from the sale of Bertucci & Keasling."

"True, and we will use some of it if needed. But I think we can find a place in Alexandria Rapids within our budget."

"Liz and Tyler found one, but there might not be anything else on the market right now. You might have to stay here."

"Nice try, Em, but Wyatt is not going to commute to Michigan."

"Emmy will pick up the kids after school," Kristen said.

"I assumed that would be the case," Wyatt replied.

"I hope they all get along."

"You don't need to worry. They will have fun together."

"I hope Kayla sleeps most of the way." Kristen took a look around the kitchen. "Okay, I am ready."

Wyatt made sure the oven was off.

They arrived at Tyler and Liz's home in Alexandria Rapids four hours later.

"I forgot about the time change," Kristen admitted.

"It's good to see you," Liz said. "Tyler is at the church. He will be home for dinner, and the older kids are at school. David is with my parents in Wisconsin. It's his first trip without us."

While Wyatt took the suitcases upstairs, Liz and Kristen sat in the living room.

120

Liz held Kayla on her lap. "This little girl is so much bigger than the last time I saw her. Do you want to know about Mrs. Marras? We used her when we bought this house."

"What can you tell me about her?" Kristen asked.

"Her husband passed away several years ago from complications of Alzheimer's. She has been selling real estate in the area for over thirty years and will know about every available property."

Wyatt and Kristen visited with Liz until the real estate agent arrived.

"Thank you for taking the time to show us around, Mrs. Marras. We realize there aren't many houses for sale in town."

"I have selected five properties that fit, more or less, your needs."

She used her laptop to show Wyatt and Kristen the properties.

"That one looks interesting," Kristen said.

"It needs some love and care on the inside," Lillian said.

They chose four listings to see. Liz offered to watch Kayla, but Kristen hesitated.

Liz finally said, "She will be fine. I do have four kids of my own, Kristen. Phoebe will help me when she gets home. Natty and Grayson won't be home until five. They have quizzing at the church today."

"I will drive," Lillian offered.

After seeing three properties, Wyatt and Kristen realized they might have to compromise more than they thought if they wanted to find a home in their price range.

"This final property only came on the market this morning, and it won't last long," Lillian said.

She smiled as she headed to the older part of Alexandria Rapids. Wyatt realized where they were and grinned. Lillian parked in the street and they stared at the front of the house.

"It looks pretty good," Kristen said. "I like the mature trees."

"It's such a new listing there isn't a sign in the yard yet," Lillian said.

121

Wyatt tapped Kristen's shoulder and pointed down the block. "That's Tyler and Liz's house."

"Get out! For real?" Kristen shouted.

"You didn't know, huh?"

"I had no idea. I would have gotten lost if I was driving."

Kristen became more excited about the house with every room she entered.

"What do you think?" Lillian asked as they returned to her car.

"It feels like home," Kristen said.

"Maybe we should take another look in the morning before we make a decision," Wyatt said. "I like it, but I want to see it again."

"I will schedule it right away," Lillian said.

Lillian dropped them at the Hammond's and promised to return in the morning.

"Did you find anything you liked?" Liz asked.

Kristen smiled and let Wyatt tell Liz the good news.

"I've never been inside the house, but one of the neighbors said it was immaculate," Liz said. "I don't want to influence your decision, but..."

"It would be great to live so close to each other," Kristen said as she hugged Liz.

Phoebe walked into the living room, smiled and said, "I sang to Kayla and read her stories. She grinned and jabbered at me. It's been so long since I was a baby." Phoebe threw her hands in the air. "I feel like I'm ninety-eight years old now."

After seeing the house for the second time, Lillian took Wyatt and Kristen to her office.

"Do you still like the house? Does it feel like home?" Wyatt asked Kristen.

"Even more than yesterday. I don't usually make important decisions so quickly, but I think we should make an offer."

"So do I."

The contract offer was filled out and faxed to the listing agent.

"The sellers have some time to decide, and they might want to wait for other offers. Your offer is more than the asking price and very enticing since you can pay cash."

Kristen looked at Wyatt. "I didn't want to take so much money out of our investments, but I really don't want to lose this place. It is smaller and older than the Bristol Ridge house, but I would love to live in that neighborhood."

By eight o'clock that night, Wyatt and Kristen learned the sellers accepted their offer.

"I promised Emmy I would call her if we found anything," Kristen said.

Wyatt laughed and said, "You miss Zach and Gracie and this is your excuse to call and talk to them. I know you better than you realize."

"It's an hour earlier in SoHam, so they should still be awake."

"Call her," Liz said. "I talked to her a few days ago. I know your move will disappoint her, but she will be happy you found a place."

Kristen called Grace's cell phone and talked to the kids first.

"Mom wants to talk to you now, Aunt Emmy," Grace said handing Emmy the phone. "She said Phoebe and Kayla are having fun."

"Phoebe is the perfect big sister," Emmy said then walked into the den and closed the door. "Tell me you didn't find a house already."

"That would be a lie," Kristen said.

Emmy plopped onto her recliner. "Okay, tell me the bad news."

"I was hoping you would think of it as good news, Em."

"Oh, I do. I'm just having a little pity party. Tell me about the house."

Kristen described the house and the neighborhood in great detail.

"How many house are there between you and Liz?" Emmy asked.

123

Kristen paused to mentally picture the street. "Four. We are on the same side of the street."

"How old is the house?"

"It was built in the fifties, but remodeled about ten years ago. Tyler came with us this morning, and he brought a man from church who is a contractor. Building contractor. He took a look at the furnace and everything. He said the wiring was updated and the roof is pretty new. He said it was a solid house and would be here long after we are gone."

"How many bedrooms did you say?"

"Four, but they are smaller than the Bristol Ridge house. I don't mind. I can easily live in a smaller house."

"Not as much to clean, huh?"

Kristen laughed, "I can clean this one myself."

"How much?"

Kristen told her the price.

"That sounds like a good deal. How are you going to pay for it? Are you going to look for a job?"

"Wyatt didn't want to take money out of our investment fund, but I convinced him otherwise."

"Are you going to pay cash for it!?" Emmy shouted.

"Yes, but I will put the money back when our house sells."

"I'm so happy for you. I hate the fact you are moving away, but I thank God for providing a house so close to Liz and Tyler. Now I can visit both of you when I come to Michigan."

"Phoebe has offered to babysit Kayla when she is older. I think she forgot I already have two babysitters. Grace and Zach."

"I miss Phoebe so much," Emmy said. "Since you already bought a house, are you coming home sooner?"

"Why? Have Zach and Grace been fighting?"

"No way. They are angels compared to Tony's kids. The younger boys, I mean. I don't mind keeping Zach and Grace. They get along so well with my kids."

"The original plan was to come home Saturday morning. Wyatt needs time to review his message."

"That's fine. I don't mind if you stay a little longer."

The entire Howe family traveled to SoHam Friday in order to take a look at Tyler and Liz's house. Roger Goldman met them and opened the house.

"Take as much time as you need. I'll be at the church for an hour. After that you can reach me on my cell phone."

"Thanks, Roger," Grady said. "We will lock up when we leave."

They stood in the entryway for a moment.

"It's more formal than I expected," Piper said standing in the entrance to the living room.

"There's a dining room over here," Asher said.

Grady rubbed the hardwood banister. "The stairs are wider than normal. It makes it easier to get furniture upstairs."

An hour later the family gathered around the kitchen island.

"What do you think?" Grady asked.

"I like the backyard," Asher said. "All it needs is a pool. It's got a hot tub and that screened-in room."

"I want the pink bedroom," Ashlyn said.

"You can have it," Corey said. "It's such a girly room."

"I like the large laundry room," Piper said. "The kitchen is open to the dining area and the family room. I won't have to cook in a cave anymore. Can we really afford it?"

"It's at the top of our budget, but we couldn't have built a house more suited to our needs," Grady said. "It's on a quiet street and close to the church." He looked at everyone. "I don't think we can pass it up. We did pray for a home close to the church. Does anyone object to making an offer?"

"I hope there are some girls my age on the block," Ashlyn said.

"You don't get a vote, Ashlyn," Corey teased.

"Corey! Don't tease," Piper ordered.

"It's okay, Mommy. I don't pay any attention to him," Ashtyn said then made a face at her brother.

Asher made a thumbs-up gesture. "I vote yes."

Grady took Piper and the kids to the hotel before meeting Roger Goldman at the church.

"I can tell you liked the house," Roger said.

Grady nodded and smiled. "We would like to place an offer on it. How do we proceed?"

"I will talk to Lennie Strohmeyer. He is the church's attorney. He will draw up a contract and present it to Tyler and Liz. I'm sure they will accept your offer."

"How can you be so sure? Maybe my offer will be too low."

"Tyler could list it with a Realtor and increase the price, but he and Liz hoped to sell it to the new pastor. If that didn't happen, the church is in a position to buy it outright."

Grady rubbed his jaw. "So, I have two options. I could let the church buy it as a parsonage and live there, or I could buy it and build equity in it."

"Or you could keep looking."

"I seriously doubt we could find a more suitable home," Grady said.

Roger nodded. "My advice would be to buy it as long as it fits your budget."

"Where do I sign?"

"Zach! Your mom and Wyatt are here," Kevin hollered down to the basement. "They want to take you and Grace home."

"Do you have to yell?" Emmy asked. "We do have an intercom system, remember?"

He shrugged and said, "I know, but it was easier to yell."

"Why is Zach downstairs by himself?"

"He wasn't. I came upstairs to grab a bag of chips," Kevin explained.

Emmy used the intercom to let the girls know Kristen and Wyatt had arrived.

"We'll be down in five minutes, Mom," Heather answered using the intercom.

"What are you doing?" Emmy asked but didn't get an answer. She heard a knock at the mudroom door and hollered, "Come on in."

Kristen and Wyatt came in and Emmy met them at the end of the hallway. "Tell me everything. I want details."

"I will do better than tell you," Kristen said. "Wyatt took pictures."

The girls came downstairs ten minutes later. Emmy used the intercom to remind Kevin it was time for Zach to go home. She heard a muffled yell from the basement and a moment later heard the boys stomping up the steps.

"I want to hear about our new house," Grace said hugging her mother.

"Okay. Did you have fun with Heather and Isabella?"

Grace nodded. "Yes, and Kevin was even nice to me. He didn't tease me the way he usually does."

Kevin grinned and said, "That's because Mom paid me twenty bucks."

Emmy put her hands on her hips. "I did no such thing, Kevin Michael." She turned to Kristen. "Do you have time for coffee, or are you in a hurry?"

"We would like to get home, Em," Kristen answered. "We are supposed to meet with Heidi Knapp at three to sign papers."

"I'm glad you're using her. She will get it sold quickly," Emmy said. Then she tilted her head. "On second thought, maybe you should use someone else."

Chapter Seventeen

"Are you sure you don't mind running to the airport?" Emmy asked Saturday afternoon.

Fez chuckled and answered, "I don't mind. It's the least I can do for them."

"Thank you, Fez. Tell them I will be there tomorrow. Oh, Kenny is coming home Monday instead of today. The band wanted him to sit in on a gig Sunday night."

"Do you want me to pick him up, too?" Fez asked.

"Thanks, but I'll do it."

"Hey, Kristen, what's up? Don't tell me you sold the house already," Emmy said the next morning.

"No, the house hasn't sold yet, but Heidi has two couples interested in it," Kristen answered.

"No way! If that's the case, you better raise the price."

"That will not happen. I called to tell you it is official."

"What's official? You aren't pregnant again, are you?" Emmy asked as she sat at the island with her devotional book.

"No! Why would you think I am pregnant?"

"Because... Never mind. What are you talking about?"

"Daryl and Brenda have accepted the position in Indianapolis."

"What position? I didn't know about it."

Kristen sighed and added, "Indianapolis First Church hired them to open a new church on the east side of the city. You did know Pastor Grady was bringing his own teen pastor, right?"

"I guess I forgot," Emmy said. "Well, I'm glad they found a job at least. Weren't they from Indiana originally?"

"Maybe. I don't remember." Kristen tapped her chin. "Yes. They were from Indianapolis, but had been serving in Kansas City before they came to Crest Ridge."

"You have a better memory than me, Krissy. Do you know who the new teen pastor will be?"

"I don't, but Wyatt might. He and Grady have been emailing each other often. Wyatt is helping with the transition."

"I don't think I could be as accommodating as Wyatt. I wouldn't feel like helping after being let go for someone else. Pastor Flores and Pastor Jonah might be the only staff members who make the cut."

Kristen laughed. "Is that a football term, Em?"

"Yeah, but I didn't mean it that way. Pastor Grady will have to hire several new people," Emmy answered. "I'm going to make meat loaf tomorrow. Would you like to come over?"

"Thanks, but my parents are in town because of Memorial Day, and I promised they could see the kids."

"Okay, no problem. We'll see you at church."

"Uncle James, did you hear we're getting a new pastor?" Kevin asked.

"Your mother mentioned it. Have you met him?"

"Not really. He was here a couple Sundays ago with his family. Pastor Wyatt is still in charge, but he and Aunt Kristen are moving to Michigan."

"Your mother told me. Where is she?" Father James asked as he checked the stove. "Is this chili for lunch? It's almost Memorial Day."

"Yeah. Isabella requested it. I think Mom's in the den talking to Dad, or else she's in her bedroom. He was supposed to come home today, but now he's coming back tomorrow."

"I'm going to stir the chili. Please tell your mother I'm here."

Kevin moved to the hallway and shouted, "Mom! Uncle James is here, and the chili is done. Can you hear me?"

Emmy walked out of the den. "I heard you, and all the neighbors probably heard, too. Is the chili really ready?"

"Uncle James says it is."

"Would you find some crackers in the pantry then tell your sisters lunch is ready, please?"

He sighed, but obeyed. He found a bag of oyster crackers and tossed them onto the island. Then he ran upstairs and informed his sisters about lunch.

"How was your week?" Father James asked Emmy.

129

"Long and lonely."

Father James looked at her then laughed. "How long has Kenny been in London?"

"Too long." She made a face at him. "He will be home tomorrow. Are you busy, or are you coming over for the holiday. I thought about grilling some steaks, but decided on meat loaf instead."

"I have things to do in the morning, but I might come for lunch. I stopped to see Mrs. Bertucci Thursday. She's doing better and is in good spirits."

"She won't take her pain meds unless Sloane forces her. She claims the pain is tolerable, but I know better."

"What are your plans for the summer? I assume you are going to Idaho."

"We are going to the ranch sometime next month." She opened a package of shredded cheese. "Not sure when exactly."

"Who's watching the house? Carson?"

"He's done it before, but he's working part-time. He will spend the nights here, I guess. I don't think we'll worry about it since Bobby is living in the guesthouse. Did I mention I met the new neighbors?"

"You mentioned it. Have you talked to them again?" He sat at the island. "You said the wife is from Puerto Rico, right?"

"Yeah, and the kids are a mixed bag."

He laughed. "What does that mean?"

"There are four kids. The daughter and oldest son look like their father, and the two middle boys look like their mother. If you saw them on the street, you'd never know they were siblings."

"No one could ever say that about your kids. You and the girls could be triplets."

"Please," Emmy turned it into a multisyllable word.

"Kevin looks like his father except his hair is lighter."

"Thankfully, Kevin didn't inherit his father's goofy ears."

The kids were talking about the last week of school as they entered the kitchen.

"Daddy doesn't have goofy ears," Isabella said. She walked to the stove and sniffed the chili. "Did you put jalapenos in it?"

"A few, but you can add more to your bowl if you want."

"I thought you were going to make cornbread," Heather said.

"Shoot! I'm sorry, Heather. I forgot. I could make some for later."

"That's okay, Mom. I doubt if there's any chili left after the guys finish. Kevin is such a pig." She grinned as she hugged her uncle. "Did I mention Peter wants to go to the Riverwalk this afternoon?"

"No, you must have conveniently forgotten," Emmy said. "It's all right with me as long as you're home by ten."

"Mom! Tomorrow's a holiday. Can't I stay out later?"

"No! The city has a curfew for teens your age."

"That is so Middle Ages," Heather said.

"Deal with it," Emmy said.

"We don't mind coming to your house," Elly Colwell said. "I'm sure the kids are busy."

"They aren't too busy to see you," Emmy said.

"I promise we won't stay long, but Carter wants to get out of the house. Don't tell them, but I think he wants to see Lassie as much as the kids."

Emmy laughed and spotted Lassie sleeping under the breakfast nook table. "The kids won't mind. James was here earlier, but got called away. He wouldn't say, but I think one of his parishioners passed away at St. Bart's."

"I wouldn't want to do his job. Has it been difficult to manage the children by yourself? Teens can be a handful."

"I'm fortunate. Some of the families in the neighborhood are having issues with their kids. Drugs and alcohol abuse."

"We will come over after Carter takes his nap. We won't stay for dinner, so don't worry about feeding us. I know you don't normally cook on Sunday night."

"We could order pizzas. I made chili for lunch, but there wasn't enough left to feed a bird."

"We will figure it out later," Elly Colwell said.

131

"Did you have fun in Florida? Are you glad you're home? I'm glad you're back." Kevin met his grandparents outside. "We had more snow this winter than I can remember." He hugged them and opened the service door. "Dad is flying back in the morning. Don't tell Mom I said so, but she's been kinda cranky lately. It's because she misses him if you know what I mean."

"Hi, Grandma. Hi, Grandpa," Isabella said. She hugged her grandmother, and allowed her grandfather to smother her with a hug. "We're so happy to see you. Heather will be down soon. She is getting ready for her date."

"Her what?" Carter Colwell asked.

"Her date with Peter Bertucci, Grandpa. Mom is freaked out by it, but they like each other."

Carter stared at Elly for a moment.

"The girls are growing up, Carter."

"They are still babies," he replied.

"Dad was totally against letting Heather go on dates, but Mom reminded him she was the same age when she and Daddy started dating," Isabella said.

"I thought she was older," Carter said.

Elly shook her head. "She was older when they started dating seriously."

"I know they were friends almost their whole life," Isabella said. "It's the same for Heather and Peter."

"Isn't he quite a bit older than you and Heather?" Carter asked.

Isabella grinned. "He will be eighteen in July, so he's two and a half years older than us. The same age difference as Mom and Dad."

"I suppose the age difference is not as important now as it was in the past," Elly said.

"Please explain that to Dad," Isabella said. "He doesn't have a clue."

Lassie chose that moment to race down the hall with her tail wagging as fast as possible. She slid to a stop in front of Carter and barked once.

"Have you been a good doggie?"

132

Lassie barked again.

"I can see you are pleased to see me." He reached down to scratch her ears and rub her head. "I missed you, too, Lassie."

Heather and Emmy walked into the kitchen. Heather hugged her grandparents.

"What's this I hear about a young girl dating an older boy?" Carter teased as he squeezed her. "Are you wearing makeup?"

Emmy looked closer at Heather and sighed.

"Oh, Grandpa. They're not serious dates. We enjoy each other's company."

"Yeah! Especially when he kisses you," Kevin teased.

"I bet Peter thinks the dates are serious," Elly said.

"Mom, they're just friends," Emmy said.

Elly smiled. "You and Kenny were friends for years and look how that turned out."

"That was different," Kevin said imitating his mother's voice. "That's what you always say, Mom."

"Are we going to order pizzas before I leave?" Heather asked.

"I placed the order online. They should be here within the hour."

Heather ate quickly and kept looking at the clock. She was hoping her grandparents would leave before Peter arrived. It didn't happen. Peter knocked on the mudroom door, waited a couple seconds, then walked in.

"Does everyone in the neighborhood walk in like that?" Carter asked.

"Not everyone," Emmy said. "One of the ladies from church stopped by the house last week, and she came to the front door. I was so embarrassed because I hadn't swept the front porch in months. There were cobwebs everywhere."

"I'll be ready in a second," Heather said. She dashed upstairs.

"She has to check her makeup," Kevin teased.

"Peter, it's good to see you again," Elly said. "You look so grownup now."

"It's good to see you and Mr. Colwell, too," he replied.

"We heard about your grandmother. I hope she's feeling better."

Peter nodded. "She's getting better." He looked down the hallway and Heather appeared within seconds.

"I'm ready."

"Take a jacket, and be home by ten," Emmy said.

"I will have her home in time, *Aunt Emmy.*"

Kevin laughed, grabbed another slice of pizza and laughed again after Peter and Heather left.

"What is so funny?" Isabella asked.

"Peter calls Mom Aunt Emmy and Heather calls his parents aunt and uncle. If a stranger heard it, they would assume Peter and Heather are cousins. Kissing cousins like the old Elvis movie. It's weird."

Lassie whimpered at Carter from under the table. He patted her head and gave her part of his pizza crust when no one was watching.

"Does anyone want to ride to the airport when I pick up your father?" Emmy asked while frying bacon.

"No, I'm going back to bed," Heather said. "I'm exhausted."

"Why?" Kevin asked. He grabbed two slices of wheat toast and sat at the island. "What did you do?"

"How late were you up last night?" Emmy asked the girls. "I thought I heard you come upstairs in the middle of the night."

"We watched movies until three," Isabella said.

"Was Peter here?" Emmy pointed the spatula at Heather.

"Yes, but he texted his father before midnight and let him know where he was."

"That's not the point. Three in the morning is too late for him to be here. You should have known better," Emmy said.

Kevin grinned at his sisters. "I'll go to the airport with you, Mom. I can listen while you and Dad decide how long Heather and Isa are grounded."

"Mom! Are we going to be grounded?" Heather whined.

"Probably."

Emmy parked the Odyssey, and she and Kevin headed to the International Terminal to wait for Kenny.

"There he is!" Kevin shouted. He looked at his mother. "Should I close my eyes so you guys can be mushy with each other?"

"We won't do anything more than kiss," Emmy said.

"Yeah, right, Mom," Kevin teased.

Kenny spotted them, opened his arms, and she held on tightly while he kissed her and twirled her in a circle.

Kevin waited until his father set his mother down before racing over and hugging him.

"I missed you, too," Kenny said.

"I've got a lot of stuff to tell you, but I'll wait until later."

Kenny insisted on everyone eating together at lunchtime, so he could tell them about his time in London.

"Dad, we've been there before," Heather said.

"When?" he asked.

"When we were babies," Isabella answered with a grin.

"We should go back sometime. I took a couple days and explored outside of London. I loved Hampton Court and Windsor Palace."

Heather looked at Isabella and rolled her eyes.

"Mom, don't let Dad drag us across the ocean to look at old houses," Isabella said.

"I'll go if I can see old castles and dungeons," Kevin said.

"When the pandemic is over, we should take a long trip to England and Ireland," Kenny suggested.

Emmy smiled and the kids groaned.

Emmy forgot about disciplining the twins, and Kevin didn't bring it up. Heather thanked him later.

"Yeah, I could have been a rat, but I figure now you owe me a favor."

Chapter Eighteen

"I am so glad school is over," Kevin said. He tossed his backpack on the island and opened the fridge. "Do we have any snacks?"

"Yes, and please put your backpack where it belongs," Emmy said. She waited for Heather and Isabella to come out of the mudroom. "Was a year at the Barclay Academy as bad as you thought it would be?"

The twins looked at each other. Shrugged, made faces and grunted.

"Was it?"

"I liked it better than going to Reagan High. I heard the classes there were like being in solitary confinement."

Emmy smiled and asked, "Can I assume you and Heather won't mind going back?"

"I hope next year we will have in-person school all year," Heather said. "Peter graduated from St. Raymond's and has been accepted at North Park College."

"Is he commuting, or does he plan to live in a dorm?" Emmy asked. "Carson is considering a dorm next semester unless the pandemic gets worse. He didn't mind commuting this year."

"I don't know what he's decided," Heather replied.

Emmy looked at Kevin. "You and Ben better not behave like a lot of eighth graders and act like you own the school. I will put you in your place if you do."

"We won't pick on the younger kids, Mom. It's too bad Gracie is moving. I didn't mind being in her class."

"She and Natalie will be in the same class in Alexandria Rapids," Emmy said.

"Mom, Dad said I should ask you about tonight." Heather walked into the laundry room carrying a basket of her clothes. "These are all the clothes from my room."

"What about tonight? Are you going somewhere?" Emmy looked at one of Kevin's sweatshirts and sighed. "This is new, and he's got grass stains on it already."

"Peter and Carson were invited to a party. Dotty is going and Peter wants me to go," Heather explained.

"Where is it?"

"Here in Bristol Ridge."

"Whose house?" Emmy looked at Heather. "Why do I get the feeling you're holding out on me?"

"It's at the Grandison house."

"Which house is that? I'm not familiar with the name."

"It's next to the Osborne's. They moved in during the holidays, and they have two kids. Mason and Maxwell. They attend Reagan, so I don't really know them, but Peter and Carson kinda know them."

"What time is the party? Is it for anything special?" Emmy loaded the washer and turned back to Heather.

"One of the guys graduated, so I guess it's a graduation party. Peter wants to go around six because there will be food."

Emmy thought about it for a moment. "Okay, since you will be with Peter and Carson, you may go. Wasn't Isabella invited?"

"Yes, but she doesn't want to go because she would be by herself."

"Is Carson taking Dotty to the party as a date, or is she going because of Peter?"

"Probably a little of both. She doesn't like Carson in that way, but they're friends. How late can I stay out?" Heather asked.

"Since the party is in the neighborhood, you can stay until ten thirty. Tomorrow is Sunday, and you can't skip church because you're tired."

"Thanks, Mom. I doubt if we stay later than eight or nine."

"Is Peter picking everyone up?"

"Yes. We didn't want to walk even though it's not that far. Uncle Tony said Peter could take us since we won't be leaving the neighborhood."

"This is it," Peter said when the house finally came into sight. "It's different than all the other houses here."

"That's for sure," Heather said. "It looks like a bunch of metal and glass rectangles piled up and stuck together."

137

Mason Grandison opened the front door. "Come on in and make yourself at home. There's food and beverages in the kitchen." He smiled at Dotty but ignored Heather.

Peter held the door open and followed everyone inside.

"Nice place," Carson whispered to Peter. "Have you been here before?"

"Once briefly. This is one of those contemporary houses architects like to build because it makes them a lot of money. It's different inside than what you might imagine from the outside. It's more open."

Carson looked to his left. "All the furniture in there looks modern. That couch looks like it belongs in a spaceship."

"And uncomfortable," Dotty added. She spotted Mason watching her from the other end of the room as he talked to a couple guys.

"Those are the snotty kids who live here, right?" one of the athletically built guys asked.

"Yeah, they live here. I think they're all related somehow."

"Is the girl in the red top the one you said was hot?" the other guy asked. "Is she the one you've been lusting after?"

"Keep it down, Hodges. I don't want her to hear us," Mason told him.

"Do you want us to get her drunk for you? I know you want to get in her pants."

"Don't even think about it, you idiot. Her father played for the Bears. He would kill me if I tried anything."

"Good luck then." Hodges elbowed his other friend, walked away and whispered, "I think we should get both of those rich girls drunk. I bet they'd be pretty wild."

Carson and Dotty checked out the large open area taking up the entire side of the house. Dotty glanced over her shoulder and noticed Mason and his friends were gone.

Carson pointed. "Even the stairway is glass and steel."

Heather followed Peter toward the kitchen.

"I'm thirsty," Peter said. "Are you?"

"Not really, but I would take a bottle of water or a Coke," Heather answered. "I thought there would be more people here."

Peter looked for something to drink but didn't see anything other than two kegs of beer and several packages of red, plastic cups. "Maybe we're early. It's only six thirty."

"At least there is pizza," Heather said.

Peter filled plates for both of them, and they stayed in the kitchen until Carson and Dotty appeared.

"What is there to drink?" Carson asked.

"All I see is beer." Peter hooked a thumb over his shoulder at the kegs.

Maxwell Grandison heard them and pointed to the fridge. "I'm sorry. I should have put some water and pop out, but I assumed everyone would want beer. Help yourself to whatever you'd like." Maxwell adjusted his dark-framed glasses. "There will be more pizza later. Mason didn't know so many kids would show up, and he skimped on the order."

"If there are more kids here than he thought, where are they?" Carson asked.

"Didn't he tell you everyone was hanging out on the deck? The weather is perfect for an outdoor party."

"Is this his graduation party?" Heather asked. "Are your parents here?"

Maxwell shook his head and made air quotes. "It's not *technically* his graduation party. More like an excuse to invite some of his friends from Reagan to the house. We don't know a lot of kids in SoHam yet."

"Where did you live before?" Dotty asked.

"Chicago. The North Shore area in a high-rise. My father's company moved their headquarters to Newcastle, so we moved here."

Maxwell explained how his father started a company that made plastic parts for the automotive industry.

"The company has factories in Mexico and Brazil."

"Sounds like they're doing well," Peter said.

"Come on outside whenever you want. I'll introduce you to everyone."

Peter led the way. Heather followed, but Carson and Dotty stayed behind.

139

"Do you ever sneak any of your parents' beer?" Dotty asked. "Mom won't allow any alcohol in our house anymore, but Dad used to keep beer around."

"I've had a few, but Mom keeps track of how much is in the fridge. Brady doesn't drink beer, but he has a liquor cabinet with the other stuff."

"Have you tried any of it?"

Carson shook his head. "It's locked up. Mom and Brady have a glass of wine with dinner occasionally. They only keep it around for entertaining guests."

"I've never tasted beer, but I don't think it's a crime to drink it as long as you don't get drunk."

Carson stared at her.

"Does that surprise you?" she asked looking at the two kegs on the floor.

"Yes, because doesn't your church prohibit alcohol?"

"It doesn't prohibit it now exactly, but it did back in the old days."

"If someone offered you a glass of beer tonight, would you drink it?"

Dotty took another bite of pizza then shrugged.

"I won't tell anyone if you do, but how would Peter react? He is your brother, and he's rather protective."

"He would be pissed."

"I don't blame him. I would be mad if someone offered Heather anything," Carson said. "Are you ready to go outside?"

"Okay, but if his friends are jerks, I might want to leave."

Carson opened the sliding door, and they could hear the sounds of a party coming from beyond the shiny metallic wall.

"There must be a deck over there," Carson said. "Probably a pool, too."

Mason came around the corner with a few friends. He introduced them to Carson then leered at Dotty for a second and walked back to the party.

"It's nice to meet you, Dotty. Didn't your father play for the Bears? I played varsity football for Reagan High, but we sucked."

"Yes, but he retired several years ago," Dotty replied.

"I'm Jafar Foran, by the way. I saw him play a few times. He was ferocious on the field. I saw him make some wicked tackles on players." He offered a hand to Carson.

Carson shook Jafar's huge hand. "He was pretty physical on the field, but he's not like that in real life."

"Do you need something to drink?" Jafar asked. "I was heading back into the kitchen."

"We're good for now," Carson answered.

"Let me know if you want anything." He smiled at Dotty and wondered if she was on a date with Carson. "Come on out and meet everyone."

Carson and Dotty followed him to the large deck.

"Wow! Even the deck is made of metal and glass," Carson whispered.

"There's Peter and Heather. Let's join them," Dotty said.

They walked over, stood next to Peter and Heather and listened.

"Does your father's band plan to do another world tour?" one of the girls asked Heather as she hung onto Mason's arm.

Heather nodded and backed away as the girl sloshed beer around in a plastic cup.

"I've heard his music, and it's okay. My parents like it more than me. Can I get you a beer?"

Heather shook her head. "No thanks. I don't drink."

"Why not?" the girl asked, spilling some of her beer, then looking around. "There are no adults here. No one will care if you have a beer."

"I don't think it's right." Heather looked around. "I seriously doubt if anyone here is legally old enough."

"So what? Life is short. Have some fun." The girl waved her arm and splashed beer onto the deck.

"I can have fun without it."

One of the other girls took Heather's arm and pulled her away from Peter. "You went to school at that church in Crest Ridge, right?"

"I did, but now my sister and I go to the Barclay Academy. At least until our church starts a high school."

141

"I heard that church is really strict. They have all kinds of rules about what you can and can't do. That would suck. I'm old enough to make my own decisions without being told what to do."

"I don't see it that way," Heather said. "I consider myself a follower of Jesus, and I let His spirit guide my life."

Several of the kids stared blankly at Heather. One girl dropped her cup of beer. A couple boys laughed. Peter moved back to Heather's side and frowned when he heard one boy whisper to another, "She's one of those Christians who always reads the Bible and doesn't do anything fun. She must suck as a girlfriend."

"Does that mean you aren't going to kiss a boy until you're married?" one of the girls asked then laughed and locked her lips onto the boy standing next to her. "You don't know what you're missing if you do."

Peter leaned closer to Heather and asked, "Do you want to leave? I don't mind if you do. Those guys are jerks."

Heather looked up at him. "Not yet. I don't care if they make fun of me for what I believe."

"Hey, Peter! Didn't you go to that school, too?"

"Yes, I did until high school."

"Then why did you go to St. Raymond's?"

"My family is Catholic. Used to be. Whatever. I chose St. Raymond's over Barclay and Roosevelt."

"Why didn't you attend Reagan?"

"Are you too good to attend public school?" one of the guys asked. "I know everyone who lives in Bristol Ridge is made of money."

Mason stepped between Peter and the guy antagonizing him. "Knock it off, Mike. I live here, too."

Mike frowned at Peter, took another sip of beer then poked a finger in Mason's chest. "You're no different. You only invited us to your party because you're trying to buy friends."

Jafar clamped a hand on Mike's shoulder. "Leave him alone, Hodges."

Mike grimaced as Jafar increased his grip. "I didn't mean to start anything."

"Good idea," Jafar said.

142

The tension broke and Mike and his friends headed to opposite end of the deck.

"Thanks, Jafar," Mason said. "He can be a jerk at times."

"It runs in the family," Jafar said.

"Are you going to play football in college?" Dotty asked. "You're big enough." She cringed when she noticed Mason's lewdful stare.

"Yes. I'm going to Paul Frank for two years. If I do well at the junior college level, I might get an offer from a small college to play." He shrugged and added, "If not, my grandmother wants me to go into medicine. Like that's a possibility."

"Is your grandmother a doctor? What do your parents do?" Dotty smiled as she looked up at Jafar, who was a foot taller then her.

"My parents are gone. My mother split years ago, and I never really had a father. I've always lived with my grandmother. She works at Coventry Shield Healthcare and wants me to go to college."

"Do you want to be a doctor?" Dotty asked.

"No, but I could see myself studying pharmacology. I had a cousin who did that until he was robbed a few times and quit."

"My mother is a teacher at Crest Ridge Nazarene."

"Do you want to be a teacher, too?"

"Probably not, but I don't have a clue what I want to study in college," Dotty said.

"How old are you? Did you graduate already?"

Dotty shook her head. "I will be a senior in the fall. Peter is a year older."

Jafar looked at Peter, who was talking to Heather. "He's your brother, right?"

"Yes."

"Mason said most of the families who live in that part of Bristol Ridge are related." He pointed to the east. "Is that true?"

"Some are related by blood, but all the families are close."

Jafar laughed. "The families in my neighborhood are close, too. I live one of the housing projects. The city wants to bulldoze the area and build new *affordable* housing."

143

"I don't know much about certain parts of SoHam," Dotty said. "Especially the area east of the river."

"That's good. You wouldn't want to hang around my neighborhood, but I don't live on that side of the river."

"Where is your neighborhood? I assumed it would be across the river."

"Most people think like that, but I live in Taylorville."

"I've never heard of it."

"It's a small neighborhood almost due east of here. It's a few blocks from the river next to an old warehouse district."

"But you went to Reagan, right?" Dotty asked.

"Yeah. I would have gone to Roosevelt if they hadn't built Reagan." He shrugged and added, "I think the school board included Taylorville in the Reagan district because of political pressure."

"Tell me what it's like to live there."

Jafar laughed. "Have you ever seen the movie *Brooklyn Streets*?"

"I don't think so," Dotty answered.

"There are gangs in our neighborhood. It's not uncommon to hear gunshots and sirens. One of my closest friends was caught in the crossfire when a rival gang did a drive-by."

"Was he killed?"

"No, but he was in the hospital for a while."

Carson noticed the Reagan High kids were avoiding them, so he joined Peter and Heather as Dotty talked to Jafar.

"Hey, Mason, I thought you wanted to make a move on that girl talking to Jafar," Mike Hodges sneered. "You better do it quick because he's moving in pretty fast."

Hodges' buddy laughed and asked, "Are you afraid of Jafar? Do you want us to take him out for you?"

Mason stared at Dotty for a moment, then he shrugged and muttered, "She's not worth the trouble."

Hodges high-fived his buddy. "Like we thought, he's afraid of Jafar."

"Peter, can we leave now?" Heather asked an hour later.

"Sure. I was ready to leave earlier." He looked around. "Have you seen Dotty? The last I saw her she was talking to Jafar."

"I saw them in the kitchen a few minutes ago," Maxwell said. "There are a few slices of pizza left if anyone is hungry."

"Thanks, but we are going to head out," Peter said. "Thanks for inviting us. Maybe we will run into each other over the summer."

They found Dotty in the open, great room sitting on one of the futuristic couches talking to Jafar.

"We are going home, Dotty," Peter said. He walked up to Jafar.

Jafar stood up quickly not knowing whether Peter might be angry or not.

Peter offered a hand. "It was nice to meet you."

Jafar shook the offered hand. "Yeah, you too. I hope you don't mind me talking to your sister."

Peter noticed two red plastic cups on the glass table next to the couch. "Of course not. Take care."

Peter dropped Carson off first, then took Heather home. He talked to her by the garage service door for a moment. He got back in the car and looked at Dotty. "I saw the cup. Did you have a glass of beer?"

Dotty frowned at him. "Had you looked closer, you would have noticed it was still full. I had one small sip. Is that a crime?"

"I guess not. Did Jafar get it for you? The beer, I mean." Peter started the car and headed home.

Dotty shook her head. "No way. That other guy brought the beer to us. We didn't ask for it, and Jafar didn't have more than a few sips."

"He seemed like an all right guy."

"Jafar is, but that Hodges guy was a real jerk."

Peter scratched his ear. "I've heard that name before."

"Jafar grew up in a section of SoHam called Taylorville. Have you ever heard of it?"

"Maybe, but I don't think I've ever been there. Where is it?"

Dotty told him about the area as Peter stopped the car.

"Doesn't sound like a neighborhood I'd want to visit."

"Jafar's had a rough life, but he's pretty smart. He finished in the top ten at Reagan. He asked a lot of questions about our church. He told me his grandmother goes to Friendship Baptist Church, and he used to go when he was a kid."

"Did he ask for your number?"

"He did," Dotty answered.

Peter crossed the street and pulled up the driveway. He stopped before he got to the garage.

"Did you give it to him?"

"As a matter of fact, I did."

"What would you say if he asked you out?"

Dotty turned and looked right into Peter's eyes. "I would invite him to church, so we could meet in a safe environment. I am not ready to date anyone if you must know."

"How was the party?" Emmy asked. She checked the time. "You're home sooner than I expected."

Heather sat beside her mother on the couch. She didn't spare any details.

"I'm proud of you for taking a stand and telling them how you believe."

"I could have caved to the peer pressure, but I thought about what you've taught us and that gave me the strength to resist."

Emmy pulled Heather closer and hugged her.

"Have I ever told you about Derrick's high school graduation party?"

"If you did, I don't remember."

Emmy explained why she was invited to Derrick's party.

"I knew you went on a few dates with him. Did you ever kiss him?"

"Once, and it was like kissing a brother."

Heather giggled. "How would you know? You didn't have a brother until Uncle James came to SoHam."

"I could tell it wasn't a romantic kiss," Emmy explained. "We didn't think of them as dates like you might."

Heather stared at her.

"I can't explain it, but you just know the difference."

"Whatever."

"So, these kids brought beer to the party. Do you remember anything about Kristen's parents' house?" Emmy asked.

"I have a vague memory of it."

"It was one of the first times I was there. The house was like a mansion to me. There was a tennis court, a pool and a poolhouse out back. Anyway, these kids were drinking on the far side of the poolhouse out of sight of the adults. This guy, Bert Hodges, gave me a beer..." Emmy paused and thought about it. "No, it wasn't Hodges. It was Dawn Matuzak. She gave me the opened beer hoping to get me in trouble. I didn't want to drink any beer."

"Why? You told us you used to sneak an occasional beer from Grandpa."

"I did, but that was a long time ago, and I didn't know any better."

"Did Uncle Rory offer you beer when you were older?"

"Yes, but he made sure I never drank more than one, or maybe two. You have to remember I wasn't a Christian then. Rory was like a big brother. He was kinda wild back then, but he looked out for me."

"So what happened at Derrick's party?"

"Dawn handed me a beer, and it spilled on my dress just as Mr. Keasling and Kristen's uncle walked around the building. He made those kids leave."

"Did he think you were drinking?"

"No. I was with Barry Newton, and Barry explained what happened. Then he took me into the poolhouse to dry my dress."

"How?"

"There was a bathroom, and we went in there. He used paper towels, but it wasn't working."

"I don't get it. I'm confused. Where was Derrick? Why wasn't he with you?" Heather asked.

"If I remember correctly, he was talking to family. It was a party for him, so he had to be a good host. Whatever."

"I still don't get it, Mom. You wore a dress to the party, and Grandma used to tell us how you hated to wear dresses."

"I probably wore one because the party was supposed to be formal. Kristen wore a dress. Maybe she convinced me to wear one. I can't remember." Emmy shrugged. "I wouldn't expect you and Isa to wear a dress to a party now."

"We wear dresses to church, but that's about it."

"Yes, and I think you look so beautiful when you do."

"Would you have been mad if I drank some beer tonight?"

"I don't think so, but I would be disappointed if you did and lied about it." Emmy paused then waved a hand. "No, I would be furious if you lied."

"I would never lie to you, Mom."

"I hope you never have a reason to lie to me the way I lied to my mother."

"I won't, and I won't go to anymore parties like tonight's."

"That might not be a promise you can keep, Heather. You will find yourself in situations where you have to make choices. You can count on Jesus to give you the wisdom and strength to make the right choice."

Chapter Nineteen

"What is the weather like in the summer?" Kristen asked as she watched Emmy packing for the trip to Idaho.

"The ranch area never gets too hot. The average high in July is slightly above eighty degrees."

"It probably snows a lot on the mountains in the winter."

Emmy grinned and said, "Yes, but it rarely snows in the valleys in summer."

"Stinker!" Kristen peeked into Emmy's closet. "You can't take all your clothes. The plane would never leave the ground."

"I told the kids to only take enough clothes for a week, and we would do laundry. Whatever they take should be something they won't mind leaving there."

"I suppose that makes sense. I heard a rumor there are stores in some of the more civilized parts of Idaho."

"True, and our ranch even has running water," Emmy said with a straight face.

"I know this joke. You send Kevin to the river and he runs back carrying the water. Very funny."

"Is there any way I could convince you not to move until we get back?" Emmy closed her suitcase and looked up at Kristen.

"Wyatt's last Sunday is the Fourth of July, and you can't come back that soon. It is not like we will never see each other again, Em. We will only be four or five hours away."

"I thought it was four and a half hours to Alexandria Rapids."

"For a normal driver. If Kenny drives it would be five hours..."

"I get it. You still think I drive like a maniac."

"Not a maniac. A Formula One driver. There is a difference," Kristen teased.

"Ha! Ha! I've never gotten a speeding ticket."

"Because you flirt with any officer who stops you."

"Do not."

"I suppose it doesn't hurt to be friends with the chief of police. What time do you need to be at the airport?"

"We plan to take off at ten unless it's storming."

"Are you renting a car in Ketchum Forks?"

"A Jeep Wrangler actually. It's supposed to have a roof rack."

"You might need a trailer to haul everything."

"We could always make two trips. It's only fifty miles each way."

"So, how are you getting to the airport? Is Tony taking you?"

"He offered, but if you aren't busy..."

"I can take you, but you better not make me cry."

Lassie trotted into the room and jumped onto the bed.

Kristen scratched Lassie's ears. "Is Tony going to watch Lassie?"

"Yes. We were going to take her with, but the vet didn't recommend it."

"Why not?" Kristen rubbed Lassie's belly. "You are such a good girl. Spoiled, but a good doggie."

"She's got a problem with her blood."

"Is it serious?"

"It could be. We haven't told the kids. The vet wants to keep an eye on her."

"Where is Peter taking you tonight?" Isabella sat on her sister's bed and watched as Heather brushed her long, dark hair. "Did Mom say you could stay out later than ten?"

"I didn't ask, and Peter is taking me to the new pizza place close to the church. I forget the name, but it's not a chain."

Isabella took the brush from her sister. She finished brushing Heather's hair and quickly braided it. "Do I smell some of Mom's new perfume?"

"Did I use too much?" Heather asked turning around. "It was no more than a dab."

"It's okay."

"Mom said I could use it. Did you know Jo Malone fragrances were so expensive? I looked online and Mom's little bottle cost over $150."

150

"Get out! That little bottle was that much. It's a good thing you asked for permission. I bet Dad doesn't know."

Heather stood and smoothed out her dress. "Do I look all right?"

Isabella adjusted the collar. "You look perfect, but try to remember not to lean over too much."

"I could wear a sweater."

Isabella laughed. "It's too hot. Don't let Daddy see you when you leave and you'll be all right."

"I didn't realize the neckline was like this when I bought it."

"Maybe you've grown since then," Isabella teased. "I'm sure Peter will love it."

Heather's phone chirped. She grabbed it and answered the text.

"Was that Peter?" Isabella asked.

"He's on his way."

The girls headed downstairs and tried to sneak down the hallway without being seen.

"Heather! Where is he taking you?" Emmy asked from the family room.

Heather stood in the hallway and explained about the pizza place. "We won't be out too late, but I might go to Peter's house after we eat. Is that okay?"

Emmy scratched her knee and chuckled. "Yes. Did Tony make you promise to bring him some pizza?"

"Not that I know of," Heather answered.

Emmy got up and hurried into the long hallway. She bumped into the girls and looked at Heather.

"I didn't know you were dressing up." Emmy looked at the shorts and t-shirt she was wearing. "This is what I usually wore when I went out."

"I hope you don't mean that literally," Isabella said.

"This t-shirt might be old, but not that old."

"I'll let you know if the pizza is any good."

Emmy watched the girls head down the hallway before returning to the family room and her book.

"Hurry before Daddy or Kevin see you," Isabella said.

"Should I take a jacket?" Heather asked when she got to the mudroom.

"You won't need one," Isabella answered. "Come and see me when you get home. I'll still be up."

Isabella checked the time when she heard a soft knock on her bedroom door and Heather walked in and sat on the edge of Isabella's bed.

"Did you come up the back stairs?" Isabella asked. "It's almost midnight."

"Yes. Are Mom and Dad already in bed?" Heather picked up the book Isabella had been reading. "*Bryony*. I read this last month. It's good, but the Melissa character should have known better than to get mixed up with that crowd."

"Don't tell me what happens," Isabella said. "I think I know, but I don't want to spoil the ending."

"I'll be back after I change. I need to talk to you." Heather stood up and left the room. She returned after getting ready for bed.

"Can I snuggle with you?" Heather asked.

Isabella threw back the covers and patted the spot next to her. "Tell me how it went."

Heather scooted under the covers and sighed. "The pizza was good. Peter brought some home for Uncle Tony, and we watched a movie in the basement."

"Was it only you and Peter, or did you have company?"

"Everyone was downstairs except Noemi. She was in her room talking to Natalie. We watched the latest Avenger movie then Dotty made the boys go upstairs."

"Did Ben tease you?"

"He tried, but I ignored him. He's worse than Kevin."

"What did you do then?"

Heather turned onto her side to face Isabella. "We didn't *do* anything but talk."

"Did you want more?"

"I waited for him to kiss me, but he never did."

152

Isabella giggled and said, "You could have initiated the kiss."

"No way! If he wanted to kiss me, he needed to take the initiative."

"Did he ask if he could kiss you?"

Heather shook her head. "I wouldn't want to kiss someone who asked permission. That shows a lack of confidence in my eyes."

"Okay, what did you talk about? I can tell it upset you. Don't hold back."

Heather hesitated then blurted out, "He put me in the friend zone."

"No! Why?" Isabella sat up. "I thought he liked you."

"So did I, but he used the excuse of being close friends for so long and almost family."

"I would be crushed if my boyfriend did that to me," Isabella said.

Heather shook her head. "It hurts, but I'm not going to cry over it."

"Are you sure?"

Heather nodded. "At first I thought he was kidding, but once I realized he was serious, I got kinda mad."

"Does he like someone else?"

"He told me he met this girl when he was checking out North Park and was thinking of asking her out. He even showed me a photo and asked if I thought she was cute. Like I would care."

"What did you say?"

"I said she looked all right. It was weird. All of a sudden I was like Dotty or Noemi to him. I told him to go ahead and ask her out then he brought me home."

Isabella chuckled. "At least he didn't make you walk home."

"Yeah." Heather scooted out of bed. "Don't tell Mom or Dad." She reached the door and added, "Or Kevin Michael."

"I won't say anything, but Mom will find out soon enough. She has this way of knowing everything."

"Is that everything?" Kristen asked as Kenny and Kevin loaded three more suitcases into Kristen's minivan.

"That's it. We're ready to roll," Kevin answered. He looked over his shoulder. "That's if Grace lets Heather and Isa go."

"Come on, girls!" Emmy shouted. "We can't keep the pilots waiting forever."

"It's not like they're going to take off without us, Mom. It's Mr. Robertson's jet." Kevin climbed into the back row.

Grace hugged Heather and Isabella one more time then hopped on her bike to ride home. Everyone got in the van for the ride to the SoHam airport.

"Turn at the next right and pull between the building and that fence," Emmy said. "You can park in front of the hanger."

Kristen parked and Emmy waved to the pilots, who were standing by the Gulfstream III.

"Let me know when you get to the ranch," Kristen said.

"Yes, Mom. I will call you," Emmy teased.

"Forgive me for being concerned," Kristen replied.

They stared at each other for a moment.

"Please don't make me cry, Em," Kristen whispered.

The plane was soon loaded and everyone climbed aboard except Emmy and Kristen.

"We will come to Michigan when we get back. I can't wait to see your new house," Emmy said.

"Have a good time and don't let the grizzly bears get you."

"Did Kevin tell you to remind me about bears?"

Kristen laughed. "He did. If you see a bear, start hollering and making a lot of noise."

"I don't think there are bears around the ranch, but I'll keep my eyes open if I go backpacking."

The flight into Ketchum Forks, Idaho, took forever according to Kevin. They finally landed, loaded everything into, or onto, the Jeep Wrangler and headed to the ranch. Kevin grabbed the front seat and made his mother sit in back with his sisters. The drive to their ranch took an hour and a half because Kenny stopped at every pullout to look at the scenery.

154

"How close is our ranch to Mr. Robertson's place?" Kevin asked while they were unloading the Jeep.

Kenny handed Heather one of her suitcases and pointed. "It's thirty miles or so in that direction if you fly."

Kevin looked around. "Did you buy a helicopter?"

"No, I meant if you were a bird. It would be close to fifty miles if we drive."

"Can we go see it?"

"I think we'll have time to check it out," Kenny said.

The girls raced inside as soon as Emmy unlocked the front door.

"This is different than what I imagined," Isabella said as she looked up at the cathedral ceiling in the open great room.

"Cool! There's a fireplace and a stack of wood," Kevin said.

Heather and Emmy walked to the opposite side of the room and stared out the floor-to-ceiling windows.

"We actually have a yard with grass."

"Do we have to mow it?" Kevin asked.

Kenny grinned and said, "No, I think the cows and goats take care of it."

"Can we pick our rooms now?" Heather asked. "I want the one farthest away from Kevin."

"You're out of luck," Emmy said. "The master bedroom is at that end past the kitchen and the other three are down the hall."

"Please tell me we don't have to share a bathroom with him."

"It won't kill you to share a bathroom."

Heather rolled her eyes and muttered, "I hate this place already."

Kevin walked in carrying two suitcases. "Where do you want these, Isa?"

Within an hour, the Jeep was unloaded, the bedrooms chosen and Kenny was reading the instructions left by the seller.

"Why don't the lights work?" Heather asked.

"I need to flip a switch for the electricity and find the main water valve. I have to make sure the water heater's pilot light is on. Then I can adjust the temperature."

Kevin walked onto the back deck. "I can hear the river from here. I'm going to check it out." He hustled toward the river, stopped suddenly and waved to everyone. "Come here! You gotta see this!"

Everyone joined Kevin.

"I didn't realize we would be this high above the river," Kenny said. "It must be forty or fifty feet to the water."

"It's like our own private canyon," Kevin hollered. "I see a trail heading down. This is so cool. I think I'll go exploring."

"Maybe you should wait until tomorrow," Emmy said. "It will be dark soon, and I don't want you to get lost in the wilderness."

"There was a general store in that little town we went through Saturday," Emmy told Kenny Monday morning. "We need to buy groceries, and that might be the closest place."

"I agree. Kevin mentioned shooting something to eat if we don't go to the store. I don't think he realizes how remote this place is."

"He might like playing in the woods at home, but he's a city boy. It will take some adjusting for all the kids."

Emmy asked the girls and Kevin to make a list of what they wanted to eat.

"I'm not sure the little store carries these brands, but I'll see what they have," Emmy said.

"Just don't buy the cheap generic stuff, Mom."

"Kevin, stay around the ranch while we're gone," Kenny said.

"Dad! We aren't helpless." Heather rolled her eyes.

"I was thinking you might want him around if a bear decides to check for food."

Heather and Isabella looked at each other.

"You're kidding, right?" Heather asked.

Kevin grinned, but then looked serious. "I did find some bear poop close to the river. This might be one of the areas they hunt for food."

"Dad! Is he joking?" Heather asked.

"Maybe you should buy a rifle or shotgun," Kevin suggested. "We might need it for protection."

"We aren't buying any guns," Emmy said. She looked at Kevin. "Did you really see some bear poop?"

He shrugged. "I did see something, but it could have been from a cow or something. I don't know the difference. I said that to scare them." He turned to his sister. "I'm sorry. I'm pretty sure there aren't any bears around."

"If we see one, we're going to feed you to it," Isabella said.

While Kenny and Emmy were buying groceries and other supplies, Kevin decided to hike west along the river canyon. The girls took the opportunity to work on their tans on the rear deck.

"Make sure you add lotion often," Isabella said after the girls had rubbed sunscreen on each other's back.

"I will, but I'm a bit darker than you right now. Why is that?"

Isabella laughed. "You spent time with Kevin outdoors last week while I was inside helping Mom. I'll catch up in a couple days."

An hour later they heard Kevin yelling then saw him climb out of the canyon and sprint toward them. "Did you feel that?"

"What?" Heather asked as she sat up.

"I think we had an earthquake about fifteen minutes ago. Didn't you feel anything?"

Heather and Isabella looked at each other then back at Kevin.

"You're crazy. There was no earthquake," Heather said.

"Then why did I almost get obliterated by a bunch of boulders crashing down from the side of the canyon? How do you explain that?"

"Did you really?" Isabella asked. She got up, put a towel around her waist, stepped into her flip-flops and followed Kevin back to the edge of the river canyon. Where were you when this happened?"

He pointed to the west. "Do you see where the river turns left to go south?"

"Yes."

Heather put on a pair of jean shorts and sandals and joined them.

"I was around the bend and probably a quarter mile downstream. Farther than I've ever gone down river in that direction. I was checking out a section of rapids..."

"Our river has rapids?" Heather asked looking over the edge of the canyon.

Kevin tilted a hand back and forth. "Nothing like what you see in the Colorado River. They're small, but they are real rapids. It would be a blast to take a raft, or a kayak, down the river."

"What about the boulders?" Isabella asked again.

"I was standing on the bank a few feet above the water when I heard a rumble and looked up. There had to have been a dozen boulders and smaller rocks coming right at me."

"What did you do?"

"I thought about diving into the water, but then the boulders probably would have landed on me. I ran a few feet back this way and dove behind a boulder that was already there. I heard a couple rocks bounce off it and they all crashed into the water."

"We didn't feel a thing here," Isabella said.

"What else could it have been?" Kevin asked.

Kevin told his story to his parents at dinner.

"I'm glad you're safe," Emmy said.

"I think it was a very localized earthquake," Kevin insisted.

Kenny thought about it. "It might have simply been erosion. It's rained more than normal this summer. Maybe the dirt and rocks gave way and the boulders finally were freed from their position."

"Maybe, but can I stick to the earthquake story when I talk to Ben?"

Chapter Twenty

"Did you finish your book?" Emmy asked Kevin while she made breakfast a week into their Idaho vacation.

"Almost. I have fifty pages to go," he answered setting the book on the table and looking out the window.

"Are you still reading that old western?" Heather asked as she poured a glass of orange juice.

"Yeah. It's really good. Can I have a glass, too?"

Heather handed him the glass and poured another one for herself. "What's the name?"

"*Riders of the Purple Sage*. It's by Zane Grey and it's over a hundred years old."

"It doesn't look that old," Heather said taking the book from her brother.

"That book is new, but it was first published in like 1912 or something. This is the restored edition."

"Why?"

"Why what?"

"Why is it restored? Was it lost or something?"

He shook his head. "No it was edited and stuff was left out. This version is the way the writer wrote it originally. It's got all the good parts in it."

"Do you even know which parts were left out originally?"

He shrugged. "Not really. I never read it before."

Heather handed the book back. "I might read it when you're finished. I should have added more books to my laptop, but I didn't know we would be cooped up the entire summer. I should have gone with Mom when she went into town to buy groceries."

"The weather is supposed to clear tomorrow," Kenny said. "No more rain for the next week or so."

"Can we take the Jeep out. Let's find a trail in the mountains."

"Maybe we should wait a couple days to let the trails dry out. We don't want to get stuck in a canyon somewhere and have a landslide bury us."

After three days of sunshine and no rain, Kenny and Kevin headed out to find a trail into the mountains.

"I downloaded a map," Kevin said. He glanced out the window then back at his map. "We should come to a fork soon. If we go left, it should take us toward the top."

Ten minutes later, Kenny stopped. "Should we see how deep the water is?"

The muddy water was only a foot deep and the Jeep made it through the creek with ease. Eventually, the trail became more primitive as it gained elevation, and Kevin had to get out and guide the Jeep over some boulders. The trail was still below the treeline, and had become narrow enough for the Jeep to brush against some branches and bushes.

"That's going to leave a mark," Kevin said as another bush scraped the Jeep's side.

They reached the top, parked and got out to enjoy the view.

"Do you think there's a trail to the top of that mountain?" Kevin pointed to a snow-covered peak.

"I doubt it, and even if there is, I don't think we should try it. I'd hate to get stranded in the snow. Your mother would never let me live it down."

"That would be funny to get stuck in snow in the middle of summer."

"Mom, Dad and I are taking the Jeep on Onion Creek Road across Bancroft Pass to Mr. Robertson's ranch. It's a 4x4 trail. Do you want to join us? We'll be gone all day, and might even have to spend the night at one of the line cabins."

Emmy looked at him. "Thanks for asking, but I can tell you don't want me or your sisters along. That's okay. The men can enjoy their adventure. We will entertain ourselves here at the ranch."

"In that case, can you make us some sandwiches?" Kevin asked.

"Do you have enough water?" Emmy asked as the guys finished loading the Jeep later.

"Yes. We have enough for a week," Kevin answered.

"Sleeping bags? Enough fuel?"

"Mom! We could survive for a the whole summer in one of the cabins the cowboys use."

When Kevin wasn't watching, Kenny held up his new Garmin inReach Explorer+. He had ordered two when they arrived in Idaho. Emmy saw it and knew the satellite phone wouldn't rely on a cell signal.

"Let me know if you're going to be gone for more than a few days. I might have to rent a pickup truck so we're not stuck out here." Emmy hugged them and kissed Kenny. She watched until the Jeep was out of site before going inside.

"Mom, I'm bored," Heather said. "There's nothing to do and the Internet is down again."

"I'm going to take another hike along the river. Would you and Isa care to join me?"

"I will," Isabella said.

"I will make sandwiches and we can carry water in our backpacks. It will be fun. We can look for snakes and all kinds of lizards and things."

Heather groaned and said, "I'll pass. At least I can send emails when the Internet comes back."

"I know you're teasing about the snakes," Isabella whispered. "You are, right?"

"Yes, but I have seen a few. We can check out the wildflowers."

It took most of the day, but the Jeep made it to Mr. Robertson's ranch with only a couple minor mishaps. They needed to use the recovery traction boards to free the Jeep from mud two times.

"Are we going to stay here tonight?" Kevin asked as they knocked on the front door.

"Maybe. We'll see if there's a cabin close by." Prior to leaving Kenny had called Tobias Tawney to let the ranch foreman know they were coming. Tobias had a couple of the ranch hands check on the north line cabin to make sure there was enough firewood and supplies.

161

The door opened and Tobias greeted them with a smile and a laugh. He removed his weathered cowboy hat, ran his hand over his close-cropped gray hair and rubbed his equally gray beard and winked at Kenny. "I'm Tobias Tawney, and I'm the foreman of this ranch. Now who might you be, young pardner?"

"I'm Kevin Colwell. Mr. Robertson and I were good friends. We drove over Bancroft Pass to get here."

"Well, come on in and make yourself to home. Are you looking for work? I could use a hand up in the north pasture."

Kevin shrugged. "Doing what?"

Tobias laughed again. "I'm kidding. You can stay here tonight if you want, but you might have more fun staying at the line cabin."

"Yeah! I want to stay in a cabin." Kevin looked around. "This is a nice house, but it's like living at home. I want to stay in a primitive cabin like a real cowboy."

"That can be arranged." Tobias gave them directions to the line cabin. "None of the ranch hands are staying there at the moment. The herd is farther south. You can have the place all week if you want."

"Thanks, Mr. Tobias. I'll do some chores if you want."

"You might need to chop some firewood. It can get kinda cold up here even in the summer."

"Is there a real stove in the cabin?"

"If you mean an old wood-burner, yeah. You can use it to cook and heat the cabin if it gets too cold."

Kevin pumped his fist. "Wait till I tell Ben and Taylor about this."

Kenny parked the Jeep in front of the line cabin and Kevin jumped out. He sprinted to the door and threw it open. He let his eyes adjust to the darkness as the sun had already set.

Kenny used his cell phone to light up the cabin.

"There's a lantern over there," Kevin said.

Thirty minutes later, the stove was producing heat and two lanterns provided enough light to let them see. Kevin checked the cans on the shelves.

"Can we make this stew?" he asked. "Mr. Robertson said he liked it."

"I don't see why not." Kenny opened the can of Dinfield Miller beef stew.

After dinner they sat outside on the porch.

"I've never seen so many stars," Kevin said.

"There's not much light pollution up here."

"I should have brought the Zane Gray books. This would be the perfect place to finish them."

Kenny called Emmy after Kevin was asleep.

"Are you staying in a cabin?"

"Yes, and it is rather primitive. There's no electricity, but there is solar power. Kevin didn't see it, and we didn't use it." He mentioned getting stuck and she laughed. "How was your day, Em? Did you do anything exciting?"

"Isa and I hiked along the river. We had lunch on a bluff above it."

"Heather didn't go, huh?"

"She stayed home. Don't tell Kevin, but she started reading his books. She admitted they were okay."

"I won't tell him."

"How long do you plan to stay?"

"Three or four days. Kevin wants to explore the ranch. He's hoping to see a buffalo herd."

"I didn't know Mr. Robertson owned any buffalo."

"I don't think he owns them. I'm pretty sure they are wild, and since they're protected and living on BLM land, they have increased in number."

"If you see them, don't let Kevin get too close. Remind him they are different than cows, okay?"

"I will. Does it matter if I get too close?" he teased.

She giggled and said, "No. You have a large life insurance policy, and I am the beneficiary."

"Ha! Ha! I don't think it covers death by buffalo stampedes."

"Heather, would you like to help me cook dinner?" Emmy asked.

"What are we having? Please tell me we aren't eating pasta again."

"I want to try a new black bean and white cheddar frittata recipe. I bought the ingredients to make fresh salsa, too." Emmy showed Heather a photo of the finished product.

"That looks interesting. How long will it take?"

Emmy and Heather spent most of the afternoon in the kitchen.

"This is really good," Isabella said at dinnertime. "Did you really make it by yourself, Heather?"

"Not really. Mom helped. I did add some different spices to the recipe and a bit of fresh cilantro."

"I didn't know you were interested in cooking."

Heather shrugged and took another bite. "It will give me something to do until we get back to civilization."

Kenny and Kevin explored the trails both on foot and in the Jeep and stayed four nights at the cabin.

"I hope Brady never sells the ranch," Kevin said on the way back. "It's a lot bigger than ours, and there are so many trails to explore. I might decide to become a ranch hand when I get older."

"I think Brady and Bennett will hold onto it for a few years." Kenny slowly drove the Jeep over a medium-sized boulder.

"It's about time you got back," Emmy said when the guys returned.

"It was great!" Kevin said. "We explored all kinds of trails, and I didn't have to shower at all."

Heather and Isabella backed away from their father.

"Did you shower?" Emmy asked Kenny.

"No, but I'm heading there now."

Heather jabbed a finger into Kevin's chest. "You need to hose off outside before you set foot in our bathroom."

"But there's no hot water outside."

"Hey! Cowboys don't complain," Isabella said then giggled.

"I read both of those books while you were gone," Heather said. "The language is a bit old-fashioned, but I really liked the stories."

"Me, too. Don't tell me how they end, okay?"

"I won't." She grinned at her father and said, "I made zucchini lasagna for dinner all by myself. You better like it."

"I'm sure it will be delicious," Kenny said then moved closer to hug his daughters.

"Go! Shower first!" Heather ordered and pointed toward the master bedroom.

"I need to run into town for supplies," Emmy said. "The Fourth of July is this Sunday, and I want steaks for the grill. Do you want to go with me, Heather?"

"Thanks, Mom, but I was going to hike with Kevin. He found some pictographs along the river, and I want to see them."

Emmy grinned and thought about the change in Heather's attitude. *You have certainly surprised me lately. You didn't even scream when that snake crawled past you while you were sunbathing the other day.*

"Mom, make sure you buy some ground mustard. I want to make a meatloaf, and we don't have any."

"I'll add it to my list," Emmy said.

"I don't suppose there will any fireworks to see tomorrow," Kevin said as everyone was eating the breakfast Heather made Saturday morning.

"Ketchum Forks will probably have a fireworks display," Kenny said.

"We've seen enough fireworks over the years," Isabella said. She took a bite and looked at Heather. "This is surprisingly good. When did you learn to make quiche?"

"I got the recipe from a YouTube video. There's a channel about this family who lives in a Jeep with a little girl who is absolutely adorable. The mom made something similar. Do you really like it?"

"It's scrumptious," Isabella answered.

165

"Dad, can we take the Jeep out later?" Kevin asked. "I found the perfect place to build a fort."

"I suppose so," he answered.

"Is it on our property?" Emmy asked.

"I'm pretty sure it is. It's on our side of the river in that direction." He pointed to the east.

"Can I go with?" Heather asked.

Emmy's eyes showed her surprise when Kevin told her she was welcome to go.

"Maybe we can all go," Kevin said.

Isabella looked at her mother and shook her head. "I don't feel like going anywhere today."

Emmy looked at Isabella and understood why.

"Isa and I will pass. We need to have a chill day together."

Heather followed Isabella to her bedroom later.

"Is it pretty bad?"

"It's been worse, but I should be okay."

"You don't mind if I go with Kevin and Dad, do you?"

"Not at all. I'm glad you are having fun."

"I realized my attitude sucked, so I decided to change it. That's one thing we can control when everything else goes haywire."

Kevin directed Kenny to the spot he found and showed his father and Heather exactly where he intended to build his fort.

"Looks like a good spot. There are trees to use for anchors and a couple large boulders to use as a wall," Kenny said.

"Or to slide into the canyon," Heather said.

"Can I buy a hammer and nails the next time we go into town? I need a saw, too."

"What about lumber?" Heather asked.

Kevin shook his head. "I'll use different size tree limbs and stuff. It's going to be rustic, and it might take a couple summers to finish."

"I'm willing to help if you want."

"Sure, but that doesn't mean you can hang out in our clubhouse back home."

While they were in town, Kenny bought a drone.

"Can we fly it on our property and other places?" Kevin asked.

"I'll have to learn how to fly it and check the rules. It should be fun."

While Kevin unpacked the drone, Kenny watched several YouTube videos and read some articles online.

"Are you ready to give it a try?" Kenny asked.

"Yeah!"

"Can we watch?" Heather asked.

"The more eyes on the drone, the better we can keep track of it," Kenny responded. "We should practice in the backyard."

"Try not to land it in the river," Emmy teased.

Soon, Kenny and Kevin were capable of keeping the drone in sight and were able to fly it in the direction they wanted.

"Maybe after we practice a few hours, we could take it to the mountains," Kevin said.

"I've seen videos where the drone follows a vehicle."

"Really?" Emmy asked.

"The drone is above the vehicle. Maybe a hundred feet in the air, and follows the road," Kenny explained.

"You should watch the video, Mom. Then you'd understand what Dad means," Kevin said.

"Do we have to watch church today?" Kevin asked. "It's a holiday."

"Yes, because it's Pastor Wyatt's last Sunday. You and your father can fly the drone later," Emmy said.

They watched the livestream until their unreliable Internet cut out again.

"That's the third time this week we've lost the Internet," Emmy told Kenny. "I wish we could switch providers."

"I don't think we have that option," Kenny said. "This will teach us not to depend on modern technology."

"You don't mean the electricity and indoor plumbing, do you?" Emmy asked sarcastically.

167

Chapter Twenty-One

"How did it go at church today?" Emmy asked. "Tony said there wasn't a potluck in your honor because of the holiday. That sucks. They should do something for you."

Kristen watched ten-month-old Kayla scoot across the floor as she packed up the kitchen for the move. "The service was okay. A lot of people are on vacation. You weren't the only family not to be there. Roger Goldman presented Wyatt with a check. That was his gift from the church."

"How much?" Emmy asked then waved a hand. "No, don't tell me. It's none of my business."

"It was enough to cover the move."

"Were there a lot of people crying?"

"Not really," Kristen said. "Most of the men shook Wyatt's hand, but they didn't get too emotional."

"I meant your friends," Emmy said. "I know the men are afraid to show their emotions."

"There were some tears and a lot of hugs."

"I'm sorry I couldn't be there, Krissy. Will you forgive me?"

"Nothing to forgive, Em. How are things in Idaho?"

Emmy talked about the weather and the hikes.

"Kevin called Zach and told him about the Jeep trails and seeing Mr. Robertson's cattle. Kevin was excited, but Zach did not seem impressed. Did Kenny really buy a drone?"

"Zach's never been enamored of outdoor adventures like Kevin and Ben. Kenny and Kevin are outside flying the drone now. What time are the movers coming?"

"They are supposed to be here at seven. It shouldn't take too long to load the truck. I sold, or gave away, items I did not think would fit in the new house."

"New old house," Emmy said.

"Yes. Wyatt thought it would arrive in Alexandria Rapids around six at the latest. Tyler promised to have some men available to help."

"The neighborhood won't be the same without you," Emmy said and her voice cracked.

"Now don't get all emotional on me. We won't be that far away."

Emmy wiped her eyes. "Yeah, but you won't be five minutes away."

"Are you going to work today?" Kristen asked Tony in the morning.

"Yes, but I wanted to stop by before you left. Sloane and the kids will come over later."

Kristen glanced over her shoulder at the house. "Your mother is scrubbing the kitchen. I told her not to bother, but you know how she is."

"She will stop if her hip starts hurting." He watched the four guys loading the truck. "It's too bad they can't pull into the driveway. That would save a million steps, and probably save you a bundle of money."

Tony followed Kristen inside and convinced his mother to stop working so hard.

"I wanted to make sure the kitchen was spotless for whoever might see it." Mama Bertucci checked the oven and fridge. "They are clean enough. I hope the new owners are half as nice as you, dear, but they won't be family. You're leaving. Your brother rarely visits SoHam, and Marco is too busy to come home. I don't know what I would do if Tony and Sloane decided to move."

"I know you don't want us to move, but Wyatt needs to go where he feels God wants him," Kristen explained.

"We will give you a chance to settle in your new home before we visit," Sloane said bending down to roll a ball to Kayla.

"It won't take us long. You are welcome to visit anytime. It will be crowded, but we will manage," Kristen said.

"We will miss you," Sloane whispered as she hugged Kristen.

"I hope I don't regret leaving SoHam. I have lived here nearly my entire life."

169

Kristen drove her Acura to Michigan and took Kayla with her. Wyatt followed closely behind in the Odyssey. The older kids rode with him so they could watch a movie. Both vehicles arrived in Alexandria Rapids at four thirty Michigan time. As they waited at a traffic light, Kristen called Wyatt's cell phone.

"I should let Liz know we have arrived," Kristen said.

"Good idea," Wyatt replied. "Do you remember how to get to the house?"

"Yes, but I am using my navigation to be sure."

A minute later Wyatt chuckled and told Zach and Grace, "Look. Tyler is mowing our yard, and I can see Liz and the kids." He pulled into the driveway behind Kristen and had barely stopped the van when Zach and Grace hopped out.

"I'm so glad to see you," Natalie Hammond said as she hugged Grace. "Are you excited about moving into your new house?"

"Yes, but I will miss all my friends in SoHam. At least I have you close."

Tyler finished mowing the last section and joined Wyatt.

"You didn't have to do that," Wyatt said as they shook hands.

"It needed it," Tyler said. "Can I help unload the vehicles?"

"Okay, but we want to go inside first," Wyatt answered.

"Go on in. It's unlocked. I will start unloading," Tyler said.

By the time Wyatt, Kristen and the kids returned, Tyler had everything out of both vehicles.

"Mom, can I take Grace and Zach to our house?" Natalie asked. "There's nothing to do here but wait for the truck."

"If it's all right with Kristen and Wyatt, you can go."

Kristen gave Zach and Grace permission. "Don't go anywhere else, okay?"

"We won't," Phoebe said. She helped Kayla crawl in the grass for a moment before running after the other kids.

"I have an idea," Liz said.

Everyone looked at her.

"You guys will be too tired to unpack and get the beds put together tonight, so you should stay with us."

"We don't want to impose. Do you have enough room?" Kristen asked.

Liz chuckled and answered, "Of course. We have a guest room upstairs. You and Wyatt can use it. Grace can sleep with Natty and Phoebe and the boys can crash in the basement. Grayson likes to stay there. He calls it camping."

Kristen looked at Wyatt. "What do you think?"

"We could let the kids stay over, but I would like to sleep in my own bed."

"Let's play it by ear," Kristen suggested.

A few minutes later four men from Tyler's church showed up.

"The truck should be here soon," Wyatt said after Tyler introduced everyone.

The truck arrived fifteen minutes later, and with the help of the volunteers, the entire truck was unloaded in under two hours. Kristen directed the placement of the furniture and the boxes, which were all labeled. Liz started unpacking the kitchen gear. The volunteers from church put all the beds together and even hooked up the electronics.

"Is anyone else starving?" Liz asked.

Everyone nodded. They walked down the street to Liz and Tyler's house and ordered pizzas.

"Have you changed your mind about tonight?" Liz asked.

"Would you mind if Grace and Zach spend the night?" Kristen asked. "Wyatt, Kayla and I will stay in our new home."

"The kids are welcome to stay," Liz said. "They are having fun, and we will figure out the sleeping arrangements later."

"You can send Zach and Grace home anytime you want," Kristen said the next morning. "I don't want them to be a bother if you have things to do."

"They aren't a bother in the least," Liz replied with a dismissive wave. "The girls are doing each other's hair, and the boys are outside. I'm not sure what they're doing, but they're having fun. Do you need any help this morning?"

Kristen looked at Wyatt, who was drinking his coffee and finishing a bagel. "It's Liz. She's offering to help if we need her."

"She could watch Kayla while we clean and unpack."

"Did you hear him?" Kristen asked.

Liz laughed and answered, "I did, and I do want Kayla to get to know me."

Wyatt found Kristen in the backyard after lunch and asked, "Would you be okay if I head over to the church with Tyler? He wants to give me a formal tour and introduce me to whoever is around."

"I don't mind. I am going to go for a walk with Kayla."

"When did she learn to walk?" Wyatt asked with a straight face.

"In the buggy, silly," she replied and kissed him.

"I will be back in time for dinner." He started back into the house, but then stopped, did a 180 and asked, "Didn't we have two older children when we moved here? Have they grown up and moved away?"

"Liz said they are playing at the park. I told her to send them home soon. They need to unpack their clothes and things."

Tyler picked up Wyatt and headed through the downtown business district of Alexandria Rapids.

"It gets pretty busy at times," Tyler said as they waited at a red light. "The town hasn't allowed a Walmart, or any of the big box stores, to open. The local businesses are in good shape. Bartonsville is forty miles east, and they have all the big stores, but their local businesses have suffered. Downtown Bartonsville is a ghost town except for the county courthouse."

Wyatt pointed to a parking lot. "Are those shipping containers?"

Tyler chuckled. "The city bought those and leases them to local people to open a business. There's a floral shop, an art store and a small hot dog stand."

"I bet the town was busy over the weekend."

"We walked over here Saturday afternoon, and there were so many people it took forever to get around."

"I've noticed several people walking around without masks on," Wyatt said.

"We haven't had many cases of the virus so far. I think it's because we are kind of in the middle of nowhere."

Tyler pulled into the church's front parking lot.

"The church is two miles from home, and I could jog here if I wanted. I usually drive the Prius in case I have to make a quick visit somewhere." He opened the door and they went inside. "How much of the church have you seen?"

"I saw parts of it the last time we were here. I met a few people, but I don't remember names."

"It's okay. There are parts of the building I haven't seen yet. I've been too lazy to take the time to do a thorough tour."

"I can understand. There were parts of the Crest Ridge church I never entered."

"There are rooms under the old sanctuary I want to check out. They are used for storage now, but there may come a time when we need more classrooms."

Tyler and Wyatt toured the building for the next half hour. Eventually, they came up some stairs and entered a long hallway.

"My office is on the left," Tyler said then chuckled. "I chose the last one to be close to these old stairs. Only a few people know they are here, and I can use them to make a quick exit if needed."

Wyatt ducked into Tyler's office. "This isn't very big." He noticed the bookcases on one wall and a copy machine to his left.

"I don't need a lot of room, and this one has a large window." Tyler checked his desk for messages, read one yellow Post-it note and chuckled. "I'll introduce you to the church secretary."

They walked down the hall, and Tyler stopped at a large room.

"I thought you could use this one. Pastor Tim used it, but now it's empty. It's the closest one to the main church office," Tyler added with a grin.

"Is that an advantage or a disadvantage?" Wyatt asked with a quizzical look.

"Time will tell," Tyler replied and they entered the main church office.

"Good afternoon, Pastor Tyler," one of the two ladies said. "Is this Pastor Wyatt?

Wyatt smiled. "I am."

Tyler chuckled. "This is Mrs. Grimsley. I might be the senior pastor, but Mrs. Grimsley is the boss."

She extended a hand to Wyatt and frowned at Tyler. "*You* may call me Clara. My husband, Mitch, is mowing the yard."

"This is Kady Ahrens," Tyler said. "She helps part-time and teaches second grade at one of the elementary schools in town. She's also on the worship team."

Wyatt nodded at the younger lady.

"Mrs. Grimsley has been the church secretary for many years," Tyler said.

"Thirty-two years this month," she replied. "Mitch and I were born here, and have never lived anywhere else. If you need anything, or need to know anything about the church, please call me. Not much goes on around here that I don't know about."

Tyler and Wyatt smiled as they left the office.

"Now I know why your office is at the end of the hall," Wyatt said shaking his head.

Chapter Twenty-Two

"Dad, what are we going to do for Mom's birthday?" Isabella asked. "It's tomorrow and we haven't planned anything. We have to do something."

Kenny set his coffee cup down and turned his attention from the backyard to Isabella. "I talked to her about it last night, and she doesn't want anything special. She said turning forty-one is no big deal."

"Maybe not, but we need to do something. Since we really can't go anywhere, maybe we could make her favorite dinner."

Kenny laughed.

"What's so funny?" Heather asked as she sat beside her father with her own coffee.

"Isabella mentioned your mother's favorite dinner, and I thought about what she always asked for when she would eat dinner with us."

"Like when she was a kid?" Heather asked.

"Yes."

"What did she want?" Isabella asked.

"Mashed potatoes," he answered.

"Mashed potatoes and what else?" Isabella asked tilting her head.

Kenny shrugged. "That was it."

"There had to be more to dinner than mashed potatoes."

Kenny motioned for Isabella to sit. Then he explained, "Your grandmother, Emmy's mother, wasn't full-blooded Italian. Just half, but your grandfather was full Italian. His mother..."

"Our great-grandmother," Isabella said.

"Yes. Grandma Mary Colasanti probably never made mashed potatoes in her life. She made pasta for every meal. Homemade pasta. Not the kind you buy at the store. Your grandfather expected some kind of pasta at every meal."

"What about Grandma Isabel?" Heather asked. "She was Italian, right?"

Kenny nodded. "Her maiden name was Polmonari. Definitely Italian."

"Where was Grandpa Sandusky's family from?" Isabella asked.

"Either Scotland or Poland," Kenny answered with another shrug. "No one knew for sure. Maybe both places. He definitely was not Italian."

"So, Mom viewed mashed potatoes as something special, huh?" Isabella asked.

"Yes, and she didn't like gravy at first."

"Why not?"

"My mother's gravy was from an old family recipe. Your mother made a face when she first tried it."

"She was a kid, right? How old was she?"

"Seven or eight."

"She likes gravy now," Isabella said. "Should we make mashed potatoes for her birthday?"

"That doesn't sound like a special dinner."

"I could make that green bean casserole she likes. The one with onion rings on the top. I can Google a recipe."

"We have steaks in the freezer. I could grill steaks, and you could make the rest of dinner," Kenny said. "Make extra potatoes because your brother will eat half of them."

"No doubt," Heather sighed.

"I will bake a cake," Isabella said. "How hard can it be?"

"Happy birthday, Emmy." Kenny rubbed her hip and leaned over her as they lay in bed. "Do you need a kiss?"

"I need sleep more than a kiss," she answered.

He kissed her cheek then pulled the sheet up to her shoulder. "You can stay in bed as long as you like. This will be your day to be lazy."

"If you're trying to make me feel guilty, it won't work."

"I can make blueberry pancakes if you want."

She moved onto her back and looked up at him. "That's not fair. You know I can't pass up blueberry pancakes." She paused then stuck out her tongue. "Wait a minute! We don't have fresh blueberries."

"We might have frozen ones."

176

"Nice try, but it didn't work. Let me sleep for another hour then I will get up, and we can do something."

"Like what?"

"We could take the Jeep and explore that trail again. We could have a picnic in that meadow. It was so pretty with all the wildflowers."

"Sounds like a plan. Too bad Lassie isn't here. She would love exploring the area. Have you heard from Tony about her visit to the vet?"

"Yeah. The vet said her numbers look better."

"That's good," Kenny said. "Do we have stuff to make sandwiches?"

"Yes, and we can take potato and macaroni salad. You should check the cooler and make sure those plastic things are frozen."

"Will do."

"Are we ready to hit the trail?" Kenny asked. "Does anyone need to use the bathroom?"

"Dad, we aren't babies. We have enough sense to use the bathroom before we leave," Isabella said as she climbed into the middle seat in back.

"Does everyone have a bottle of water?" Emmy asked as she scooted in next to Isabella. "We have plenty of water in the back of the Jeep."

"Do we have enough food for Kevin?" Heather asked.

"We have enough food to last normal people a week," Emmy said.

"That means we have enough to last a day. Two at the most," Isabella teased.

"If everyone is buckled in, we are ready to start our adventure."

"Dad, we're just going ten miles from home," Kevin said. "We don't even have to use four-wheel drive to get there."

"We might if the roads are slick from the rain."

An hour later Kenny pulled into one of the dispersed camping sites along the trail.

"That wasn't so bad, was it?" he asked.

"No, but next time we should bring a chainsaw. I'm sore from sawing through that tree," Kevin said.

"It must have fallen earlier today," Emmy said. She got out and did a 360 to take in the view. "I love this. Look over there! I can see snow on those peaks."

"They are probably snowcapped all year long."

"I'm going to check out the stream." Kevin pointed to the opposite side of the meadow. "We should have brought our fishing poles. I bet I could catch enough fish to last all summer."

"From up here?" Heather asked.

"Maybe, but I could fish the river behind the house every day. I found an easier trail to get down to it."

"You're becoming quite a mountain man," Emmy said.

Kenny brought out the camp chairs and their small table. He set the cooler on it.

"Should we have lunch now, or go exploring first?" Emmy asked.

"Let's explore first," Kenny said.

Kevin took off. "I'll be by the stream."

"Where are you going to explore?" Kenny asked the girls.

"Are there bears or mountain lions up here?" Heather asked.

"I doubt it. Not in the meadow at least." Kenny pointed to some of the far away peaks. "They would be more likely to be at higher altitude."

"I'm not straying too far from the Jeep in case the bears don't know where they're supposed to be," Heather said.

It was five o'clock before Kenny pulled into the driveway, and everyone piled out.

"I'm going to take a shower before I fire up the grill," Kenny said.

"You wouldn't need a shower if you hadn't fallen into the creek," Isabella teased.

"At least we were able to make a human chain and pull him back up the bank," Emmy said.

178

"I'll start on dinner," Isabella said. "Heather, will you help me peel the potatoes?"

"Can't we use the instant potatoes? It's so much easier."

"I want to make real mashed potatoes for Mom's birthday."

"I will help peel the potatoes," Emmy said. "Just because it's my birthday doesn't mean I can't help."

Kenny grilled the steaks, and they decided to eat on the deck since the weather was perfect.

"Do they have mosquitoes in Idaho?" Kevin asked.

"Of course," Heather said. "They stay away because of our candles."

"Not all of them," Emmy said as she slapped her arm.

"Should we sing before we eat?" Kenny asked.

"No! I made a cake this morning," Isabella reminded them. "We can sing and make Mom blow out candles later."

The steaks were great!" Kevin exclaimed.

"They must have been since you ate yours and half of mine," Emmy said.

"Should we have the cake now, or wait?" Isabella asked.

"Let's wait," Emmy suggested.

"I'm ready for cake," Kevin said an hour later.

Isabella brought it out, set the candles in the frosting and used a charcoal lighter to light them.

"Make a wish first, Mom," Kevin said.

"We have to sing."

"Now you can blow out the candles," Isabella said.

Emmy blew out the candles. "I made a wish." She squeezed Kenny's hand and whispered, "For Lassie to get better."

"What did you say?" Kevin asked.

"I wish Lassie was here," Emmy said.

Heather scooped the ice cream while Isabella cut the cake.

"We ordered a book for you, Mom, but I accidentally sent it home instead of here," Heather said.

"That's fine. I don't need presents, but thank you. It's been a wonderful day."

Heidi Knapp called Kristen Friday morning with good news.

"It's a cash offer for the full listing price. The only downside is their request for a quick closing," Heidi said.

"We don't mind a quick closing," Kristen replied. "The name is unfamiliar to me. What can you tell me about the buyers."

"Dr. Hittleman is a chemical engineer. He started his company about thirty years ago, and it's one of the most successful in that field in the country."

"So, it's an older couple, huh?" Wyatt asked.

"Yes."

"No kids?"

Heidi checked her computer. "According to the info online, they have three grown children and several grandchildren. Maybe the grandchildren live in the area, and that's why they want a home in SoHam."

"When can we sign the contract?" Kristen asked.

"I will fax it right away."

"This will give us an excuse to come back to SoHam for a couple days," Kristen said. "Thank you for everything, Heidi."

"Let me know if I can be of further assistance."

Kristen set the phone down and looked at Wyatt.

"We need to decide what to do with the proceeds. We should talk to Mr. Robertson's attorney."

"What would you like to do with it?" Wyatt asked.

"Invest it. Maybe we could set up trusts for the kids' educations. I could talk to Derrick, and see what he recommends."

"I will go along with whatever you decide."

Chapter Twenty-Three

"Emmy, it is so good to hear your voice. How is your vacation going? We miss you at church," Rebecca replied when Emmy called Saturday morning.

"We miss being there, and we're having a great vacation. The weather has been perfect, other than some rainy days. Kevin is loving Idaho, but I think the girls are a bit homesick. They miss their friends."

"And now some of their closest friends have moved to Michigan."

"I'm sure that is a factor in how they feel," Emmy said. They talked about Rebecca's kids for a moment then Emmy brought up the new pastoral staff.

"Everyone has arrived in the area, and they have all moved into their housing. Pastor Howe had a staff meeting Wednesday, and I met the new people."

"How did they seem?" Emmy asked.

"They are all uncommonly nice. You knew Grady was bringing people from his old church with him, right?"

"Yes."

"In addition to them, he has already hired new pastors for the children and seniors. He is going to interview a new intern next week."

"That was fast. Doesn't the board have any say in who he hires?"

"Not really. The board sets a budget for staff, and the senior pastor is allowed to hire who he wants."

"I knew he was bringing someone to replace Wyatt and you. Who was the third one?"

"The teen pastor. Youth pastor. You know what I mean. The older kids."

"What are their names?"

"I wrote them down because I knew people would be calling and asking."

"I didn't mean to bug you, Rebecca. Have you gotten lots of calls this week?"

"A few, and I don't mind." She pulled up the names on her phone. "Grady's senior associate is Cole Miller and his wife is Valerie. They have two kids, but I didn't write down the names."

"That's okay. Who else?"

"Keegan Lochner is the worship pastor."

"I remembered his name."

"The other one is... let me find it... Tarrell Robinson. I'm not sure how he spells it, but he is the new youth pastor. I don't think he's married."

"Is he African American?" Emmy asked.

"Yes, and he's maybe thirty at the most."

"How old are the other ones?"

"Keegan and Pastor Miller are in their mid-thirties," Rebecca said. "They knew each other in college. I remember that from the meeting."

"And Pastor Howe already hired a children's minister and someone to replace Pastor Milhuff, huh?"

"Yes. Monica Sanchez is the children's pastor, and Darrell Norton will be the pastor for the seasoned members as Tyler liked to call them. He's in his late fifties at the most, but he should be a good fit. Pastor Flores and Pastor Jonah are still here, and Pastor Howe didn't make any changes in the office staff."

"Except you," Emmy said while carrying laundry. .

"I was hired before he came. I don't think Mr. Goldman was going to give him the option of not hiring me."

"He will make sure the church takes care of you and Ryan. I made him promise."

"I appreciate that," Rebecca said.

"So, how did rehearsal go this week?" Emmy asked. She got a whiff of Kevin's dirty clothes and wrinkled her nose.

"Thursday's rehearsal was longer because Keegan took time to get to know everyone. He insists we call him Keegan and not Pastor Keegan or Pastor Lochner," Rebecca said. "He likes to keep things rather informal. Oh, we switched the schedule around since your family is gone."

Emmy set the basket on the washer. "I'm sure the girls will be anxious to rejoin the team when we get home."

"Keegan chose familiar songs to make the transition easier this Sunday. He gave us a list of several new songs he would like to use in the next couple of months. He emailed the list with links to each one. He would like the team to begin writing original material and offered to work with anyone interested. He mentioned you, Emmy."

"I'm not part of the team anymore."

"Yeah, well, he might try to persuade you to sing once a month and be part of the creative effort to write original material."

"I would have to think about it," Emmy said. "Do you think the team resents Keegan coming in and taking your position?"

Rebecca thought for a moment. "I can't think of anyone who might feel that way. Last week at practice I talked to them about the transition. I assured everyone I was okay with the switch. Keegan assured me I would still have input. In a way, this will be easier for me. I will be working almost as many hours as before but during the day. I can bring the kids to church with me, and not have to find a babysitter or place them in a daycare center. I'd rather not have strange people watching them." Rebecca laughed. "I should have said unfamiliar people."

"I get your point even if you made it sound weird," Emmy chuckled.

"Are you going to watch the livestream Sunday?"

"I will make sure everyone gets up in time to watch. We might be in our pajamas, but we will be at church with you in spirit."

"Who was on the phone?" Piper Howe asked her husband early Sunday morning.

"It was Dr. Schofield. He was supposed to be here to install me, but was called away for a family emergency."

"Is it serious?" Piper asked. She adjusted Grady's tie. "That's better."

"His father was taken to the hospital back in Michigan. Or was it Indiana? I can't remember. Whichever state he is from, I guess."

"So, are you on your own?"

183

"No. His new assistant will be here." Grady chuckled and said, "This is his first week on the job. What a way to start."

"You have to stay awake for church," Emmy said when Kevin yawned and closed his eyes.

"But it's too early," he complained. "Why does church start so early?"

"Time zones, you goof," Heather said poking her brother in the side.

They watched the countdown timer reach all zeroes and the screen changed from the announcements to the live shot in the sanctuary.

"That's the new pastor, right?" Kevin asked.

"Yes, but I wonder why no one is introducing him," Emmy mentioned.

"That is strange," Kenny said. "I would have thought Dr. Schofield would be there to formally introduce him."

Pastor Howe welcomed everyone in the sanctuary and also those watching the livestream. He explaining the reason for Dr. Schofield's absence and then opened the service with a prayer. He left the platform and the worship team took over.

"I thought Pastor Rebecca was fired," Kevin said. "She's still playing the piano."

"There is a new worship pastor," Emmy replied. "Pastor Rebecca is working in the office now.

"Is that the new worship leader?" Isabella pointed to a man with a guitar. "I've never seen him before."

"That's Keegan Lochner."

"He better get a haircut, or the old ladies in the church will be after him," Kevin said with a laugh.

"He's pretty tall," Isabella added.

"He looks skinny," Heather said.

"He probably has tattoos," Kevin joked.

The worship team sang four songs before leaving the stage.

"Who is that?" Kevin pointed.

"If you listen, perhaps he will introduce himself," Kenny said.

"As you can tell, I am not Dr, Schofield. My name is Anton Curbelo, and this is my first Sunday as your assistant in the district office. I received a text from Dr. Schofield a few minutes ago. His father has passed away..."

"He didn't preach as long as Pastor Tyler," Kevin said later.

"Maybe he cut his message short because of what happened," Isabella said.

"I liked it when he introduced the new staff members and reintroduced the ones who stayed. He even introduced Pastor Flores."

"Does the Spanish church do a livestream, too?" Kevin asked.

"Yes," Emmy answered.

"You can't watch it because you don't speak Spanish," Heather told her brother.

"I know a few phrases."

"Yes, but I doubt they use them in church," Isabella teased.

"So, we have a Hispanic pastor for the children. An African American youth pastor..."

"And an old white guy for the old people," Kevin interrupted. "It fits since they're mostly old white ladies, who do nothing but complain about stuff."

"Pastor Norton is not an old white guy." Emmy frowned at Kevin. "He's in his late fifties."

Kevin shrugged then chuckled. "Like I said. An old guy."

Isabella added, "I thought Dr. Schofield's assistant did a good job of *installing* Pastor Howe and the staff. He might not be as excitable as Dr. Schofield..."

"No one is," Emmy said.

"Daddy, I thought you did a good job today,"

"Thank you, Ashlyn." Grady pulled his daughter onto his lap. "Why do you look sad?"

She snuggled closer to her daddy. "I'm sad because that man's father got sick."

"Me, too."

"Mommy said it's okay because he gets to be with Jesus all the time now. Maybe he can talk to Grandpa in heaven," Ashlyn said.

Grady hugged her and blinked away a tear.

"Who were those old ladies you were talking to after the service?" Corey, the younger son, asked.

Grady chuckled.

"Please do not refer to them as *old ladies*," Piper insisted.

"But it's the truth," Corey responded.

"That may be so, but please use a more proper term to describe them." Piper looked at Grady. "What were they telling you? They were rather animated and had you surrounded for several minutes."

"They gave me a few pointers about how I should conduct the services. They want to hear more hymns."

"Not those old songs!" Asher, the older son, said with a roll of his eyes. "They belong in funerals."

"One of the ladies chastised me for not keeping Pastor Wyatt on the staff. She explained how they didn't care for him when Tyler first hired him, but after they got to know him, they really liked him."

"Are you going to fire Pastor Cole and hire the other guy?" Corey asked.

"That's not in the plan," Grady answered.

Chapter Twenty-Four

"How are things in Bristol Ridge?" Emmy asked.

Diane switched the phone from one ear to the other, sighed and said, "Lonely. You guys are gone. Andy Walker is somewhere in Australia or New Zealand. Marissa stopped by to brag about her new *cottage* as she calls it. She must think she's a Vanderbilt. I talked to Mona on Tuesday."

"How is Mona doing? Where is she now?" Emmy asked checking on the cinnamon rolls in the oven.

"She's fine. She took a couple of the grandkids to Hawaii. Mona told me it will be impossible for her to live with either of her children, but she loves her grandchildren."

"She doesn't have to live with anyone. She can buy a place of her own. She has the ranch in Idaho, the one in Hawaii and she can buy a place in Arizona or somewhere."

"She mentioned buying a condo in Santa Fe."

"Have you talked to your new neighbors much?"

"Not really. I see the kids outside once in a while, but the parents are busy traveling with work."

"Who takes care of the kids? Grandparents?"

"No, there's a couple who live in the house..."

"Kinda like Rosco and Teresa?" Emmy asked.

"Maybe. Oh, Bennett and Marissa moved in a few days ago."

"Really?! I didn't think Marissa would ever be satisfied. She made the builder redo the entire kitchen after seeing something better in a magazine. I don't know why Bennett puts up with her. She's worse than the character in that old movie."

"Marissa still believes she should be living in the old South with a dozen servants to take care of her," Diane chuckled.

"Kristen and Wyatt are closing on their house Wednesday. They are coming home for that."

"Where will they stay?" Diane asked.

Emmy turned off the oven and pulled out the pan of warm, gooey cinnamon rolls. "She didn't say. They might stay with Tony, or they might stay in a hotel," Emmy said with a shrug.

"How is Tony's mother doing?"

"Better than her doctor expected. I talked to her Sunday. She said the pain is manageable, and she doesn't need to use her walker or a cane anymore."

"Oh, did I tell you Brady took the boys to the Upper Peninsula for a week?"

"No. Why? What are they doing?"

"He rented a house close to Lake Superior, and they are fishing and spending time on the boat."

"What boat?"

"Brady bought a fishing boat. He wanted to take them to Canada, but there are issues with travel. He might take them to Alaska instead."

"How long are they going to be gone?"

"Mid-August. Give or take."

"So it's just you, Lily and Conor at home, huh?"

"At least the house is easier to keep clean," Diane said with a laugh. "Should I check on your house?"

"You can if you want, but Bobby is keeping an eye on it. I told him to use the pool as often as he wants. We're paying the pool company, so someone should be enjoying it."

"What about Tony's kids? They like to swim."

"I told Tony they could use it whenever they want as long as an adult is there. I'd hate for the boys to be swimming and have an accident."

"When are you coming home? I forgot. You are coming back to SoHam eventually, right?"

"Yes. I used to think I could never live anywhere else, but I like Idaho. I don't think I'd want to stay here in the winter, but we could come out here for a week of skiing. Kenny said he'd like to learn how to ski."

"Next thing you know, you guys will buy a place in Arizona and spend the winter there."

Emmy giggled and added, "Maybe Hawaii, or New Zealand, or one of the Caribbean islands. The pandemic changed my mind about a lot of things."

188

"Your law practice must be doing well since you have an office in Illinois and Arizona," Kristen told her brother Wednesday morning. "How is Amber? I haven't seen her in forever."

"She is doing well. You do know she is teaching at the University of Arizona, right?"

"Yes. She is still taking care of her parents, too."

"We had to hire a full-time caregiver. Actually several. A local company does it all. The scheduling I mean." Derrick quickly perused the contract and legal documents for the closing. "You know you could have signed everything in Michigan and saved a trip home."

"I know, but we are using this as an excuse to come back for a day."

"I would let you stay in my condo, but Amber is having it repainted, and workers are updating the kitchen this week."

"That is okay. We checked into the Lincoln Hotel downtown. I haven't been there in ages."

"Do they still book weddings and receptions there?" Derrick asked.

"Why wouldn't they?"

"The virus thing," Derrick replied.

"Right. I don't know for sure. People are still getting married."

"Occasionally," he joked. "I have set up the trusts per your instructions. Unless tuition costs increase dramatically, you are covered. Are you going to go back to work soon?"

"Not until Kayla is in school all day. We can live on Wyatt's salary."

"You could take money from your investments if needed."

"Yes, but I want to live a simple life now. I do not need a big house..."

"Are you going to keep driving your old Acura? It must have over a hundred thousand miles on it by now," he teased.

"Okay, point taken. I like to drive a nice car."

"You should lease your next vehicle."

"Why? Isn't that like renting? I would be throwing money away."

189

"Not necessarily. You like to trade your vehicles in every few years rather than keep them until they fall apart. Since you budget for a car payment, leasing would be a way to either reduce that payment, or drive a fancier vehicle."

"I don't need anything fancier. The next time I trade cars, I should let you do the negotiating."

"How did the closing go?" Tony removed his jacket and tie and plopped onto the couch.

"My hand is still cramped from signing my name a thousand times," Kristen answered.

"Are you crashing here tonight?"

Kristen explained their plans.

"I thought that place closed because of the pandemic."

"It did, but we are squatting in the bridal suite."

"You should have been a comedian, Kristen."

Kristen watched Coby, the youngest Bertucci son, walk into the family room.

"Hi, Aunt Kristen. Mom said dinner will be ready in ten minutes."

"Thank you, Coby."

"You're welcome," he hurried away.

"I remember when he was born, and look at him now. He is taller than me," Kristen said.

"I don't think he's taller than you, but he's probably taller than Emmy," Tony said. "He's shot up three inches this summer. He can wear some of Taylor's clothes."

"Does it make you feel old?"

"I'm younger than you," Tony said with a grin.

"Where is Peter?" Wyatt asked.

"He's working for Two Bears Landscaping this summer," Tony answered. "He wants the experience because he wants to be a landscape architect. He wants to redesign all the parks in SoHam and Crest Ridge."

"It must make you feel very old to have a son going to college in the fall," Kristen teased. She saw Tony's look and put a hand to her mouth. "Sorry, I forgot."

"It's all right," Tony said with a wave. "Sometimes I forget he and Dotty were Heather's kids first.

Heather Bertucci Khryzman was Tony and Marco's sister and Peter and Dotty's birth mother.

"How long ago did she pass away?" Wyatt asked.

"It was early October of... What year was it?"

"2005," Mama answered. "October 2, 2005."

Tony glanced over his shoulder at a photo on the fireplace mantel and clenched his jaw.

Dotty carried Kayla up to Kristen. "She needs a new diaper."

"Let me have that child," Mama said. She got up from her recliner and took Kayla from Dotty. "I can still change a messy diaper."

Kayla jabbered at Mama, and Kristen handed the diaper bag to Dotty.

"I plan to spoil this one more than the others," Mama said.

"I will let you," Kristen said. "It is good to see you getting around better now."

"I surprised my doctor. He thought I would be using a walker for the whole year," Mama replied.

"Dinner is ready!" Ben yelled from the kitchen.

"Benjamin! I told you to tell them without yelling." Sloane frowned at him. "Would it hurt you to walk to the family room?"

"Fine," he answered swiping one of the dinner rolls. He marched into the family room, bowed and announced in a semblance of a British accent. "Dinner is served in the dining room. Please follow me." He strutted out of the room with his head high and shoulders thrown back.

"Why didn't Zach and Grace come with you?" Ben asked with a mouthful of mashed potatoes. "I could show Zach the pictures Kevin sent, and I kinda miss Gracie."

"They wanted to stay and help at church," Wyatt answered.

"What's going on at church? Are we going?" Coby asked.

"The church in Michigan," Wyatt explained. "They are having an outdoor Vacation Bible School."

191

"Are they staying home alone?" Taylor, now twelve and still the quietest of the Bertucci children, asked.

"They are staying with Liz and Tyler," Kristen answered.

"Where will they go to school?" Noemi asked. "I will miss not having Zach in my class."

"There is only one high school in Alexandria Rapids," Wyatt replied. "The junior high is only a few blocks away, but the new high school is at the west end of town."

"Will Grace have to walk to school?" Ben asked.

"If the weather is nice, she might walk. Otherwise, Liz or I can take her. Natalie will be at the same school, so they will have one friend to start the new year."

"I don't know which high school I will attend," Ben said. "The coach at St. Raymond's wants me to play football for him, but Mom and Dad might make me go to Reagan. The Barclay Academy doesn't have a football team anymore. They sucked when they had one. They lost almost every game."

"I think there were more people in church today," Piper said on the way home.

"You could be right," Grady answered.

"Hey, Dad! Did you make Keegan sing that old-fashioned song to keep those old ladies off your back?" Corey asked.

"I almost never interfere with Keegan's choice of songs. I tell him what the focus of the message will be, and let him decide what fits best."

"Yeah, you totally caved," Asher said.

Chapter Twenty-Five

"Who is picking Emmy up at the airport?" Sloane asked Monday morning. "What time are they supposed to arrive?"

Tony added a healthy dose of ketchup to his scrambled eggs and hash browns before answering, "She texted me earlier. They are supposed to land around four thirty. I told her I would swing by the airport after work to pick them up, but it would cost her more than a taxi."

"You would try to charge her." Sloane stared at his plate. "Would you like something to go with your ketchup?"

"I like ketchup. Do we have any more bacon?"

"Not until someone goes to the store," she answered.

"Am I supposed to do that? You're home in the summer. You teach school, remember?"

"Is that what I do? I thought I was merely a face on the computer."

"You might regret saying that later when you have a room full of rowdy students."

"Have you been waiting long?" Kenny shook hands with Tony.

"Fifteen minutes. How was your vacation?"

"It was awesome, Uncle Tony!" Kevin shouted. He waved his arms and added, "Idaho is the perfect place to live. It's got mountains, rivers, wild animals and the kids don't have to go to school."

Emmy walked up shielding her eyes from the sun. "I saw you leaning against the van when we landed. Did you leave work early?"

"I can leave whenever I want since I'm the boss." He smiled then hugged Heather and Isabella. "How did you like Idaho?"

Heather shrugged. "It's okay. I got bored at first, but I found some things to do. There aren't any kids within fifty miles of the ranch. If it wasn't for my phone and laptop, I would have been totally cut off from civilization."

"It wasn't that bad, Heather," Isabella added.

"It was great!" Kevin exclaimed. "Did Ben tell you about the river canyon right behind the house? It was a thousand times better than the creek running through your woods."

"He mentioned the river. What was the name?"

"The Big Lost River. There's a Little Lost River not too far away. I found an old Indian trail leading down the cliff. Ben and Taylor would love it. Maybe Coby, too."

"Maybe I'll send them with you to Idaho next summer," Tony said.

Thirty minutes later Tony was on the way to Bristol Ridge.

"I brought the van because I assumed you would have a ton of luggage," Tony said as he looked at Emmy in the rear-view mirror.

"We left a bunch of stuff at the ranch," Emmy explained. "I figure each year we will take more gear with us and leave it there."

"What are we gonna do for dinner?" Kevin hollered from the back row. "There won't be any food in the house."

"We can order pizzas," Kenny said.

"Can we go swimming?" Isabella asked. "I missed the pool."

"You can use the pool after you unpack."

Tony parked by the service door, and Bobby O'Connor strolled up a moment later. With everyone pitching in, the van was quickly unloaded.

"Thanks for your help, Bobby," Kenny said. "Did you have any issues with the house? You didn't mention any in your emails."

Bobby shook his head. "No problems. I checked it every two or three days. We used the pool when we had time, and I used the grill. I might have to buy something like yours. Maybe smaller though."

"How are Shay and Karissa?" Emmy asked. "I bet she's grown a lot since I saw her."

Bobby shrugged. "Not really. Shay's pretty much the same size."

Emmy smacked his arm. "I meant Karissa."

"Well, she finished junior high while you were away..."

Emmy rolled her eyes. "Why do I ever expect a straight answer from you? I'll have to stop over and see them soon."

"Will Peter be home later?" Heather asked Tony when no one was listening.

"He should be. Should I tell him to stop by to see you?" he asked.

"No, I would rather come to your house."

"I'll tell him to hang around." Tony grinned at her. "I think he missed you, but he wouldn't admit it."

"The only bad thing about the ranch is no one will deliver food all the way out there." Kevin grabbed another slice of pizza.

"How many slices have you had?" Emmy asked.

He shrugged. "I forgot to count. Can I see if Ben wants to stay here tonight? We can swim and camp out in the clubhouse."

"Ask your father," Emmy said.

"You should wait until we have time to inspect the tree house," Kenny said. "It might not be safe anymore."

"It's pretty sturdy, Dad, and it's a clubhouse. Not a tree house. Those are for little kids."

"Are you going to live out there this year?" Heather asked. "It might get a bit cold in the winter."

"We could use one of those propane heaters."

Emmy shook her head. "No, you might start a forest fire."

"Dad, can we take the Jeep through the woods tomorrow? We should check the trails to make sure they're passable."

"I'll see. Your mother might have a few chores for me."

"I have more than a few," Emmy said. "My honey-do list is four pages long."

"Is there room for me in the clubhouse?" Kenny asked then he kissed Emmy.

She frowned at him. "If you want to live in the woods, go ahead. Just don't expect me to let you in the house until you take a long shower."

"You can stay with me, Dad," Kevin said. "No shower required."

"Mom, I'm going to run over to see Dotty and Noemi. I won't be out too long," Heather said after dinner.

Emmy glanced up from the kitchen desk as she sorted the mail. "Dotty and Noemi, huh?"

"I might see Peter, too. If he's home."

"Don't stay out too late."

"How late is too late?"

Emmy checked the time. "Be home by ten."

"Eleven?"

"Ten thirty and that's my final offer," Emmy said with a shake of her head. "Did you learn that from me?"

Heather got her bike out of the garage and hesitated because she heard the boys splashing in the pool. She rode past the deck and checked to make sure Peter wasn't with them.

"Where are you going?" Kevin asked as he ran to the wrought iron fence surrounding the pool. "Are you going to see Peter?" he teased.

"It's none of your business."

She heard the boys laughing and shouted, "You need to grow up."

She rode her bike to Tony's house and saw him in the garage unloading groceries. She leaned the bike against the house and asked, "Is Peter home?"

"He was helping me with the groceries. Go on in, Heather." He watched her walk inside, smiled and whispered, "You and Isa look so much like your mother."

"Hi, Aunt Sloane. Are Dotty and Noemi busy?"

Sloane smiled. "They were upstairs a few minutes ago, and I just now sent Peter to the basement with frozen food."

Heather felt her face turn red. "I told Mom I was coming over to see them. She didn't believe me either."

"I won't tell her anything."

"Maybe I should run upstairs first in case Mom asks about Dotty and Noemi."

Sloane put away two cans of coffee. "I will tell Peter you are here when he comes upstairs."

"Thanks."

Heather found the girls in Dotty's room. She hugged them then sat on Dotty's bed.

"Was Idaho as insufferable as you said in your texts?" Noemi asked.

"Not really, but I did miss my friends. The area is really beautiful. There are mountains on both sides of the valley and the river is in our backyard. Well, not in the yard. It's behind our yard in a canyon."

They talked for ten minutes before Peter knocked on the door.

"Mom said you were here." He smiled at Heather.

"Are you finished with the groceries?" she asked.

"All done."

"Would you like to go for a walk?"

"Sure. Where?"

"Outside," Dotty teased with a grin.

Peter took Heather's hand once they were outside.

"Did you miss me, Heather?"

She answered by kissing him long and hard.

"I guess that's a yes," he said with a grin.

"Did you miss me?" she asked as she backed into his arms and held them tightly around her.

He kissed her cheek. "I screwed up. I never should have put you in the friend zone like that. Dotty found out and got on my case. She told me I was an idiot, and I guess she was right."

"Did you see many other girls while I was gone?"

"Do you want the truth?"

They made their way to a hanging, wooden love seat under a tree at the edge of the yard.

"Yes. The whole truth."

"Okay. I went out a few times with that girl I told you about."

"How did it work out?" Heather edged closer to him.

"She was cute and I liked that, but once I got to know her better, I realized she was only interested in herself. She was definitely high maintenance," he said with a chuckle.

"Were there others?"

197

"Two others, but I only took them out once and it was with a group of people."

"Are you glad I'm home?"

He answered with another long kiss.

"I'll take that as a yes." She stood up, faced him and added, "No more kisses tonight. I know it shouldn't matter, but it does."

"What matters? It was only a kiss."

"The difference in our ages. I know Mom and Dad are... you know."

"Dead set against us dating?"

She shook her head. "No, they're getting used to that. I meant there's the same difference in their ages. They trust me and you."

He stood up and pulled her close. "Would they still trust us if they knew about the kiss?"

"Daddy would lock me in my room until I'm thirty-five."

Peter laughed. "My dad threatens to lock Dotty and Noemi up, too."

"Fathers can be very protective."

They walked through the yard to the front of the house holding hands.

"I should go."

"I could walk you home."

She pointed to her bike. "I'll take a rain check."

"You're home early," Emmy said.

Heather sat on the couch next to her mother. "I didn't want to stay out too late on a school night," she said with a grin.

"I will hold you to that in a couple years."

Chapter Twenty-Six

"Who was on the phone, Em?" Kenny asked.

She walked into the den and stood behind him as he sat at the desk looking over their latest statement from Aberdeen Investments. "Do we have any money left after buying the ranch?"

"Actually, our account has gained half of it back already."

"Are you kidding?"

"It's been a good year so far. I know we didn't buy the ranch as an investment, but it really is. We could probably sell it next year and make a tidy profit."

"I don't want to sell it, but I don't want to buy any more properties. Two are enough."

"Who called?"

"Oh." She sat in her recliner and Kenny turned around to face her. "It was Keegan Lochner from church."

"Do I need to ask what he wanted?"

"No. He asked to meet this afternoon if I wasn't busy. He is serious about writing original material, and wants to collaborate."

"Is he coming here?"

She shook her head. "I have to run out later, so I said I would meet him at the church. I can meet Pastor Howe if he's around."

"He will ask you to sing, too."

"I know, but I can always refuse."

"Can you?"

"I do miss singing, but I still want to focus on my writing. The books. Not songs."

Rebecca was in the office when Emmy arrived at one.

"Emmy! It's so good to see you."

They caught up on news for a while.

"I'm supposed to meet Keegan. He wants to talk about writing new material."

"He was in the music suite. Should I let him know you're here?" Rebecca asked.

"Sure. I don't want to surprise him."

"Have you met Pastor Grady?"

Emmy shook her head and glanced over her shoulder. "Not yet. Is he here, too?"

Rebecca nodded to her right. "He's in his office working on Sunday's message. You should introduce yourself."

"I don't want to bother him."

Rebecca's eyes sparkled. "Too late."

Emmy did a 180.

"Hello, I am Grady Howe."

"I'm Emmy."

He smiled. "I know who you are. You did a concert at my last church years ago."

"I did?"

He nodded.

"I'm sorry. I can't keep track of all the places we played."

"I understand. Are you here to see Rebecca?"

"Actually, she is supposed to meet with Keegan," Rebecca said.

"Would you allow me to walk you to the music suite?"

She giggled then nodded. "I'll talk to you later, *Pastor* Rebecca."

"How long have you been a part of Crest Ridge?" Grady asked as they walked down the hall to the old music suite.

"I started coming here over twenty years ago. Wait! Maybe longer. I came here in the summer before my last year of high school."

"You don't have to tell me if it's too personal."

"It's not that. Lynette Jefferson invited me to come a long time ago. She was Lynette Rosas then. She's married to Paul Jefferson. He's the pastor of SoHam First Church. Have you met him?"

"Not yet, but we talked on the phone. I hope to meet the local pastors soon."

"Kenny and I were married in there." She pointed to the old sanctuary.

"I take it the Spanish congregation wasn't using it then," Grady said with a smile.

"We didn't have a Spanish service back then. Why is Keegan using the old music suite office? There is a music suite in the new building."

"He is doing some renovations in the new music suite, so he is temporarily using the old office."

"I see."

Grady opened the door for Emmy, "Keegan, you have a visitor."

Keegan bounded out of the office. "Emmy! Thank you so much for coming." He held out a hand, and she giggled as she shook it.

"Pastor Rebecca said you are like the Energizer Bunny."

"I do like to keep busy. Should we use the coffee shop to talk? It's less private."

"Certainly." *If I knew you better, I wouldn't mind using your office. But it's probably wise to use the coffee shop.*

"I've tried to follow Billy Graham's example to never be alone with a woman other than my wife."

"I was thinking of the same thing. I recently read about a pastor in Texas who had an affair with a college girl from his church. He admitted it started when he would meet with her for counseling."

"I would never counsel a woman without the presence of my wife."

"What about another lady from the church?"

"I don't understand the question." Keegan stopped walking.

"You said you wouldn't counsel a female without your wife's presence. Would it have to be your wife, or could it be another lady from the church?"

"Oh, I get it now." Keegan shook his head. "It would have to be my wife."

"I like that," Emmy said.

As they walked back to the foyer of the old building, Keegan talked about the team.

"I haven't met everyone, but I am astonished by how many talented people are available. I've have two teams before, but there are three here, and the teens."

"The teens are very talented."

"That's why I want to create original material. Scripture based material. I think we could become another church with a fantastic body of music."

"We have recorded before," Emmy said.

"I've heard those recordings." He stopped and said, "Please don't think I want to become another Chris Brewster. My talent is in organizing and leading a worship team. My voice is all right. I don't claim to be anything special. I can play the guitar well enough to lead worship, but I will never be good enough to record." He began walking again and she had to hustle to keep up with his long strides. "The two most talented people in the church aren't on the worship team at the moment."

"Really?"

"You do realize I mean you and your husband, don't you?"

"Okay, God has blessed us, but you can't really believe Kenny is talented, can you?"

"I have heard most of the Fridays At Five CDs."

"He only knows three chords, and just turns up the volume to compensate for a lack of skill."

Keegan laughed. "I'll try that myself."

They sat across from each other at one of the tables and talked about the worship team's history.

"I've met Pastor Chase a number of times," Keegan said. "He's an excellent judge of talent."

"He was very influential in my development as a singer and a worship leader. The most influential other than Kenny. Pastor Chase gave me the confidence to do what God had planned for me."

"Did God's plan for you change?" Keegan asked.

"Oooh! I set myself up for that, huh?"

Keegan smiled.

"You don't need either Kenny or me on the team. You have more than enough talented people already."

Keegan shrugged and said, "What can I say? I'm greedy. I want the worship team to be the best they can be."

"I'm too old," Emmy said.

Keegan guffawed and pointed a finger at her. "That is the lamest excuse I've ever heard. Would you like to try again?"

"Not really. You hit the nail on the head when you mentioned God's plan."

"Please don't think I'm all about the best performance, or anything like that. Yes, I want to prepare the team so they are capable of giving their best effort, but my number one goal is to prepare a way for them to grow spiritually."

"If I rejoined the team, I will hold you to that."

He stood up and extended a hand. "Deal. I accept the challenge. Practice starts at six thirty this Thursday. You might as well join us since you, or Kenny, will have to drive the twins to practice."

"I don't know."

"I'm not asking you to commit to every week. I would settle for two Sundays a month."

"Okay, but my voice will need time to regain its strength."

"Yeah. I've heard that excuse before. I will let you ease back into the rotation, but I expect to hear the Emmy who made all those CDs."

"Oh, I hope I sound better than when we recorded those early projects."

"How did your meeting with Keegan go, Mom?" Isabella asked.

"Good."

"Come on. Spill it. Did he convince you to rejoin the team?"

"Yes. He made me realize God has a plan for my life, and it hasn't changed just because I wanted to take it easy for a while."

Isabella hugged her mother. "I'm glad. It will be fun to sing together."

"I would like to welcome someone new to the worship team." Keegan Lochner grinned at Emmy. "A few of you might remember her from her previous years as a member and leader of the team, but she's a new member to me. Let's make her welcome."

Bobby O'Connor stood up and waved his hands emphatically. "Wait a second, Keegan. Did she pass the audition? I know she used to be able to sing, but that was years ago. Should we make sure she can still sing on key?"

"Will somebody smack him for me?" Emmy made a face at Bobby.

Heather turned to Isabella. "I knew they would tease Mom, but it might help her relax. She told me she was nervous about coming back to the team."

"We will have to make sure she doesn't dance around like she did in the old days." Isabella giggled and smiled at Nathan Kellett, one of the young guitar players.

"She would break her hips if she tried," Heather said then laughed.

Keegan chuckled and said, "I'm pretty sure she can still sing, and I twisted her arm enough to get her to agree to help us come up with a few original tunes."

"Does that mean we don't have to keep singing her old songs?" Bobby asked. "I had to play them on tour for years."

"You don't have to play the older material anymore," Emmy said. "But the new songs might be too complex for your drumming skills. If I remember correctly, you only know how to play in 4/4 time."

The team laughed at the interaction between the two close friends. Bobby and Emmy had been a part of the worship team longer than anyone else. Almost twenty years. Bobby joined the team as a teenager, and Emmy was only twenty-one.

"That's because ninety percent of all your songs use that time signature." Bobby held out his hands and Emmy hugged him. "I knew you couldn't stay away for too long."

"Now that we've welcomed Emmy back, let's get down to business," Keegan said. "This week we are going to introduce two new songs to the congregation..."

Chapter Twenty-Seven

"Mom, are you really nervous, or are you kidding?" Isabella asked as the worship team gathered in the music suite after a quick rehearsal Sunday morning.

"I used to tell your father I had Monarch butterflies in my stomach. This morning they're crashing into each other."

"If you get too nervous, lip-synch and Isa and I will carry the tune," Heather teased.

"I might take you up on that."

Keegan gathered the team in a circle and prayed.

Emmy closed her eyes. *Lord, please give me the strength to use my voice as You intended. I've been remiss to think I needed to take time away from the team. Thank you for bringing our new team to the church, and please allow your spirit to guide us in worship today.*

The worship team made their way to the platform, and Emmy looked for Kenny. She spotted him to her right about halfway back in the sanctuary. She bit her lip and knew Kenny could see. It was her way of telling him she was nervous. Kenny smiled and blew her a kiss.

"Mom! Did Daddy just blow you a kiss?" Isabella asked quietly. "That's not appropriate in church."

"You weren't supposed to see, but it's his way of reminding me to relax."

"Are the butterflies still crashing into each other?"

"Yes, and I'm afraid if I open my mouth, they will escape."

Heather looked at her mother. "Is that a weird way of saying you're afraid you're going to puke?"

"Maybe, but I'll be okay once we get started."

They closed their eyes while Keegan prayed. He motioned to Bobby, who counted off the song as he grinned at Emmy.

"Just like old times, Em," Bobby said into his mic which was fed only into the in-ear monitors of the team. No one else could hear him.

Heather and Isabella giggled for a second, but Emmy took a deep breath and smiled.

"Emmy, it was so good to see you on the platform again. You should be singing every week," Mrs. Thompson said. "Maybe you can convince that new pastor to include more hymns. You must be old enough now to appreciate how much better they are than all these contemporary songs."

"Thank you, I think," Emmy said. "I will talk to Pastor Keegan about the hymns."

Heather and Isabella were standing next to Emmy and heard this conversation.

"Mom, are you really going to talk Keegan into using hymns?" Isabella asked.

"I only said I would talk to him about the hymns. I didn't say I would try to talk him into using them. I might tell him to never use hymns."

"You can be so devious at times, Mom," Heather said.

"Don't tell your father, okay?"

"It will be our secret."

Keegan saw Emmy and smiled as he approached. "Thank you for today. I saw a lot of smiling faces in the crowd when you appeared on the platform."

"They were probably smiling at the girls."

"No they weren't, Mom," Isabella said. "The older people were smiling at you."

"I hope they realize we have different teams, and I won't be singing every week."

"We have some overlap in the teams," Keegan said. "I can see the time when we will have enough team members to eliminate the overlap."

"Maybe, but you will discover some musicians like to play every week," Emmy added.

"In fact, I added two singers to the team this week." Keegan turned around and saw the two ladies who appeared to be waiting to talk to Emmy. He waved for them to approach, turned to Emmy and said, "Did you have a moment to talk to them?"

"Of course." Emmy smiled at them.

"Thanks. I need to talk to Pastor Miller. I'll see you later." Keegan hurried away.

"Hi, I'm Emmy. Keegan told me you have joined the worship team, but he didn't tell me your names or anything about you."

The taller one looked over her shoulder at the quickly retreating worship leader. "He always seems to be scurrying to the next item on his list."

"He is extremely energetic. Probably too much coffee. These are my daughters." Emmy introduced Heather and Isabella.

"We heard you today. You harmonize perfectly."

"Thank you," Isabella said. "Mom, we're going to talk to some friends."

"Okay, but try to find your father, please." Emmy couldn't see Kenny, so she turned to the new ladies. "Have you been coming to Crest Ridge long?"

"About a month," the taller one said flipping her long red hair over her shoulder. "My name is Sara Kupla, and this is my roommate Kate Leone."

Emmy shook hands with both ladies. She grinned because Kate was only a couple inches taller than herself and had dark, curly hair. Kate's gray eyes reminded Emmy of smoke.

"How did you find our church? From your accent, I would guess you aren't from around here."

"We were both born in New York City, and grew up on Washington Place. Then we were roommates at Asch College where we studied fashion design, and worked in the garment district to help pay for school."

"How did you end up in SoHam?" Emmy asked looking directly at Kate.

"We were hired by a start-up company in the Gordon Hill area. Harris Blanck. They manufacture women's clothing, and we are on the design team."

"I'm familiar with the area. My husband and his partners own a warehouse there."

Kate grinned and said, "We know who he is, and we work down the street from their building."

"They don't use it much anymore other than to store gear. Do you live nearby?"

Sara answered, "We live in one of the older homes on the edge of Raynor Park. We live upstairs, and our landlady lives on the first floor. She used to attend this church years ago, but she doesn't get out now."

"That's amazing. I grew up on Fifth Street in Raynor Park. What street are you on?"

"Triangle. 146 Triangle. You might know our landlady. Her names is Rose Freedman."

Emmy shook her head. "The name doesn't sound familiar, but I haven't lived there for ages. It's possible my parents might have known her."

"She turned 107 on February 22 this year," Kate said.

"Are you kidding me?"

"No," Kate replied.

"We had a party for her," Sara said. "Oh, her grandson bought the house across the street about a year ago. He's her only living relative, and he was the one who suggested this church. He comes when he can. He plays guitar and sings. He writes folk songs and likes to sing old Irish ballads. We tried to talk him into coming with us when we auditioned for the worship team, but he claimed he wasn't good enough."

"What's his name? Would I know him?" Emmy asked. "I used to know most of the local musicians."

Kate shrugged. "His name is Dave Kincaid, and he would be a perfect fit."

"Maybe we can convince him to join. Keegan is looking for more musicians."

Emmy heard a commotion and her name mentioned.

"We won't take up more of your time," Sara said.

"It was a pleasure to meet you." As they turned and walked away, Emmy noticed Sara's fiery, red hair reached almost to her waist.

"Hey, Mom!" Kevin tried not to appear to be running, but he scurried toward Emmy. "Mom! Uncle James is here. He wants to see you."

"Where is he? Did something happen? Why isn't he at St. John's? Is Mama Bertucci okay?"

"Geez, Mom. He just wants to see you. He didn't mention anything bad happening."

Emmy looked toward the back of the sanctuary and saw her brother talking to Kenny. *At least he's not wearing his priest robe or his clerical collar. He looks like an ordinary man.*

Kevin took her hand and pulled her through the crowd.

"Here she is, Uncle James."

"Why are you here? Did something happen?"

He shook his head. "No. Why would you assume that?"

"You never come here on a Sunday."

"I finished early and came to hear you sing."

"Really?"

"Yes. Isabella invited me." He hugged his nieces and ruffled Kevin's hair.

"What did you think?" Isabella asked. "Didn't Mom do a great job?"

"She sounded angelic. Was there something wrong with her microphone?" he teased.

Emmy made a face at him and was about to stick out her tongue when Pastor Howe walked up and shook hands with the men.

"This is my brother," Emmy said. "He doesn't come to this church very often."

Grady smiled at Father James. "You are welcome to join us every Sunday."

Kevin laughed and said, "He can't because he's a priest at St. John's. They might fire him if he docsn't show up for mass."

Grady laughed. "Please forgive me."

Father James laughed and replied, "It's okay. I didn't come to steal any of your parishioners. It's not often I get a chance to hear my sister and nieces sing together in public."

"We should thank Emmy and the girls for sharing their talents with the church," Grady said. "Excuse me, but I should talk to those people before they leave. I am still learning who is a regular and who might be new to the church."

"How much of the service did you see?" Emmy asked. "Are you busy for lunch?"

209

"I missed the announcements at the beginning, but I saw the worship team come out from wherever you hang out before the service, and I would love to have lunch with you."

"Would you mind stopping to pick something up? Kenny can take the kids home."

"Where would you like to go?"

"Do you have to ask?"

They ended up going all the way to Darby's.

"About time you got home, Mom. I was so hungry I ate the leftovers from last night," Kevin said.

"Too bad. We stopped at Darby's, but if you're too full to..."

"I've got room for a chili dog and fries." Kevin opened one of the bags. "This is a salad. Why would you go all the way to Darby's and order a salad?"

"Salads are good for you," Emmy said.

Kevin made a face and stuck a finger down his throat.

"Don't worry. This is for me and James. The other bag contains the dogs and burgers."

"You should come to Idaho with us the next time we go," Kevin told Uncle James later as the guys sat on the deck. "Dad and I watched some YouTube videos about these guys who modify their Jeeps and go on these awesome trails. They climbed straight up these huge boulders and through mud and water. It was so awesome. We took the Jeep on some gnarly trails. We got stuck a couple times, but it was so cool."

"Sounds like you had fun."

"We did. I can't wait to go back. I'm going to convince Dad to modify his Jeep. He should get bigger tires and upgrade the suspension. That way we could take it anywhere."

"You're going to have to wait for that," Kenny said.

Father James sounded totally serious when he said, "I need to talk to your mother."

"Okay, I'll tell her to come out here. I think she's in the family room."

Kevin dashed inside and Emmy came out a couple minutes later.

She sat across the table from her brother. "I knew there was something wrong. Is it your father? Did he have another stroke?"

"He is fine. There's a chance I might be reassigned to a different parish."

"Why? Did you piss off the bishop again?"

"Emmy! Do you have to be so crass?" Kenny asked.

"I didn't upset the bishop, but there are ten new priests coming into the South Hampshire diocese.

"Wow! I thought there was a severe shortage of priests. Did the bishop double your salaries?"

"I have taken a vow of poverty," Father James said piously putting his hands together.

"Yeah, cut the crap. What's up?"

"Since my position is basically that of a hospital chaplain, and with the current situation being what it is, I really can't do my job properly..."

"What are you getting at? I don't fully understand all this incardination and excardination stuff you told me about before."

He explained it to her again.

"Sounds like slavery to me."

"Emmy!" Kenny shook his head.

"It's the church's way of making sure there are no rogue or freelance priests. We are all assigned to a bishop or an ecclesiastical superior."

"What does that mean?"

"You know a bishop is in charge of a diocese, right?"

"Yeah."

"Well, there are other religious orders in the church. The Jesuits and Franciscans are examples. These different orders have a hierarchy like the rest of the church. Your church is divided into districts with a person in charge of that particular district."

"Yeah, I get it," Emmy waved a hand. "Where is the bishop thinking of moving you to? Kansas? Alaska? Siberia?"

Father James looked at Kenny then back at Emmy. "I might be assigned to Divine Resurrection."

"Where is that? Is it a real church, or did you make it up?" Emmy asked.

Kenny grinned. "It's a real church, Em."

"Where is it? Out in the boonies somewhere? It's not actually in Siberia, is it? I was trying to be funny."

"You could say that," Kenny grinned again. "The boonies, I mean. You have driven past it a million times."

"I have?"

"It wasn't always called Divine Resurrection."

"What was it called?"

"St. Willibrord."

"I've heard that name before." Emmy tapped her jaw. "It's a strange name for a saint."

"Do you remember the church on Hough Street that burned down about five years ago?"

"Yeah. It was arson, right?"

"Yes," Father James replied. "The site was razed and a new church was built last year."

"I remember it now." Emmy's eyes sparkled. "Are you getting transferred down the street? That church is less than a mile from here."

"It's a possibility."

"Does it have a rectory?"

"No, I would have to live on the street, or maybe I could live in Kevin's fort."

"Real funny!"

"Yes, there is housing provided, and I would be one of four parish priests, so my load would not be too strenuous. I would be more of an advisory priest."

"Dear Lord! The Catholic church must be in dire straits if they need you to be... a whatever."

"How do you feel about me living so close?" Father James asked.

"I suppose I could get used to it, and I might come to hear you do mass sometime, but there's no way I'm converting back to being Catholic."

Chapter Twenty-Eight

Ronald Delaney stretched his arms over his head as the train pulled slowly into the SoHam station. He ignored the mother and small child sitting opposite him and stared out the dusty window.

"Do you live here?" the child climbed out of his seat and asked. "I live here with Mom and Grandma. I'm going to be in second grade when school starts. I'm glad we can have real school again. It sucked last year."

Delaney took a deep breath. "I used to live here, kid, but I left after high school."

"Are you planning to move back?"

"Stevie, don't pester the man." His mother gathered up her belongings and stood up as soon as the train stopped.

"It's okay," Delaney responded. "I'm only gonna be here for a few days."

"Do you have a job?" Stevie asked.

Delaney grunted. "You might say that." He waited until everyone exited the car before grabbing his backpack containing everything he owned in the world. He stepped off the train and shielded his eyes from the sun. He followed the crowd toward the exit of the elevated platform. Upon reaching the bottom, he glanced around.

"It looks different from what I remember. There wasn't a ballpark here before."

He crossed the street and headed toward downtown SoHam. He noticed some improvements along Rialto Avenue and stopped to admire the nearly finished, ten-story courthouse. He walked all the way to the Kinmundy River and stood on the concrete embankment. He watched a tugboat pushing six barges downriver. He observed two deckhands walking along the edge of the barges and muttered under his breath, "That might be a good way to get out of SoHam after I finish what I came for."

He stared at the bluffs on the other side of the river for a time. He closed his eyes and pictured neighborhood where he grew up. Raynor Park.

213

He smoked a cigarette as he watched another tug for several minutes. He tossed the butt into the river as the boat disappeared around the bend.

Delaney crossed the river, trudged up the hill and walked until he reached his destination. He paused at the southeastern corner of East Fifth Street and Clement Street. He smoked another cigarette as he stared at the large, two-story brick house set back from the street kitty-cornered from where he stood. He tossed the butt away, crossed Clement and walked along the cracked sidewalk on the south side of the street. He noticed the tall trees inside the black, wrought-iron fence of the large house and watched as someone mowed the yard. He hustled along when the person looked in his direction for a moment. He glanced over his shoulder to make sure the person working in the yard was no longer watching. He checked the number of the house on his side of the street.

"16302."

He lit another cigarette, turned to look across the street and chuckled.

"That's the place. 16301 East Fifth Street. I remember Todd telling me about the place. It was smaller than the dump we lived in."

Delaney slowly smoked his cigarette. He tapped out the last one, lit it and tossed the empty pack toward the street. It landed at the edge of the grass. He drew in a deep puff and pulled a wrinkled photograph from the back pocket of his faded black jeans. He frowned as he stared at the slightly out-of-focus photo of Emmy and the twins.

"I know you don't live here anymore, and haven't for a long time. I don't know exactly where Bristol Ridge is, but I'll find it. I have unfinished business with you, Emmy Colasanti."

Check out these other titles by the author. Visit the website:
kennethleemcgee.com

The Emmy's Story Series

1. We Were 'posed to Get Married
2. One Of The Guys
3. A New Friend
4. Did You Like the Ravioli Tonight?
5. Completely and Forever: A Wedding
6. It's Time To Go!
7. How Difficult Can It Be?
8. Forever... Isabella... Forever
9. The Forgettable Year
10. Turning Thirty
11. Hello, I'm James
12. Remember The Struggle
13. But God! I Write Songs
14. A Lifelong Dream
15. Gideon's Tree
16. New Priorities
17. Christmas Surprise
18. God Is In Control
19. Life Goes On

The Annie Mercer O'Dell Series

1. Roosevelt High
2. North Park College
3. Smoky Mountain Summer

The Rex Ford & Clay Horn Books

1. The Amazing Adventures Of Rex Ford & Clay Horn

The Stockton Woods Series

1. Sounds Like a Mournful Train Today
2. Sounds Like a Happy Train Today
3. Sounds Like a Cheerful Train Today

Stand Alone Books

1. Growing Up In Kinmundy Junction
2. Grandpa, Lions and Kitty Cats: A Collection Of Short Stories For Children Of All Ages
3. The True Stories Of Ol' Melvin, Obadiah, Perkins MacGhee and other Characters
4. Grandpa, Lions and More Kitty Cats: A Second Collection Of Short Stories For Children Of All Ages
5. Random Thoughts of a Strange Mind